THE GRAVE DIGGER'S BOY

R.R. NEWMAN

BLOODHOUND
— BOOKS —

Print ISBN 978-1-912986-73-6

PART ONE

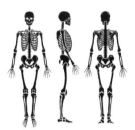

CHAPTER ONE

In the blue light of a late autumn afternoon the single-decker bus throbbed, fumed and steamed under the cold war concrete canopy of its bay at Exeter Central Bus Station.

The driver was a young, slim, red-haired man in scarf and gloves who stared straight ahead, his breath clouding about him as he chewed a piece of gum. In the single seat behind his cabin sat his son, Ben – a pale, freckled boy approaching adolescence. His jaw was slack with boredom and the copy of *2000 AD* in his cold hands was creased, read from cover to cover several times that day as the bus went back and forth, back and forth. He shivered in the chill, looking forward to the delicious moment when the doors would close and the warm air from the radiator at his feet would envelope him.

With almost every seat taken and the scheduled 3.35 departure time seconds away, there came the sounds of shoes slapping through puddles on paving. A dark-haired teenage girl in an Our Price record shop uniform and well-worn duffel coat launched herself aboard with a laugh. She turned to wave at someone, and handed her ticket to the driver.

'Ta,' he said, and the doors jerked shut behind her.

As the bus began to judder backwards, she moved carefully along, swaying with its motion. Ben stared at her over the top of his comic.

She gave a sweet, silly smile as she passed, trying to make him laugh. He blushed, blinked and looked down at Judge Dredd.

There was only one seat left for her to take. It was next to a young man whose legs were splayed and who had a transparent carrier bag filled with papers across his lap. His cropped hair was plastered to his forehead with gel and his mouth was surrounded by raw skin. He didn't move to make room for the girl but instead gave her a challenging look. From the corner of his eye Ben watched as the girl lowered herself into what little space the young man had left her. He was just the kind of person Ben would cross the road to avoid – he broadcast aggressive intent.

The bus rumbled out of the station and onto the open road, its sound pitching up as it got into gear. Its windows were fogged and the interior smelled of rain-soaked clothing, mossy and rank. Outside, the blue deepened, broken in waves by passing yellow lights. Someone sniffed, someone else coughed, and the treble end of a piece of repetitive dance music playing on a Walkman insisted on being heard over the beating of the engine.

Ben looked at the roof, letting his gaze pass over the girl on the way. As his eyes drifted from roof back to comic, they settled on her for almost a full second. She provoked a feeling that was new to him. He enjoyed looking at her. The skin of her cheek looked so soft, her lips so ripe. As if she could feel his gaze, her eyes flicked in his direction and she smiled again, this time showing a line of glistening white, baby-straight teeth. Ben fought the urge to respond in kind and instead chewed at his chapped lip and looked away, embarrassed.

The bus stopped and more people got on, shuffling and sniffing, filling up the aisle until his view of the girl was blocked. He didn't know if he was relieved or frustrated.

As the bus headed out of town, his father wrestling the wheel and wet roads, the blue settled to black and lights became less frequent. The windows turned into hazy, distorting mirrors.

There were more stops and some departures, first in suburbs, and then in villages, and slowly the bus emptied until there were only six passengers including the girl and the fierce young man in the seat next to her. They had struck up a conversation which Ben couldn't hear but he could see that the girl, pulling away, was answering only briefly, making herself cold. The young man compensated by leaning in, speaking behind his hand.

'No,' said the girl, her voice changing register and becoming audible above the engine, though she stopped short of shouting.

'Come on,' said the young man with a throaty, suggestive laugh, and then rested one of his rough hands on her thigh.

She stood up as if he'd touched her with a branding iron and began to move quickly towards the front of the bus, not looking back.

None of the other passengers spoke or did anything to help. They just stared at their own reflections in the windows, or down at their newspapers, curling in on themselves in fear and shame.

This time as she passed she didn't look at Ben but he couldn't stop himself from staring up at her. He noticed that her eyes had become yet darker, her lips blue and bloodless.

'Fuck you, then,' shouted the young man from his seat, throwing his arms in anger. 'Frigid bitch.'

The girl folded her arms, pinning shaking hands to her sides.

Ben's father changed gear and the bus began to slow in the approach to the Berebroke junction. Ben heard his voice through the Perspex window, low and calm, 'You all right, love?'

She nodded and gave a short smile that dimpled her cheeks and made her eyes shine momentarily.

Ben held his breath as the bus swung around and then downhill into Berebroke itself. After a few hundred metres the engine gave a climactic rumble and the heavy vehicle lurched to a halt. The doors hissed and clattered open. The girl stepped out into the white light of the single street lamp which illuminated the country bus stop. Without stopping she pulled the hood of her duffel coat over her head. She did not go along the pavement into the centre of the village but instead took the path behind the bus stop. It led away into a small wood – the last remaining part of what was once a great forest – and the way was unlit, and overgrown with oaks, brambles and hawthorn. She seemed to know the way and within seconds had been folded up in the dark.

The bus jolted and the doors crashed shut but before it could pull away the young man came striding forward, brushing past Ben with the swinging carrier bag.

'Open the door,' he said. Ben's father hesitated, holding his foot on the clutch. Ben couldn't breathe. 'Open the fucking door.' The young man pressed his face against the cabin window so that his breath fogged the Perspex. 'I've got to fucking get off here, haven't I.'

The beating of the engine filled the silence.

'For God's sake, let him off,' said someone.

The young man turned his head to look at them and, in so doing, noticed Ben. He leaned in close, enveloping Ben in a cloud of deodorant spray and alcoholic bad breath 'What are you looking at?' Ben, rigid with fear, felt spittle hit his cheek.

'All right, keep your hair on,' said Ben's father. He sounded calm and unflustered, as if oblivious to the threat of violence. He activated the door mechanism and the young man swung out onto the pavement, landing heavily. As he stalked away, he flipped his middle finger back at Ben's father. The door closed and the bus bolted away.

The passengers who remained on the bus exhaled together in relief and someone tutted.

Ben heard his father's muffled voice. 'All right, son?'

At first, Ben nodded, and then realised his father couldn't see him.

'Yes,' he said, though it came out weakly.

'Didn't want him to know we were together in case he decided to take it out on you.'

'I know.'

'Gave that poor lass a good head start though, didn't we?'

'Yes,' Ben replied, and felt his chest swell with pride – pride in himself, but especially in his father, who always seemed to know what to do.

CHAPTER TWO

Ben was woken by the sound of the doorbell in the hall downstairs playing the first two bars of the Blue Danube waltz over and again. As he lay in the dark on the metal-framed cot bed he heard his grandmother, May, coughing violently, and then the scuffing of her slippers along the hall carpet. A sliver of light appeared under the box room door. As she negotiated the stairs she shouted, 'All right, all right, I'm coming,' before another coughing fit took hold.

The front door creaked open and Ben heard a deep, warm, male voice. May responded and then there came the sound of shoes being wiped on the coconut mat as the door slammed shut.

'Peter!'

In the bedroom next door, mattress springs creaked.

'Wake up and come down.'

'I'm bloody coming,' said Ben's father. Ben listened as his father moved around, got dressed, used the toilet, and then thumped downstairs, groaning.

Ben couldn't lie in bed any longer: he counted to three, threw aside his blanket to let in the icy air, and hurriedly dressed in jeans, T-shirt, tracksuit top, and trainers, before stepping out onto the landing.

It felt oddly like Christmas, only he knew there were no presents waiting downstairs. Nobody called at this time of day unless it was bad news.

He walked slowly down the stairs, placing each foot carefully to avoid creaking boards, and as he drew nearer the hum of conversation crystallised into words.

'...any information whatsoever, however insignificant it might seem to you, can be very helpful at the early stages of an investigation like this.'

Ben hovered in the hallway, smelling cigarette smoke and instant coffee, and then edged into the doorway. May was sitting in her usual seat, its arms stained and marked with burns, her nicotine-tinted white hair disarranged, and a cigarette pinched between her lips. Peter was on the sofa, leaning forward with his arms on his knees, brow furrowed as he looked at a sheet of A4 paper in his hand.

'She got on at Exeter,' he said, his voice hoarse. 'I've seen her on the route a few times before, coming and going, like.'

Someone out of sight spoke next – a woman with a London accent. 'She went to school and worked in Exeter, but lived in Berebroke.'

Ben moved into the room and the two police officers standing in front of the window came into view, coffee mugs in hand. The man was in his mid-thirties, square-jawed, with gelled hair and the build of a footballer. He wore a crisply pressed grey suit. There was something of a suppressed snarl about his mouth and nose. The woman at his side was shorter and a little older, with broad hips, cropped blonde hair and a long, sharp nose. She wore sagging black trousers, a brown jacket and a dull-grey blouse.

'Who's this, then?' said the male detective, winking at Ben and curling up one side of his upper lip to reveal a glistening canine tooth. Ben blushed.

Peter glanced over at his son and gestured for him to come nearer. 'This is my boy, Ben.' Ben leaned against his father who pulled him close with a calloused hand.

'Nice to meet you, Ben,' said the strange man. 'I'm Detective Inspector Sweetland – you can call me Steve.'

Ben couldn't stop staring at Sweetland. He was perfect, like an actor, and he wore some kind of aftershave which made him smell of orange peel and freshly-planed wood, rather than cigarettes and sweat.

The female detective raised a hand in greeting and her bracelets rattled, but she didn't introduce herself.

Ben smiled weakly and then looked down at the paper his father was holding, and felt his legs weaken. It was a school photograph of the beautiful girl from the bus reproduced in black and white. She'd been caught half-laughing and her eyes creased. The studio lamps picked out white highlights on her glossy lips.

'I saw her,' Ben whispered, his voice catching in his throat.

The short-haired woman tilted her head. 'Say again, love?'

'He comes on the buses with me sometimes,' said Peter.

'What happened?' said Ben, looking first at his father and then at the female detective.

'This young lady didn't come home last night, love,' she said. 'We're trying to find her and make sure she's all right.' She attempted to smile, baring yellow-grey teeth.

Ben pressed his lips together and his face grew pale.

'Well, like you said, she got off down Berebroke and that's that,' said Peter. He released his grip on Ben's waist and waved his fingers at May, who passed him a packet of cigarettes and a lighter.

The male detective stepped closer and knelt down in front of Ben. The smell of his aftershave grew stronger and his leather shoes creaked. 'If you can think of anything, son, anything at all.'

Ben shook his head furiously.

Sweetland showed his canine again, raised an eyebrow, and sighed. 'We heard from someone else, you see, that she got in a bit of bother on your dad's bus.'

Ben looked at Peter, who blew smoke from his nostrils and picked a flake of tobacco from his tongue with a fingertip.

'I don't remember every bit of trouble on every shift.' He coughed into his fist.

A sad look passed over the detective's face and he glanced down at the floor. 'I find it so disappointing when people keep things from me. Things that could help.'

Ben looked to the female detective and found her expression hardened.

'What are you on about?' rasped May. 'He's telling you–'

'Mum!' snapped Peter, holding up a hand. 'Fucking hell. It's a bit embarrassing, is all. There was this lad.'

Sweetland rose to his feet in one smooth, well-balanced move and returned to his spot by the window next to his colleague.

'He got on at Exeter and I could tell he was a bit sketchy – sort of twitchy, sniffing, you know. He gave me one of those looks, like he wanted me to say something so he'd have an excuse to kick off.'

'Did he say anything?' asked Sweetland.

'No, just "Berebroke", and when I asked if he wanted a return or a single, he said "Single". Then she got on, that girl, whatshername.' Peter pointed with the orange tip of his cigarette at the photograph he was holding in his other hand. 'She went and sat next to him and so I tried to keep an eye on them, like – make sure she was okay.'

'Very gallant,' said Sweetland sarcastically.

Peter ignored the dig.

'When she wanted to get off, I opened the door, and I saw her going into the woods.' His face contorted with unease and regret. 'I did wonder why she did that – why she didn't stick to the main road, with the lights.' He shrugged. 'Mind you, when I was young, I used to walk all over the place in the dark. You get used to it when you grow up in the country.'

Sweetland gestured for Peter to hurry along.

'Then, when he wanted to get off after her, I held him as long as I could.'

'Why didn't you come out of your cabin? Or drive on a bit further?' asked Sweetland.

Peter rubbed at his knuckles. 'Dunno.' He glanced at Ben. 'Worried about the boy, I suppose.'

Sweetland pursed his lips and slowly nodded. 'Is that how you remember it, Ben?'

'Yes,' said Ben, barely audible.

The other detective was staring at his father, slowly shaking her head in disapproval.

Sweetland sighed again. 'What's done is done,' he said.

Peter's eyes were fixed on the carpet as smoke curled around his bowed head.

Ben put a hand on his father's shoulder and leaned to whisper in his ear.

'Go on, then,' Peter replied aloud. 'Tell them.'

'The man who went after her had a bag with him,' said Ben. 'It said HMP Exeter and it had one of those gates, like off a penny.'

The two detectives locked eyes and then looked back to Ben.

'A portcullis,' said Sweetland, snapping off the words with a fierce grin.

'It had papers in it,' Ben went on.

'Release papers.'

Ben didn't know what that meant.

Sweetland beckoned him with a crooked finger. 'Come here a minute,' he said.

Ben looked at his father who gave his reluctant approval with a shrug. Ben got up and crossed the floor. Sweetland crouched in front of him and put his warm hands on Ben's shoulders. 'Now, this is important: did you see him touch her?'

Ben nodded.

Sweetland's eyes flared. 'Good lad. When was that – when they'd got off?'

'No, sir,' said Ben, guessing that police officers were to be addressed like teachers. 'On the bus – he touched her leg. That's when she got up.'

Though his expression barely changed, Ben was able to detect that Sweetland was disappointed. 'Now, you're young, aren't you?' he said. 'And you've got good eyesight, haven't you? Think about it now, son –

did you see him touch her after they got off the bus? In the woods? Maybe he ran after her?'

'No, sir,' said Ben. 'He didn't run.'

Sweetland's grip tightened on Ben's shoulders and his eyes seemed to bore into Ben's skull. 'See,' he said, now almost whispering, 'we think he did touch her but we need to be able to prove it. Do you know what proof is?'

'Yes.'

'Right, well then.'

Ben's mouth opened and closed and he looked at his father and grandmother. She seemed to have transported herself from the room and was staring blankly.

Peter said, 'Tell the man, son.'

What did that mean? Ben didn't know what to say. He didn't want to lie and could feel the urge to cry rising from his chest, up his throat, forcing tears into his eyes. 'I didn't see him touch her.'

Sweetland sprang up, grim-faced.

Slapping a hand onto Ben's shoulder, he said, 'Good lad,' but it sounded like an insult. He seemed tightly wound, disgusted.

Peter cleared his throat. 'I, uh...' He looked down at his slippers. 'I saw him running after her, into the, uh...' He twirled a finger, trying to loosen the words. 'Into the trees, the, uh, wood, there.'

Sweetland smiled tightly. 'There we go,' he said. 'Did you see him touch her?'

Peter squirmed under Sweetland's gaze and squinted.

'It was dark.' He nodded. 'But I think so.'

'We don't like "think",' said Sweetland. 'Yes or no?'

'Yes.'

'Okay then,' said Sweetland with a reassuring half-wink. 'Then I'd like you to go to the station in Exeter and give a statement as soon as possible.'

He looked at his watch and made a decisive move towards the door. 'Goodbye, Mrs Hodge,' he said to Ben's grandmother as he stepped out into the hallway. His colleague followed him, nodding and making a gesture somewhere between a wave and a salute.

The front door slammed and they were gone.

Ben stared at Peter who refused to look back. He was chewing on the inside of his lip and picking at a nail, his eyes fixed on the net curtains.

'Did you really see him touch her, Dad?'

Peter nodded as if half asleep, averting his eyes. 'I wouldn't tell a lie to a policeman, son,' he said.

Ben lay prone on the front room floor, kicking his scuffed black trainers together, mesmerised by the television while the house filled with the smell of roasting meat and boiling cabbage.

The female newsreader said, with practised solemnity, 'On *West Country News* this Sunday: the hunt for a Devon girl missing since yesterday afternoon is intensifying as police fear she may have come to harm. From Berebroke near Exeter, here's our crime correspondent, Alison Kent.'

The reporter had a high-pitched, uncertain voice. 'It was on this footpath in a sleepy Devon village that 16-year-old Esther Garrett was last seen, and this is where police are concentrating their efforts.'

Leaves blew across the ground as the camera zoomed on a dog and handler rooting in the undergrowth, tossing aside ripped plastic bags and drinks bottles.

Cut to Detective Inspector Sweetland, the collar of his black overcoat pulled up around his face, handsome and earnest as he addressed the reporter off-screen. 'We would urge Esther to come forward as soon as possible if, for whatever reason, she has felt the need to leave the area voluntarily. But I'm afraid to say at this stage we do not believe that to be the case. We would also like to hear from any members of the public who might have seen her after 4.15 yesterday afternoon, or if they have any other information whatsoever.'

Then the reporter, on-screen, windswept in front of a line of police cars and vans in Berebroke's market square, apparently live: 'In the last few minutes, we have heard that police are eager to speak to nineteen-year-old Aaron Greenslade who they believe might be able to help them with their enquiries. Though they are unable to provide details at this time, they have warned members of the public not to approach him but to call the emergency hotline.'

A photograph of Greenslade appeared against an electric blue background.

'Evil,' said a voice over Ben's shoulder. He looked round to see his grandmother drawing on a cigarette. She hesitated and exhaled smoke. 'It's all about sex these days.' She frowned. 'What are you watching the news for, anyway? Ain't there no cartoons on?'

Ben shook his head.

'Dinner's ready anyway,' she said, stubbing her cigarette out in an orange plastic ashtray.

They ate in the kitchen, the three of them arranged round a table pushed against the wall over which hung a crude oil painting of a herd of charging elephants.

'Do they think she's dead?' asked Ben.

'Maybe,' said Peter, putting down his fork and rubbing his eyes with a shaking hand. May blew smoke in his direction and tutted.

'Poor thing,' he said. 'Poor little thing.'

Ben begged to be allowed to watch the evening news broadcast before being driven back to his mother's house but there were no new developments except that the passing of time and the fall of darkness increased the sense of inevitability.

'It won't be good news now,' said his grandmother, looking up from the *TV Times*.

Ben, sports bag in hand and ski jacket on, ready to leave, shuddered.

'Maybe she just stayed over at her friend's house,' he said. 'Perhaps she fell down and hurt her leg or something, or she might have run away.' He looked at his grandmother with wide eyes. 'She was too...' He couldn't complete the thought: too special, too beautiful, too alive, to be a victim.

Peter stamped into the room and shook a set of car keys.

'Right,' he said, his face set colourless and grim.

In the car Ben was silent as pop music came from the radio on its lowest volume setting. He could hear his father's every sniff and sigh, and smelled the tang of his sweat and coffee breath.

'You all right, son?' he asked.

'Yeah,' said Ben.

The silence resumed, growing heavier and more uncomfortable as the journey wore on. Eventually, Ben decided to break it by telling a lie. 'I've got to go up in assembly tomorrow.'

He didn't know where the idea had come from – sometimes, he just opened his mouth and let the words come out. It was exciting.

'Yeah?' said Peter, failing to sound interested.

'I saw an old man fall over outside the school and I went to help him. He broke his arm but I told him not to move and picked up his shopping – all these oranges and apples went in the road. Then I went and got a teacher and they called an ambulance. And I stayed with him until the ambulance came.'

There hadn't been an old man or an ambulance, but the more Ben spoke the more he convinced himself it was true.

Peter glanced across at him, eyebrows raised in appreciation. 'Good lad.'

Ben shrugged. 'It was instinct, really.'

Peter gave him a nod. 'It's good to help people – always try to help, if you can, especially the old ones.'

That reminded them both about their failure to help Esther Garrett and the conversation died. This new silence was darker.

They pulled onto the estate where his mother lived. It had been built over the preceding decade in several units and was called Orchard Meadows after the landscape it had replaced. The houses were all peach-coloured brick and white trim, some looking unfinished and unlived in, while others were already peeling and tatty. The roads were scattered with grit and sand from passing construction vehicles working on the final phase, out towards the motorway junction.

As the car cruised along the main artery road, Orchard Avenue, Ben and his father repeated their standard dialogue for want of anything else to say.

'All right?'

'Yeah.'

A voice began to murmur in the background – the hourly news on the radio. Ben turned it up.

'In the last few minutes, police searching for missing Devon school-girl Esther Garrett have begun searching a disused military airfield near the village where she was last seen–'

Peter switched it off. 'Morbid,' he said.

Ben chewed a nail. 'I want to be a policeman when I'm grown-up,' he said.

'Yeah?' said Peter, distracted and barely registering what Ben had said. He pulled the car into the side of the road and honked the horn.

Ben moved to get out, popping the door, but his father stopped him by wrapping a hand around his head and pulling him close so that he could plant an awkward, cold kiss on Ben's temple. 'Look after yourself, son,' he said. 'Give me a ring on Wednesday, like usual, all right?' He shoved Ben's head away with a half-push, half-caress, and Ben smiled as he climbed out of the car.

On the doorstep, his mother, Ellie, was waiting – a silhouette haloed with cigarette smoke in the light from the street. As the car pulled away, she raised a hand to display a middle finger at its red rear lights.

She took Ben's shoulder and pushed him into the warmth of the house.

'Mum–' he began, but she interrupted, pressing a hand to her temple.

'I've got a headache.' She tugged her long cardigan round herself and shuffled barefooted into the dimly-lit front room. The TV was on and he could see a glass of wine balanced on the arm of the sofa. Ben put down his sports bag, took off his coat, and removed his shoes. She curled up on the sofa, tucking her feet under herself, and picked up the wine glass.

'Dad said I had to tell you something.'

She closed her eyes. 'What now?'

'It's about the girl who's gone missing.'

She frowned, squinting. 'What?'

He hesitated, trying not to sound proud. 'I saw her on Dad's bus. We both did.'

Her head slumped to one side with exhaustion. 'Oh, God. What's he done now?'

'Didn't you see?' Ben said, and gestured at the TV.

She shook her head wearily and held the wine glass up to the light, swirling it, her eyes glazed, shut off from him.

When he realised she wasn't going to say anything, he stepped back-wards out of the front room and slipped upstairs.

He didn't turn the light on in his room: there was enough from the moon and the orange street lights. Gunshots sounded from the TV downstairs. He dragged his plastic swivel chair to the window and sat on it, looking over his folded arms over the windowsill and out into the street. From the other houses came flickering blue from television screens, or the steady yellow-white glow of house lights. He couldn't see beyond the close but knew that he was looking towards Berebroke.

Clamping his eyes closed, he muttered a prayer. 'Please let them find her tonight.' He blinked and then gave a small, startled gasp, before whispering, 'Alive, I mean.'

CHAPTER THREE

T he rattling of the milkman's float woke Ben up and the cold
stopped him going back to sleep so he went downstairs in his
pyjamas, barefoot and shivering.

He noticed that three wine bottles were lined up by his mother's end
of the sofa and that the ashtray Nan had won at bingo was overflowing
with cigarette ends. The front room smelled stale, like the British
Legion club in a Portakabin to which his grandfather sometimes
took him.

He turned on the TV and quickly jabbed at the rubbery keys on the
remote to get the volume as low as it would go. He watched the second
half of the national news with drowsy disinterest but sat upright when
the local bulletin began.

'Police have been searching through the night at the former RAF
Medleigh near Berebroke, Devon, in the hunt for missing schoolgirl
Esther Garrett.'

There was a shot of a plain of broken concrete under portable flood-
lights; another of black-coated men swinging sticks through undergrowth. Esther's school photograph filled the screen.

'The sixteen-year-old was last seen leaving a bus on Saturday afternoon and police are increasingly concerned for her safety.'

Detective Inspector Sweetland, buffeted by wind, grimly determined. 'We would urge anyone who knows anything whatsoever that might help in our investigation to come forward—'

Ben noticed that Sweetland was no longer addressing Esther directly.

'—and we are increasingly keen to talk to Aaron Greenslade.'

The mug shot appeared on screen and the news reporter said, 'The public are urged not to approach Mr Greenslade who *West Country News* understands has a history of violent behaviour and might be armed with a knife. Instead, police are asking them to call this number.'

White digits scrolled across the screen.

'In the meantime, Esther's family can only wait. And hope.'

He turned off the TV and, with a sigh, set about making his own breakfast and packing a lunch for school. Then he showered and dressed. He hovered outside his mother's bedroom door for a moment listening to the sound of her snoring before creeping out of the house.

'We would seriously urge you to come forward,' he muttered to himself in the gruffest voice he could manage. 'Freeze – Detective Inspector Hodge, CID.'

Mist made the sounds of traffic on the main road sound soft and distant, and diffused the weak morning light, sapping the colour from everything. Ben could hear his own clothes rustling and the sound of his breath as he walked with his sports bag over one shoulder. At the end of the close, he hesitated and then, instead of turning right towards his school, headed left and downhill, in the direction of the arcade of shops at the centre of the estate. A delivery truck was mounted on the pavement in front of the brightly-lit Spar convenience store. The building was designed to resemble a wayside Tudor inn with black and white faux half-timbering and a free-standing post cast in concrete, at the top of which a signboard swung in the wind.

He approached the door on which a sign read: 'POLITE NOTICE: No more than two unaccompanied under-sixteens at any time. Thank you.' He pushed it open and stepped inside, avoiding the gaze of the bleary-eyed woman behind the counter who was cutting open large bundles of cigarette packets with a pen knife. The newspapers were on a wire rack at the end of a row of shelving. The best picture was on the cover of the local newspaper, the *Exeter Chronicle*, which had reproduced the school photograph in colour, but *The Sun* was cheaper, and had a small version of the same picture. His sweaty fingers felt the coins in his pocket and, reluctantly, he snatched up a copy of the red-topped tabloid.

'You're too young to be looking at page three,' said the woman behind the counter.

Ben blushed. 'It's for my dad,' he said.

She smirked. 'I'm only joking with you, love.' She held out a hand and Ben reached up to drop his coins into her palm.

Outside, he looked around, peering into what had become a dense fog, from which rose children's voices. He placed the newspaper carefully inside his jacket and began to walk towards school, but veered off as he passed the small park behind the shops. He climbed the stile and felt wet grass around his ankles, soaking through his black trainers. The park was empty and silent, apart from the tap-tapping of condensing fog dripping onto leathery fallen leaves. Breathing heavily, he headed to the picnic table at the centre of the park and placed his bag on it. He unfolded the newspaper and placed it flat on the slimy, green, dew-wet wood. A breeze gently lifted but then dropped the front page.

He looked at her for a long time, waiting for her to complete the gesture in which she had been captured by the photographer – the smile turning to a laugh. Even on paper, in the dull ink which now covered his fingers, she seemed to him as bright as a star. 'Don't worry, miss,' he said, making his voice as low as it would go. 'I'm on the case now.'

A crow cried and startled him out of his daydream.

Realising the time, he unzipped his bag and rummaged for a ruler which he used to tear carefully around the photograph. He held it for a moment, his lips twitching in confusion at a combination of guilt, fear and excitement. Then he folded it and tucked it into his shirt pocket.

At school, he had more immediate problems to deal with – getting from one class to another without a dead arm or having his bag taken, and finding a safe corner of the playground where no one would bother him as he ate his sandwiches. In a few quiet moments he remembered the slip of paper in his pocket and touched it anxiously, his cheeks turning pink, as he was certain that everyone knew it was there. After school, with the light already dimming, he dawdled in the school library, hoping to avoid the boisterous crowds around the school gates, and then wandered home, stopping to throw stones on the wasteland until it really was dark.

At home, he let himself in with a Yale key, and went straight to his room without turning on a light. He drew the curtains and then took the picture from his pocket. He looked at it for a lingering moment before slipping it into an envelope and then into the space beneath the bottom drawer of the rickety wardrobe – his favourite hiding place.

Changing into jeans and sweatshirt, he ran downstairs, made himself a salad cream and cheese sandwich, poured a glass of orange squash, and turned on the TV. On ITV, the national news was just beginning.

Ben held his breath.

'In Devon, fears grow for a missing sixteen-year-old schoolgirl who, police now suspect, may have been abducted.'

He exhaled and, for a passing moment, felt relieved that she hadn't turned up safe and well. Immediately, a wave of shame hit him – he didn't want her to be hurt, or to be dead. He didn't understand what he wanted.

'A nineteen-year-old Exeter man, Aaron Greenslade, was arrested this afternoon in connection with Esther's disappearance, but has not yet been charged. Police have forty-eight hours to question him.'

He heard footsteps on the driveway and then a key in the latch. Instinctively, he reached for the control to switch channels.

'Meanwhile, Esther's parents have made an emotional appeal–'

The bright colours of an Australian soap opera filled the screen as his mother stepped into the hallway and turned on the lights. 'What are you doing sitting in the dark?' She dropped her sagging, scuffed handbag and collapsed onto the sofa next to him. He looked up at her and took a bite from his sandwich, his eyes wide.

She was thinner than ever, paler than ever, and her eyes looked sunken. Her hair was dark and fine, tied back untidily into a limp ponytail.

'I got a call from that policeman today,' she said. 'He told me that there's no need for you to give a statement.'

Ben took another bite.

'I spoke to your dad, too.'

Ben stopped chewing and licked crumbs from his lips.

'I don't want you on that bus anymore,' she said. 'I've told him that. Either you stay with me at the weekend when he's on shift, or you stay with your Nan.' She and May Hodge had never liked each other and she couldn't help turning her lip.

'But Mum—'

'It's not a debate,' she snapped back. 'It's not safe.' Her features softened. 'You must get bored, anyway, don't you?'

Sulking, Ben nodded. 'Suppose.'

As she began to search her bag for a packet of cigarettes, Ben put down the plate with the half-finished sandwich and spoke with almost theatrical mournfulness. 'Mum?'

'Yes?'

'Can we have a newspaper delivered?' He looked away. 'It's for a school project.' He could have stopped there but the urge to lie creatively overtook him. 'We've got to cut out stories about wildlife and nature and the environment and that and then we're going to make a big display for the library.'

She looked in pain. 'I'm not sure we can afford it – don't they have them at school?'

Ben scowled, red spots forming high on his cheeks.

'Oh, God, don't sulk – I'll pop round to the newsagent in the morning.'

Ben smiled. 'Thanks Mum.'

'Funny you should suddenly be interested in newspapers, though, because as it happens you've got newspaper ink all over your face.' She grabbed his arm to hold him still, licked her fingers and began to rub at his face.

Ben raised a hand to fend her off and then began to scrub frantically with his own bunched sleeve. He didn't cry – he had just reached the age where tears no longer came easily – but he blushed and began to breathe heavily.

'Oh, for God's sake!' she said, 'It's not the end of the world.'

Ben struggled free and ran upstairs, boiling over with shame.

He locked himself in the bathroom and washed his face until every trace of smut had gone. He stayed there, sitting on the closed lid of the toilet, until he heard the distant sound of a jazz LP, and his mother's breathy, wordless singing accompanying it.

Ben sat cross-legged on the front room floor with a book open in front of him. His mother was reclining on the sofa in her dressing gown, her hair wrapped in a towel, a glass of wine in her hand. Ben's grandfather, Dennis, was in the armchair with his bony, arthritic hands on his knees, wheezing in and out. Dinner plates were stacked on the coffee table along with three empty yoghurt pots. All three of them had their eyes fixed on the TV screen.

'She'll be dead, sure enough,' said Dennis.

Ben looked at his grandfather who was shaking his head, peering from beneath wild, still-dark eyebrows.

'It's only been a couple of days, Dad,' said Ellie, wearily. 'She might just have run away, or–'

'No, she'll be dead, and it'll be her dad, or an uncle, or a brother who did it. Keep it in the family – that's what they say, isn't it, these country-side types?'

'Oh, for heaven's sake.'

Dennis rolled the next word around his mouth like brandy. 'Incest.'

'Dad!'

'She hasn't got a brother anyway,' said Ben.

Dennis raised his eyebrows, then raised himself up on the arms of the chair and, smiling, said, 'How the hell do you know that?'

'Newspaper,' said Ben.

'Newspaper, he says! Bloody hell.' Dennis shook his head and laughed to himself.

Ben felt a creeping sensation in his gut. When he was only six he'd been forced to sit through a film about 'strangers' at school which had given him nightmares. He'd also heard children at school tell stories about a local man called Kenny Brown who was supposed to be in prison but, before he was sent away, had lured a girl into his mother's shed and molested her. Ben didn't quite understand what that meant, not exactly, but he knew it was bad, and that Kenny Brown was a kind of bogeyman.

On screen appeared Esther Garrett's mother and father, pale and shaking as camera flashes assaulted them in a rolling wave. Her father, round-faced, with a wispy blonde moustache, spoke for both of them in a fragile, stilted voice with a heavy local accent. 'Every morning we wake up without our Esther—'

'I wouldn't leave *him* alone with any kiddies, personally,' said Dennis.

'—brings new heartache, but we remain hopeful that we will have her back with us by Christmas.'

'Fat chance,' Dennis said.

'If you know where Esther is, we ask you, please, please tell the police.'

Esther appeared on the screen. It was grainy VHS camcorder footage, slowed down to a series of still images. It had been filmed somewhere sunny. She was wearing a huge white T-shirt and her hair was tied up in a knot. She was bent over with laughter, dimpling her cheeks, her eyes gleaming.

'Been fed to pigs, I daresay. They leave nothing behind.'

'Dad!' hissed Ellie, 'Do you have to talk like that in front of Ben?'

Dennis laughed, grim and knowing. 'Don't be so soft – kids love a gruesome story, don't they, Ben? Eh?'

The report on Esther Garrett ended and Ben looked back down at his book, pretending to read.

When Ellie went upstairs to get dressed, Ben cleared his throat. 'Grandpa?'

'Yes?'

'Can I have your newspaper, if you've finished with it?'

His mother had started getting *The Sun* but Dennis always read the *Daily Mirror* and Ben was interested to see if it had different pictures or details. Dennis looked down at the ragged roll he'd wedged between his leg and the arm of the chair.

'For the cartoons,' said Ben.

NEW WORLD NEWS

Since 2000

№ 768365569

CLUES IN SEARCH FOR MISSING GIRL

Police in Exeter have appealed for witnesses after clothing and a bag belonging to missing 16-year-old Esther Garrett were found in the city early yesterday morning.

At a press conference, Detective Inspector Steven Sweetland of Devon and Cornwall CID asked members of the public living and working in the Marsh Barton area of the city to come forward and report anything suspicious they might have seen.

As hopes of finding Esther alive begin to fade, DI Sweetland also confirmed that Aaron Greenslade, the 19-year-old Exeter man arrested last week, is still being held for questioning, and that no other suspects are being sought.

CHAPTER FOUR

The pub was called The London Coach but everyone knew it by the name of the national chain to which it belonged, the Maltsters Feast. Until a few years before, it hadn't been a pub at all but a nursing home, though the brewery's designers had done a good job of making it look like an old coaching inn with fibreglass fittings and horse brasses bought by the kilo. A sign outside promised 'Family Fun', two meals for £10, and a ball pit presided over by a children's television character. Inside, it was brightly lit, wipe clean, and smelled of hot chip oil. It rang with the laughter of children, backed by the sound of a looping tape of recent pop songs.

A long silence had hung between Peter and Ben as they sat opposite each other at a small table out of the way in a tacked-on conservatory, during which Ben read one of the comics his father had brought him.

'Is that good, then?' asked Peter eventually, stubbing out his cigarette and blowing the last of its smoke away over his shoulder. He picked up the pint of Guinness on the table, next to his empty plate, and took a swig which coated his upper lip with off-white foam.

'It's all right,' said Ben. His cheeks reddened. 'I don't really collect Marvel.'

'Oh, right,' said Peter.

'I like *2000 AD*, mostly. Judge Dredd.'

'Blimey — is he still going?'

Ben nodded.

There was another long silence. Peter sipped his drink, scratched his head, and craned to look around the pub. Ben noticed him looking at the waitresses who hurried back and forth.

'You must get bored, hanging round with me all the time,' said Peter after a while, patting his pockets.

Ben shook his head. 'I like it.'

Peter smiled unevenly and, for a moment, his eyes sparked.

'I like it too.' He'd found a packet of cigarettes in the pocket of his black Harrington jacket and picked at the cellophane with his long nails.

Ben cleared his throat and said nervously, 'I keep thinking about that girl.'

Inspecting the cigarette he'd pulled out, Peter nodded with his lips pressed together. 'Me too, son — me too.'

His father reached over the table and put a hand over Ben's entire face. 'Exterminate!'

Ben giggled, and Peter laughed too.

'We did what we could. I did, anyway — you're only little, so you couldn't do anything. I just wanted him off the bus.'

Peter lit the cigarette, leaned back and put his arm over the back of his chair so that he could look around the pub. 'I have to deal with people like that all the time — junkies, alkies, fucking arseholes—' He checked himself. 'Sorry, son.'

'They should give you a gun.' Ben squinted as he considered the problem. 'Or a cage you could put them in while you drive them to the police station.'

Peter raised his eyebrows and gave a quiet, dry laugh. 'They don't pay me enough for any of that.' The laugh stopped abruptly and he leaned forward. 'Look, don't worry about it — you know what girls are like anyway,' he said. 'She's probably run off with a boyfriend or something.'

Ben frowned. 'They said that she wasn't like that.'

'Oh, you'd be surprised,' said his father. 'Bonny-looking lassie.'

A blush crept over Ben's cheeks.

'Do you want an ice cream, then? Sundae, banana split — whatever you like. Special treat.'

Ben reached for the menu and then, a moment later, looked up from its pages. 'Can I have a scrapbook, too?' he asked.

With a baffled shrug, Peter said, 'All right.'

As they drove home along the main road, they passed a lay-by full of white Leyland police vans. Peter slowed the car and glanced across. Ben pressed his face against the window and saw over the low stone wall a field of tall reeds. A row of black-clad policemen was moving across it in a slow ripple, their heads down, shoulders hunched. They were swinging sticks, probing the vegetation, heading towards woodland which filled the hillside rising across the field. Though he couldn't see them, Ben could hear dogs splashing in the water, and see the leads stretching out from the grips of their handlers.

A policeman in a high-visibility jacket, breathing steam, stepped from the side of the road and waved them on with visible irritation. Ben's father pulled over instead.

'Wind your window down,' Peter said to Ben, who did as he was told.

The policeman leaned down. 'It's not a show for your entertainment, sir — move along.'

'No, listen,' said Peter softly. He gestured at Ben. 'I'm a dad myself. Is there anything I can do to help, like?'

The policeman spoke more warmly. 'Oh, I see. We're not asking for help from the public at the moment, sir.'

'All right then,' Peter said. 'Good luck.' He gave a quick salute — the kind he gave other bus drivers when they passed on the road — and pulled away.

'I wish I could help, too,' said Ben.

'Careful what you wish for, son. It might not be so good to find her now, after all this time.'

'What do you mean?'

Peter looked across at him. 'Never mind,' he said.

As the car climbed the hill, Ben looked back down over the field with its black line of men and imagined Esther lying in the grass with her eyes closed and a smile on her dark lips, waiting to be discovered.

NEW WORLD NEWS

Since 2000

MAN CHARGED WITH ESTHER GARRETT MURDER

Police have taken the unusual step of charging 19-year-old Aaron Greenslade of Exeter with the murder of the missing Devon schoolgirl Esther Garrett even though she has yet to be found dead or alive.

Esther, 16, was last seen on 11 November entering woodland near Berebroke, a village between Exeter and Okehampton, only yards from her family home.

In a statement, a police spokesman confirmed that the ongoing search is now focused on finding a body and that specialist dog teams have been drafted in from outside the county. Speaking to reporters outside the central police station he said: 'We have a compelling case against Mr Greenslade and hope that he will be able to tell us where we can find Esther and bring some peace of mind to her family.'

CHAPTER FIVE

Under the harsh light of a low wattage, unshaded bulb, Ben sat on the edge of his bed watching his cousin rifle through the cardboard box in which he kept his comics. Chelsea wasn't really his cousin but he called his mother's best friend Auntie Jeanette, and Chelsea was her daughter. She was six months older than him, taller, and much less shy. She had long white-blonde hair and a face which, when resting, looked pinched and bullish.

'These are so boring,' she said, throwing a comic at him with force. He flinched as it hit him and then gathered it in his arms. She'd creased it and he tried to straighten it out without looking as if he cared too much.

She stood up, put her hands in the pockets of her jeans, and puffed out her cheeks. 'You're boring,' she said. 'I might go downstairs with the grown-ups.' She turned her head to the door and listened, a strand of stray hair falling over her cheek.

From beyond the hallway came the sound of Jeanette's shrill laugh as the man she had brought with her spoke in a bassy, resonant murmur that rose through the floor. One of Ellie's LPs was on, turned up too loud for a Monday night, with pattering drums and occasional squeals from a trumpet. As always when Jeanette visited, there was the smell of something sweet, earthy and green on the air.

Ben stared at his feet. 'Do you want to see my scrapbook?'

Her head snapped back and she snorted. 'Scrapbooks are for girls.'

Ignoring the intended insult, Ben leaned back and rummaged in the crack at the side of his bed, and then pulled out the oversized book with its lurid orange cover and dark green sugar paper pages.

Suspicious but intrigued, Chelsea took a step closer. 'What's in it?'

'Do you know that girl that went missing?'

Chelsea wrinkled her nose. 'What girl?'

'Don't you even watch the news?'

Chelsea responded with a solid downward punch to his arm which he received with an open-mouthed but silent wince.

'Show me,' she said, snatching the book from him and sitting down next to him.

She turned to the first page and, at once, he felt his cheeks begin to burn. The portrait shot of Esther Garrett was centred there with her name written neatly underneath in felt tip ink.

'Is she dead?' asked Chelsea, placing an extended finger on the picture as if trying to reach through it.

'I don't know,' said Ben. 'She's just missing.' He took the book back and turned to the last page. 'The police think she's dead, though.'

After a moment, Chelsea said, 'They thought my dad disappeared, but it turned out he'd just moved to Wolverhampton with a woman from work. Anyway, why do you care?'

'I was the last person ever to see her alive,' said Ben, and then frowned at what had sounded like a boast. It was the kind of story he might have made up when the need to lie overcame him – only this time it was completely true.

Chelsea smirked. 'Don't be stupid – that must be whoever killed her.'

'Because she was on my dad's bus and she got off and walked into the forest—'

'Like Little Red Riding Hood.'

Ben gave the smallest of nods and looked away. He took a breath and then hesitated before speaking. 'How could someone hurt a person like that?'

'Like what?' Chelsea said, loading the query with scorn.

Ben blushed. 'She was just a nice person, that's all.'

'Like a goody two-shoes?'

'No,' said Ben, defensively.

'There's a girl in my year, Kerry, who's really square. Even though she's quite pretty, she's never had a boyfriend.'

Ben blushed and looked sideways at Chelsea. Did that mean that she had had a boyfriend? He couldn't imagine her kissing anyone.

'And she never gets in any trouble. Doesn't talk in class. Reads at playtime. She never even hands her homework in late. I think her family are Bible-bashers or something.' Then, with a grunt, she snatched the scrapbook and began to flip through its pages.

'Maybe you should go out with Kerry – you're both weird. And this thing is totally weird,' she said, meaning the scrapbook.

Ben wondered whether being weird was better or worse than being boring.

She raised her left eyebrow and smirked. 'I'm going to tell your mum,' she said.

'No!' said Ben and leapt up, grabbing for the scrapbook.

She giggled and turned away from him, forcing him to circle her, and then jumped onto the bed. When Ben tried to follow her, she kicked him away, taking the breath out of his lungs, and his eyes began to water.

'You're such a baby,' she said, rolling her eyes, and shoved the book at him. 'I'm sorry, all right?'

The music downstairs stopped and Jeanette's voice rose up the staircase, 'Chelsea, love – we're going.'

'Good luck finding your girlfriend, weirdo,' Chelsea said as she left the room.

NEW WORLD NEWS

Since 2060

MEMORIAL CEREMONY FOR MISSING GIRL

The family of Devon schoolgirl Esther Garrett, who disappeared early in November, are to hold a memorial ceremony in Beretroke next Tuesday, 1 December.

Her father, Edward, 41, told us in an emotional interview, that he and his wife have given up hope of seeing Esther alive. 'What we have been told by police,' he said, 'leaves us in no doubt that our darling daughter is dead. We know we're not supposed to say that, but it's true, and it's destroyed us. She was the light of our life and a truly wonderful person who shone brightly for all of her 16 years.'

The ceremony will be held at St Leonard's Church and members of the public are welcome to attend.

Esther's school, King Alfred's, held a special assembly in her memory, at which her fellow pupils shared their recollections of their friend and classmate. 'Esther was always the first person there if you needed help,' Melissa, 16, told our reporter. 'She wanted to be a doctor or a nurse when she left school,' said the school's headmistress, Edith Martin. 'Her kindness and her smile will be sorely missed.'

CHAPTER SIX

B en was lying on the sofa in his pyjamas reading a comic in the milky morning light that bled through the net curtains.

His mother entered the room, moving quickly, muttering to herself as she looked for her car keys. She was wearing a freshly cleaned blue tunic and her hair was tied back into a tight knot. She found the keys on the windowsill, dropped them into her bag, and stepped over to stand beside him. 'Right, well. You know where the sandwich things are. If you get cold, put the heating on. If you go out—'

'Yeah, I know – don't forget the key,' he said, rolling his eyes.

'I'll be home at seven. If you need anything, ring granddad at work.'

'Okay,' he said, flatly.

She hovered. 'Right, well, bye then.'

'Yeah.' He kept his eyes fixed on the page of the ragged, year-old issue of *2000 AD* he had propped against his knees. He became alert when he heard the front door close, the rusting Ford Fiesta start on the second attempt, and the thin yowl of its engine disappear into the mist.

Certain he was alone, he threw down the comic, leapt to his feet and ran upstairs, taking them two at a time. He dressed in cords, T-shirt, tracksuit top and trainers. He opened a red lockable tin on his desk and took out £7.50 in change, saved from his pocket money over several weeks, augmented with coins his grandfather had found behind his ear. He tipped the contents of his school sport bag out onto the bed and took the bag downstairs where he made two sandwiches and stuffed them inside with two cartons of juice, a packet of crisps, and two chocolate bars. He put the front door key in his trouser pocket, put on his anorak, and left the house, slamming the door behind him.

Glancing at his watch, he broke into an ungainly run – the bus that passed on the main road was almost due. The dampness in the air, poised between fog and drizzle, caught in his lungs and, unused to exercise, he was out of breath within seconds. As he rounded the corner, he saw that Chelsea was waiting for him at the bus stop, her padded jacket gleaming white. He waved as he jogged and she waved back.

'Hi,' he panted, dropping his bag on the damp pavement and bending double.

'You're not right in the head.'

'Did I miss the bus?' he asked, panting between each word.

'No, it's always late,' she said.

Crows cried, echoing across the empty streets of the new estate from the twisted old apple trees which marked the line where farmland began.

The 11b finally slid out of the mist ten minutes late, its headlights on, and with almost no passengers: it was a once a day, village crawling, back route bus, little used and heavily subsidised. Chelsea boarded first, smiling brightly. 'Two child tickets to Fox's Cross, please.'

'Bit young to be travelling on your own,' said the driver. He had long grey hair, a yellowing white moustache which hung over a mouthful of teeth almost the same shade, and was wearing tinted glasses, just like Ben's father usually did.

'Oh, it's okay,' said Ben. 'Our granny is meeting us at the other end.'

Chelsea looked surprised and then smirked, almost sniggered, not being as used to lying as Ben. He was worried the bus driver would notice, but he didn't – he just grunted and punched a button on the ticket machine which spat out a length of purple-printed paper.

'Two forty.'

Ben leaned forward and counted the money out of his sweating palm while Chelsea tore the tickets free. The doors slammed shut and the bus floated free from the kerb as they stumbled towards the back, observed warily by an elderly woman on one side and a serious-looking Chinese woman in work overalls on the other.

They sat in silence at the back of the bus for a few minutes. Ben was anxious and still out of breath, and there was something deadening about the view from the window – trees with a few last rusty leaves and rain-blackened bark; hedgerows reduced to tangles of thorn and shredded litter; hillsides ploughed terracotta red.

Chelsea spoke first. 'Say that she is dead, right?'

'Yeah?'

'Well, how do you make a dead body just disappear anyway?'

'There's loads of ways,' said Ben. He shifted to face her, gripping the chromed bar of the seat in front, his eyes widening. 'I got some books out of the library – books about murders and that. One man *immersed* his victims in acid.'

The old woman in the seat ahead of them turned to stare disapprovingly. Ben ducked his head and lowered his voice. 'All that was left of them was teeth.'

'Gross,' said Chelsea. 'What else?'

'Well, look outside,' said Ben. Chelsea glanced over his shoulder. 'All those fields and ditches. You just need to be careful and you can bury a body so it never gets found.' They passed a field which rolled down into a valley where five or six decrepit caravans were parked, green with moss, and surrounded by deserted pig pens.

Chelsea wrinkled her nose and shook her head. 'Someone would see you, and you'd get covered in mud. I bet it takes ages to dig a properly deep enough hole.'

'Or you can do it in a house. Reginald Christie–'

'Who?'

'I'm telling you now. He's in the book I read. He killed loads of people and just hid them in the walls of his house.'

At this, Chelsea looked troubled. 'It's like a horror film.' She gave a cackling laugh. 'Have you seen Simon Capp's death video?'

'No,' said Ben. 'Who's Simon Capp?'

'Oh, he's this boy in my year. His brother gave him this video with loads of deaths. I think it's called the *Face of Death* or something.'

'Is it like…' Ben had never seen any horror films and racked his brains. 'Is it like *Nightmare on Elm Street*?'

'No, it's actually all real, and you can go to prison just for having a copy of the tape, apparently. There's this one bit, right, where this man shoots himself in the head–'

'That's horrible.'

Chelsea looked deflated. 'Actually, it's really wicked.'

Biting his lip, Ben looked out to see that they were passing a sparse row of houses behind which loomed skeletal farm buildings. The bus entered a small market square with a war memorial and two pubs, all built from the same grey stone, with the same sharp gothic features – conceived as a piece 400 years ago, the fancy of an aristocrat, and a meeting place for the hounds and horses of the hunt. The bus swung round to face back the way it had come before the driver called out, 'Who wanted Fox's Cross?'

Chelsea leapt up and bounced, half-dancing, down the aisle, with Ben following behind with his bag over one shoulder.

'Thanks, mister,' she said, as they jumped down onto the tarmac.

The driver peered out from behind his dark lenses and shouted after them, 'Where's your granny?'

'She'll be here in a minute,' said Chelsea and stared back at him, smiling, but challenging.

With a grunt, he closed the door and the bus pulled away. They waited until it was out of sight, surrounded by blank windows and a mist that was thicker than it had been in town. The air smelled sickly, fruity – a pungent mixture of manure and vegetation. That smell was overlaid with woodsmoke and the lingering exhaust fumes of the bus.

After almost a minute of pretending to wait, Chelsea pointed to the lane at the side of the pub.

'It's up there. I reckon it will take us twenty minutes.'

Ben looked at his watch: it was just after quarter past ten.

As they strode past unoccupied holiday cottages, phone numbers displayed on cards in dark panes, Chelsea looked at Ben with a frown. 'If she is dead, she won't look like the picture in your scrapbook anymore, you know. She'll be rotten.'

Red spots appeared high on Ben's cheeks under his eyes. 'Shut up,' he said. 'Stop being disgusting.'

She lashed out with a fist, which he dodged, neither of them breaking their stride. 'You were the one who started going on about people going in acid and dead bodies in ditches.'

The lane petered out, becoming a dirt track with vehicle ruts and a line of lush grass down its centre, running past a row of cottages hidden behind high wooden fences. Soon, that became a turning place where a pick-up truck and van were parked, and then stopped altogether at a wooden stile where a green sign that read PUBLIC FOOTPATH pointed away into a gloomy tunnel of vegetation. Chelsea was over the stile in an instant, almost vaulting it, but Ben considered it for a moment before clambering across, hesitant and ungainly.

'It's another fifteen minutes now,' said Chelsea. She was red-cheeked, not through exertion, but because it was cold, and perhaps also because she was excited. Ben nodded and followed her silently as they passed under the strangely twisted stems of denuded hawthorn and the silvery branches of sloe. Beneath their feet was a slippery mixture of mud and rotting leaves, while from over their heads came constant and numerous crow cries so loud they might almost have been electrically amplified.

'I didn't know there were so many paths,' said Ben. 'What happens if we get lost?'

'We won't,' said Chelsea. 'Do you remember Bruce, my old stepdad? He used to work out here and he took me and mum on loads of walks. I know it quite well.'

Ben recalled meeting Bruce once or twice – an unshaven, wax jacket-clad figure lurking in the garden at a Christmas Eve party, smoking roll-ups; or sitting in the dining room with Peter, sharing cigars and downing cans of cider, talking half-heartedly about cars and rugby.

Over their heads, the scrawny trees and tangled branches began to thin, and soon they were walking across a clearing towards a ridge.

'Look!' cried Chelsea, stopping dead as she reached the edge. Ben fell in beside her, panting. They looked out from one hillside across to another, with Berebroke settled in between, the remains of the morning mist sitting in the valley around it like a smoke circle. From on high, Ben could make out the squat grey tower of a church and row after row of houses, car headlights weaving among them. A dog was barking, uttering the same sound over and again like a tape loop.

'Come on then,' said Chelsea, half-jumping, half-sliding on the wet grass, making for the stile at the bottom of the field, on the edge of the churchyard.

The other side of the path was tarmacked but still muddy and scattered about with empty cider cans and ancient, faded crisp packets. As they passed the church's side gate, Ben stopped and looked across the churchyard, over the crumbling stumps of old headstones and a lichen-covered stone angel, half-fallen through subsidence. The crows in the treetops above entered a frenzy. Ben pictured Esther Garrett's family and friends walking up to the door of the church.

'Have you ever been to a funeral?' he asked.

Chelsea shrugged. 'I was too little for my granny's.'

'I don't ever want to go to a funeral,' said Ben.

'You'll come to mine though, won't you?' she said. 'I'll come to yours.'

Ben squinted. Was it a joke?

She stamped onward.

The path took them onto The Street — the central artery around which Berebroke had been built. There was a row of shops and a decrepit-looking pub, its windows dark and flyblown. Cars were parked along either side of the road. In the distance, dark figures in hats and gloves were unloading a lorry, sending reverberant booming sounds into the gloom.

'Jesus. Who'd want to live here?' said Chelsea.

Ben felt a tightening in his stomach. 'We should have told someone we were coming,' he said. He looked around and wiped his cold, red nose. 'If there's someone taking children, I mean.'

A silver car crawled by almost silently and the driver, a middle-aged man in smoked glasses, turned to look at them as he passed.

'Do you want to see this stupid wood or not?' said Chelsea, attempting bluffness, but too quiet to pull it off, her voice wavering.

'Of course,' said Ben.

'Then it's this way,' said Chelsea, pointing to a turning off The Street, past a plain chapel with a chained gate and crumbling plaster.

Soon, they were walking through a new estate which seemed to have been lifted from the edge of a larger town and transplanted into the countryside. The houses were built from generic red brick with white-painted wooden trim and faux-Victorian porch lanterns. It looked almost like the set of a soap opera – as if each house was only a shell, blank beyond the front door. The front gardens were sparsely planted, gravelled over, or, in some cases, had been used to store rubbish – rolled-up carpets, stripped-down motorbikes, rotting cardboard boxes. Christmas lights twinkled in windows, and the front door of number eight had a large holly wreath hanging from its brass knocker.

'We're almost there,' said Chelsea. She moved purposefully having studied a map. Ben trailed behind her, nervous of what lay ahead but equally anxious not to be left behind in the fog so far from home.

They followed the path between the dead-end walls of two houses and, after a sharp bend, found themselves on the edge of Dodd's Wood. The track ran in a straight line through the trees, reaching the main road after a hundred metres or so at an arch formed by two tall, old apple trees. The ground was black with decaying leaves and laced with tendrils of ivy. Here and there were lurid red spots – fallen berries, like bright spots of blood. The wood smelled ripe and rotten.

Ben wasn't sure what to do next but kept walking, looking up and around, hoping that the wood, or perhaps Esther Garrett herself, would somehow communicate with him. But there were no leaves to whisper.

'I don't like it,' said Chelsea in a shivering, hesitant whisper.

'I do,' Ben replied, sucking in a deep lungful of cold air. He reached out to touch a silvery branch as they passed and the tree trembled at the brush of his fingertips.

Halfway along the path, at the deepest point of the narrow sliver of woodland, they stopped and stood side by side staring solemnly downward as if in prayer.

'Is this what you were looking for?' whispered Chelsea.

At the side of the path was the stump of a tree that had been cut down, leaving a flat, table-like surface. It was covered in cards and bunches of plastic-wrapped flowers. Some had rotted away, leaving only green-coated cellophane and stalks, the ink on their cards faded or streaked. Ben leaned closer, supporting himself with hands on knees, and read one aloud in a halting voice as he deciphered the decayed letters. 'Esther – you were always something something friend to me and I will miss your smile and never stop... hoping? Love and kisses.' He couldn't read the signature at all. There were song lyrics and verses, too. In the middle of the pile sat a teddy bear clutching a polyester satin heart on which was written 'Thank you for being a friend.'

Chelsea turned away. 'It's not right, this.'

Ben didn't hear her. He began silently to mouth words, addressing them to Esther who, for a moment, he imagined to be beneath the pile of mementoes and trinkets. *Hi. It's Ben. We met on the bus. I'm sorry, I guess.*

Somewhere nearby, a car door slammed. Ben shot upright and Chelsea started. 'What was that?' she said.

Ben was fixed in place, panicked, and it took him a moment to realise Chelsea was moving away from him, heading for cover on the other side of the path, deeper into the wood.

'Someone's coming,' she hissed.

He followed her without thinking. 'We don't have to hide. We're allowed to be here.' Despite that, he couldn't help whispering.

They slipped behind the trunk of a tree that had fallen in the great gale of 1987 and which had since grown a coat of fungus, ivy, and crawling insects. They squatted on their haunches, ankle-deep in mud and composting vegetable matter, and breathed together.

Further along the path, through the arch of branches by the bus stop on the main road, a figure emerged from the mist. Though their view was obstructed they could see that it was a man; tall, dressed in dark clothing, moving elegantly but purposefully with his head bowed.

Chelsea's fingers dug into Ben's arm and he felt her warm, irregular breath across his cheek. 'Shit,' she said.

'Sometimes the killer returns to the scene of his crime,' said Ben, barely breathing the words, reciting the library book from memory. His words ran out as the figure on the path slowed, shoes crunching on the path, and then came to a halt a few feet away in front of the shrine. Through the wild tangle of undergrowth Ben saw a sharply-cut Mackintosh, gloved hands clasped at the small of the back, and harshly-cropped, dark hair.

Ben was certain his irregular breathing was loud enough to be heard, which only made it more difficult to breathe regularly. Though the squatting position he'd adopted had seemed comfortable at first, he could feel pins and needles spreading through his foot and lower leg. He cupped his hands over his mouth and began to draw back his own carbon dioxide in an effort to calm himself.

The figure on the path knelt in front of the shrine, put a hand in the pocket of his overcoat, and withdrew something which he placed on the trunk. He began to speak aloud, soft but quite audible in the silent wood. 'You know I've done my best, don't you?'

Ben recognised the voice at once: Detective Inspector Sweetland. A thrill ran through him at the thought of being so close once again to a real detective, with a real detective's coat, and a stern detective's countenance.

Sweetland went on but now sounded almost angry. 'I've done what I had to do, Esther. I've done what needed to be done and I won't be judged for it.' His shoulders jerked forward as he made a low, animal sound, half-sob, half-grunt. He used one gloved hand to cross himself, stood up, and stepped back. He lifted the same hand to his mouth, kissed it, and waved, before spinning on his heel and striding back to his car with his hands in his pockets.

Ben looked down at the earth beneath his feet and felt an intense chill rise up his spine, up his neck and across his scalp, as if someone he couldn't see was standing at his shoulder. He was certain, all at once, that Esther Garrett was there, concealed under the soil, in a shallow grave – a phrase he'd learned from his morbid library books. His trainer, he became convinced, was mere inches from her skull – he knew it with utter certainty. The need to stay hidden was overcome by fear and he leapt to his feet, scrambled over the fallen trunk, tearing his cords, and stumbled back to the path.

Chelsea rose halfway to her feet, open-mouthed and astonished. She turned to look in Sweetland's direction and saw that he was framed by the arch of trees, and facing their way. His eyes pierced the gloom, pinned Ben in place.

'Shit,' Chelsea said for the second time.

Sweetland stared at Ben for a few charged seconds and then slipped away.

Chelsea vaulted the tree trunk and approached Ben with her fists balled. She stopped short, tensing and flexing her hands. 'Why did you do that?'

Ben's eyes drifted back to the spot where they'd been hiding. 'We should get out of here,' he said.

Pushing past him, Chelsea went to look at the shrine, bending after a moment to pick something up. She held aloft a silver chain and St Christopher's medal.

'Put it down,' said Ben with quiet intensity.

She did as he ordered.

Though he wanted more than anything to be out of the wood and on his way home, Ben forced himself to take one last look at the shrine, reading every single card one more time.

'Take one,' said Chelsea as he held the last one between his fingers. 'For your scrapbook.'

He shook his head, but didn't release his grip.

'No one will know,' she said. 'They'll think a fox took it or something.'

Ben said firmly, 'No,' and turned to walk away. 'It wouldn't be right.'

After a moment Chelsea followed, overtook him, and spun so that she was walking backwards. She stretched out her palms and stopped him with a thump in the chest. They stood facing each other for a moment. Then she leaned forward and gave him a quick, hot kiss on the cheek. The touch and faint perfume of her skin made him feel light-headed and the wood seemed suddenly full of sound and life.

He coloured and wiped his face with the back of his hand.

'We should go,' she said. 'We don't want to miss the bus.'

NEW WORLD NEWS

Since 2069   № 76831558

POLICE SCALE DOWN MISSING ESTHER SEARCH

After working through the Christmas period, Devon and Cornwall Police have announced that they are to reduce the number of officers assigned to the ongoing hunt for the body of schoolgirl Esther Garrett, who went missing in November last year.

A team of dedicated officers will continue with the enquiry, carrying out searches of CCTV, but physical searches in fields, woodland and moorland near Exeter are to stop at the end of this week.

Aaron Greenslade, 19, has been remanded in custody and charged with murder. His trial is set to begin later this year at Exeter Crown Court.

CHAPTER SEVEN

With each roll of the waves, the tide came ever nearer the concrete sea wall where Ben and his mother sat, side by side, but a foot apart. They stared out across the water as sunlight flashed upon the surface. The cries of excited children were hard to distinguish from those of circling gulls. On the horizon, cargo ships stacked high with containers made their elephantine way along the English Channel.

Ben had grown several inches from spring to summer and his red shorts and black T-shirt exposed newly gangling legs and arms, with pointed knees and elbows. His face had begun to change shape, too, growing longer, the jaw more prominent, and his eyes were cast into shade by a deepening brow. He was burning in the sun, the tip of his freckled nose already peeling.

Ellie also looked thin but not because she had grown – because she had shrunk: her cheekbones protruded and the grooves between the bones of her arms were quite visible. The whites of her eyes were no longer white, and her skin seemed grey, even in the golden light of a summer's day. She had brought a book but it sat unopened, its spine pristine, on the ground next to her.

Neither had spoken for some time and the silence between them was uneasy but when Ben tried to get up, she restrained him, grabbing at his wrist and pulling him back down.

He glared. 'I'm bored.'

'I don't want to sit here on my own,' Ellie said, angry, but also pleading.

Ben reached down to trace a shape in the dry sand that had blown up onto the wall between his feet. He pushed a black fleck of seaweed around in a circle, and lifted his fingertip close to his eye to inspect the crystals that were stuck in its whorls. He rubbed his fingers clean and looked away, further along the beach.

A family was busy evacuating the spot they'd occupied throughout the middle of the day. Dad, beer-bellied and burned scarlet, was gathering up windbreaks and picnic boxes, while Mum, blonde and pear-shaped, shooed two children, eight or nine years old, towards the steps. Ben squinted. There was a teenage girl with them, dressed in a pink one-piece swimsuit, slim and dark-haired. He lifted a hand to shield his eyes from the sun.

The more he looked the more certain he became.

Yes, he was sure of it – there was no doubt in his mind that it was Esther Garrett. She had the same sweet smile, the same accidental elegance.

He wanted to get up and walk over to get a closer look but knew Ellie would stop him. Instead, he continued staring, trying to bring the girl into closer focus. The harder he looked, and the less often he blinked, the fuzzier his vision became. He rubbed his eyes and got sand in them, making them sting.

'What are you looking at?' asked Ellie, her tone flat.

'Nothing,' he said, replying too quickly.

For the first time in as long as Ben could remember, she smiled – weak, sad, but a smile nonetheless. 'It's okay,' she said.

'What?' Ben replied, screwing up his face in irritation.

'To look at girls,' she said. 'It's normal.'

Ben groaned. 'I wasn't, not like that.' He ran his hands over his head and gave an exasperated, grunting sigh. 'Look at her,' he said, not looking himself.

'At that girl?'

'Yeah.'

Ellie leaned forward and peered. The girl was halfway up the steps now, looking back over the sea, one hand on her hip and the other covering her eyes. 'What?'

'It's her, isn't it? It's Esther Garrett?'

With a roll of her eyes, Ellie turned away from the girl in the swim-suit. 'No, Ben, it isn't.'

Ben gave a quick glance. He could see now that his mother was right. This girl was thicker in the hips, rounder in the face. Her hair was too long.

'You're obsessed.'

'I'm not.'

'I'm worried about you. You're too young to be worrying about things like that,' said Ellie. She pulled her thinning hair back tightly, fastening it with a rubber band. It tightened her face, making her look suddenly fierce and sour. 'You need to lighten up. Life is short.' She swallowed and looked away. 'Try to have some fun, please.'

Ben scowled and, this time, when he got up, Ellie was too slow to stop him. 'Like you do? Drinking too much and staying up all night?'

'How dare you!' she shouted as Ben shoved his hands into the pockets of his shorts and stamped away.

'I wish I lived with Dad,' he muttered, intending her to hear.

She opened her mouth to say something else but, instead, winced and controlled a quiet gasp of pain. Her thin fingers splayed across her abdomen and she massaged it gently through the fabric of her summer dress.

Ben didn't see; he didn't break his awkward, spindly stride, or even look back.

It was a bright day and warm for the time of year, and the sunlight beaming through the austere windows of the church cast green-tinted, black-barred shadows on the tiled floor. The walls bore naïve hand-made hangings with good news messages, and vaguely avant-garde depictions in wood of religious scenes that had been built in when the church was erected in the 1960s.

Gentle music was coming, not from the organ, but from a cassette deck set up on a chair on the dais: a compilation tape of slow, melancholy jazz recordings that his mother had made − muted trumpets, late night piano, and barely-brushed drums.

Ben was on a pew at the front, staring up at carvings around the ceiling, trying to avoid allowing his eyes to rest on the closed coffin. It was almost a year since the disappearance of Esther Garrett. He looked thinner and paler than ever, with no remaining trace of childish plumpness, and was already taller than his father. His red hair hung over his forehead and collar, thick and untidy. He had never worn a jacket before and had certainly never seen his father wearing one, but there they were, side by side, both dressed in versions of the same three-button suit from Burton's in Exeter. Ben was conscious that his trousers were a touch too short, and that the suit really ought to have been black, but dark blue was close enough, and he was at least wearing a black tie, borrowed from his grandfather.

Dennis was standing far away on the other side of the church, on his own, puffy-eyed and dishevelled. Having greeted and hugged Ben at the door, he had turned away without speaking when Ben's father had started to utter hesitant condolences.

There were only a few other mourners − some colleagues of his mother's from the hospital, a neighbour with nothing better to do, and, at the very back of the hall, Jeanette and Chelsea.

The vicar appeared and switched off the cassette player. Ben didn't take in what he was saying until he heard: 'Benjamin, her son, will now say a few words in memory of his mother.'

Ben had written the short speech himself and read it from a sheet of lined paper, swallowing the words, more nervous than grief-stricken. As he concluded, he heard Jeanette sob and glanced her way, his eyes briefly catching Chelsea's. She wasn't crying but gave a passing, sympathetic smile.

There was a small party at his grandfather's house, on the same council estate as the church, where his mother had grown up – a thousand temporary houses built in 1947 from prefabricated concrete blocks and scheduled to be knocked down by 1950. That date passed and the houses came to seem spacious and sturdy by modern standards, even as their exteriors gained rusty streaks and turned pond-green. His grandfather's house smelled of old man's sweat, mothballs and furniture polish, and even with the lights on seemed gloomy. Politics decided who stood or sat where: Ben hovered by the sitting room door, submitting himself to hugs and handshakes; his father was in the garden smoking on his own; while Dennis had slumped into his own half-collapsed armchair with its greasy arms and creaking springs.

'You never expect to outlive your child,' he said to a middle-aged woman who was standing by the fireplace eating her way through a paper plate full of sandwiches.

Ben was certain he'd heard him say this ten times already.

'I'm just glad my Irene didn't have to suffer it. She'd have been heartbroken.'

The woman with the sandwiches said, with her mouth full, 'Well, they're together in heaven now.'

Ben heard a soft laugh at his elbow.

'That's a good one.'

He looked sideways and saw Chelsea. She leaned against the wall with her hands behind her back, looking uncomfortable in a plain black dress and flat formal shoes. She had changed, too, her features sharpening and weight shifting about her body so that she seemed lean and coiled.

'How's it going?' she asked.

Ben shrugged.

'Mum says you're going to live with your dad.'

Ben swept hanging red hair from his eyes and looked down at his in-turned feet, saying nothing.

'I suppose I won't see you around the estate, then.'

'No,' he said and then, after looking around to check he wasn't overheard, added, his voice sliding a tone, near breaking, 'Unless I come back to see you.'

Chelsea gave a honking laugh and then clamped her mouth shut as the room fell silent for a moment and several people looked her way.

Ben frowned and rubbed a hand on the back of his neck, not sure what to say or what he was supposed to do with himself except keep looking sad.

'Have you been watching the news?' asked Chelsea.

'What news?' Ben said.

'You know – about your girlfriend. That Esther.'

'Oh.' He chewed at his chapped lip. 'Yeah, a bit.'

Aaron Greenslade's trial had been underway for just over a month and was inescapable. There had been little else for Ben to do at the hospital but read magazines and newspapers, or watch the TV turned low at the end of the ward. He had gleaned every small detail available.

The prosecution held the upper hand from the start. There was testimony from multiple witnesses – passengers on the bus, as well as Ben's father – stating that Greenslade had followed Esther into the wood where he had laid his hands on her, just as the bus pulled out of view. There was some attempt by the defence to argue that the evening had been too dark and wet, and the bus too far away, but convincing diagrams and photographs of a reconstruction were produced.

Dispelling any final reasonable doubts in the minds of the jury was testimony from Darren Napier with whom Greenslade had lived at a hostel in Exeter. Though he was not a sympathetic witness – a dishevelled drug addict with sores on his face and missing teeth – his account was detailed and specific. Greenslade, he said, had confessed to him, describing exactly how he grabbed Esther, overpowered her, killed her with his bare hands, and then took her bag because he wanted her money and cash card to buy drink and drugs. DI Sweetland confirmed, in his statement, that the same witness had directed them to the location of items belonging to Esther Garrett, stolen by Greenslade, and dumped in Exeter city centre.

The defence made an attempt to suggest that Napier might have murdered her himself, but it seemed half-hearted.

Eventually they resorted to portraying Greenslade as the victim of an abusive upbringing. They shared intimate details of his mother's alcoholism and his father's violence and drug use. He had begun smoking at nine years old, was drinking strong cider provided by his mother by the age of eleven, and was taking amphetamines and cocaine with his father by the time he was thirteen. His grandmother's boyfriend had repeatedly raped him over the course of years, beginning when he was six and not ending until he left home at fifteen. The family home was filthy, chaotic, and often had no food or drink. Greenslade was encouraged to mistreat animals by his father who liked to shoot cats with an airgun. He had been forced to watch his mother have sex with strangers, some of whom had also molested him after paying his parents.

That argument was supported by another line of attack – where, they kept asking, was Esther Garrett's body, if indeed she was dead? Where was the solid evidence that a murder had actually been committed? No serious search had been undertaken among runaways in London, Cardiff, Leeds, or any of the many places a young woman might lose herself.

Finally, in desperation, they played dirty, aggressively questioning Eddie Garrett. They implied that he had a violent temper and suggested that he was attracted not merely to young women but to pubescent and pre-pubescent girls, but a suggestion was all they could muster – there was no proof. They dredged up a twenty-year-old conviction for importing pornography, which was at least something concrete, but nobody cared. And then Eddie Garrett cried, in court and outside, which became the key image of the trial. Everyone agreed that it was bad form to bully a grieving father on so little evidence and the defence, rattled, backed down.

Insofar as he could bring himself to care anymore, Ben was convinced of Greenslade's guilt, not because of the cleverness of the lawyers, or the hard work of the police, but because he'd seen into Greenslade's eyes himself. He had seen them burning with anger, blazing with frustration. Nobody had ever scared him as much as that young man on the bus.

Chelsea reached into the small black handbag hanging across her chest and pulled out an envelope. She held it out but Ben didn't take it.

'It's for you. I cut out all the stories about her from the newspaper, for your scrapbook.'

'Oh,' said Ben. She didn't put it away, just let it hang conspicuously. Ben snatched the fat bundle and jammed it into his trouser pocket.

'Thanks.'

Ben stared at the house through the rain that pelted against the car window, his face slack.

'Come on, then,' said his father. 'Let's get it over with.'

For a moment, Ben's expression betrayed hot fury. He shot a look sideways, gave a grunting sigh.

'Sorry, son,' said his father. 'It's just that your granddad wants the key back and, well, there's no point in putting it off, is there?'

Ben sighed again, still glowering darkly. He flipped up the hood of his coat and climbed out into the downpour, slamming the door behind him. His father followed, pulled his jacket over his head, and dashed for the front door of the house, which he unlocked so that Ben could enter. He went back to the car and returned a few seconds later with a nest of sturdy cardboard boxes. Ben hadn't moved beyond the doormat.

The house was dark behind closed curtains, and musty. The only sound was the tapping of rain against the windows, sounding almost at times like distant jazz drumming.

Peter flicked both switches by the door and the house grew warm with yellow light.

'Right,' he said, trying to sound cheerful, but Ben didn't move. 'I wouldn't brood, son. Let's just get on.'

Ben's temple pulsed as his frown deepened, and he opened his mouth to speak, but he swallowed the words. He didn't have the nerve to say what he'd wanted to – that it was easy for Peter to say that, because he didn't care that she was gone.

'Here, have a box,' said Peter, holding one out. 'Let's go and get your stuff.'

Ben took the box and walked upstairs, slowing as he neared the top. The door of his mother's room was closed, thankfully. His father, who hadn't been allowed inside the house for some years, looked around with frank interest.

In Ben's room, Peter pulled a roll of bin liners from his coat pocket and ripped one free, shaking it out until it ballooned.

'Put anything you don't want in here.'

They began sorting through the piles of toys, books and clothing scattered around the room.

Peter stopped every few seconds to ask, 'What about this?'

Each time, Ben shrugged and said, 'I don't want it.'

His Lego, children's books, sketchpads, all went into the bin bag. Eventually, Peter stopped and ran a hand through his rain-wet hair. 'Don't you want to keep anything?'

When Ben spoke, his voice cracked, emerging as a mumble. 'It's all kid's stuff.'

'What?' said Peter, cocking his head.

Ben raised his voice to get the words through the blockage, almost screeching. 'I said, it's all kid's stuff.'

Peter heard him this time and nodded, sadly. 'Sure?'

'Yeah,' said Ben.

For a second or so, his father looked at him, as if trying to read his mind, and then he shrugged. 'All right. There's not much room at Gran's anyway, is there? I'll take this bag downstairs.'

Once Peter had left the room, Ben scrambled across the unmade single bed and reached down to where he kept the scrapbook, between the wall and the mattress. He pulled it out and held it in both hands, looking at the cover.

He heard his father's footsteps on the stairs and began to blink rapidly.

Moving quickly, he picked up a supermarket carrier bag and stuffed the scrapbook into it along with a handful of comics.

'All right, son?' said Peter, standing in the doorway.

Ben nodded and then, after a moment, said, 'Can I go round to say goodbye to someone?' He wiped a drip of rain from his nose while he thought how to put it. 'My friend. I'll only be five minutes.'

Peter huffed wearily. 'Go on, then. I'll get this lot in the car.'

Ben ran downstairs and put on his coat. He put the carrier bag underneath and zipped it up. Outside, it was still pounding with rain, and so he ran to the end of the road, turned left and jogged uphill, past house after house just like his own. He passed Winchester Close and Shrewsbury Close, and turned up Lancaster Close. At the end of the keyhole-shaped cul-de-sac he saw Auntie Jeanette's house, lights blazing against the daytime gloom. Splashing through puddles, he ran to the front door and rang the bell.

Jeanette answered, still in her dressing gown and slippers, and pulled him in out of the rain. She hugged him, squashing him against her chest, and then pushed him away. Holding him by the arms, an expression of sympathy on her face, she looked him up and down. 'Stay there.'

She bustled away and returned with a towel. Shivering, he took it and rubbed it over his hair and face. 'Take your coat off,' she said. 'Hang it on the radiator.'

'I can't stay long,' he said, anxious to avoid unzipping his coat to reveal the carrier bag. 'Dad's waiting.' He chewed his lip as a wave of melancholy swept over him.

Jeanette frowned and nodded. 'I know, love. How have you been?'

He shrugged.

'I know,' she said again.

He rubbed nervously at his eye. 'Can I speak to Chelsea?'

'Of course you can, my love,' said Jeanette. She looked at his sopping wet trainers and sighed resignedly. 'Run on up, then.'

'Thanks,' he said breathlessly, and then dashed up the carpeted staircase.

Chelsea's door was open and he could hear the sounds of pop music – a boy band, though he didn't know which one. She was lying on the bed reading a magazine. He knocked to get her attention.

She looked up and planted her chin in her cupped palms. After a moment's consideration she said, 'You look like a drowned rat.'

'It's raining,' said Ben.

'Well, yeah.'

She sat up and gestured for him to enter.

He took a couple of steps forward but no more and surveyed the room. It was better – warmer and cleaner – than his old room at his mother's house, and certainly better than the box room at his grand-mother's he was moving into. Clothes spilled out of a fitted wardrobe and there was a computer on the desk surrounded by stacks of floppy discs – pirated games swapped in the school playground.

'We can play something if you like,' she said, noticing his interest.

'No time,' said Ben, sullen and jealous. He unzipped his coat. 'I don't want to throw this out but I can't take it to my dad's house yet.'

'What is it?'

He carefully removed the bag.

'Comics? No thanks.'

'No, it's this.' He presented the scrapbook, moving a little closer so she could reach it from where she sat.

'Okaaaaaay,' she said warily as she took it in her hands.

'Look after it for me,' he said.

She held it and sat looking up at him, appraising his face. 'You're so freckly,' she said, teasing but not mean-spirited.

'Shut up,' he mumbled, irritated at her levity.

'I quite like it,' she said.

He couldn't stop himself blushing. 'I need to go,' he said and rushed, half stumbling, out and downstairs.

NEW WORLD NEWS

Since 2069

LIFE FOR ESTHER KILLER

A depraved killer has been sentenced to life for the murder of Esther Garrett in Devon last November.

Aaron Greenslade, 20, of Albert Way, Exeter, was described by Detective Inspector Sweetland of Devon and Cornwall Police as 'a dangerous young man who would undoubtedly have gone on to commit further such crimes had he not been apprehended.'

The parents of the Devon schoolgirl have described themselves as 'content' with the sentence which will see Greenslade serve a minimum of 30 years in prison. In a statement outside Exeter Crown Court her father Eddie Garrett said: 'We will never be able to forget our darling daughter but the fact that Aaron Greenslade has refused to tell us where she is only increases the pain.'

Greenslade declared his innocence throughout the trial and insists that he has no knowledge of the whereabouts of Esther's body. The presiding judge said: 'Mr Greenslade's callous disregard for the family only underlines the need for a long custodial sentence.'

Mr Greenslade's brother, Steven, 29, broke down when the sentence was announced and has since mounted a campaign for his brother's release. He said: 'My brother is a vulnerable individual who has been the victim of a miscarriage of justice, and I firmly believe that.'

PART TWO

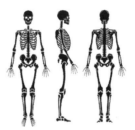

CHAPTER EIGHT

Ben was on his way to work when he saw the photograph on the front page of *The Sun* on display in the newsagent's window. He stopped and stared. Steven Sweetland was now white-haired but had the same firm jaw and was still handsome, even under pursuit by a mob of press photographers. The headline alongside his photograph read, 'KILLERS WALK FREE – Convictions collapse after bent cop revelations.' Ben bought copies of *The Sun* and *The Telegraph*, which also carried the story, and paid for them with a handful of change. He jammed them into his briefcase before hurrying on to Lewisham station to catch the London Bridge train.

Twenty years had changed Ben, too. His hair had been cut back to rust-coloured bristles, only slightly longer on top than on the back and sides, and his face had become angular and pinched, with permanent lines carved between his pale eyebrows. At six-foot-two, without any fat at all, even if he no longer looked awkward, he remained conspicuous and uncomfortable in his own body. He was dressed in a grey suit, not expensive but not cheap either, with a shirt of weighty cotton, a silk tie, and leather-soled shoes. His overcoat was old-fashioned, stylish, and made to last, but hung from his bony shoulders as if on a hanger.

At the tail end of rush hour the train into London Bridge was quiet enough that he was able to find a seat, folding his long legs and slipping his bones into a gap between two other passengers. As the roofs and treetops of South London slid by outside Ben gnawed an already savaged fingernail and read the papers.

Sweetland had just retired at the age of fifty-five, having been promoted to detective chief superintendent five years before. His reputation had begun to unravel when a man he'd helped to convict for murder in 1998 was cleared by new DNA evidence. It became apparent that the witness upon whom that case had relied was not himself reliable. He was a drug addict and paid informant who admitted that Sweetland had falsified a statement for him to sign. An internal review had looked over transcripts of all of Sweetland's investigations and discovered that several supposed confessions appeared to use the same form of words, and that processes had not been followed in recording them. More damaging, however, was the recurring appearance of the very same drug-dependent witness, Darren Napier, in multiple instances, often years apart. Napier was always willing to swear that he'd seen someone in a particular place at a particular time, or that they had confessed to him in a prison cell or hostel room.

As the train began its crawl into London Bridge, bumping over points, Ben rushed to read the last few paragraphs of the *Sun* article. Finally, there she was, among a list of other murder victims: Esther Garrett. He felt a shiver run through his limbs. It wasn't quite the first time he'd thought of her since the days of the scrapbook but reading her name in print made him feel twelve years old again.

At the station, the train gave up its passengers, and Ben was pulled along in the flow. As he went through the familiar actions of swiping his season pass, crossing the chaotic concourse, and leaving the station, he felt as if he was hovering over his own shoulder. What was going on? What was he, a boy from a housing estate, a boy from Devon, doing in this city?

Halfway across London Bridge he broke from the crowd and stopped. He pressed his hands on the flat metal of the balustrade and looked down at the grey-brown water as it swept by. A tug slipped under the bridge, fighting the tide, and oily discharge from its exhaust drifted up, filling Ben's nose and throat with its tang. He breathed out unsteadily and shook his head before glancing to his left, towards the glass tower where he worked. Reluctantly, he heaved himself away from the rail and began walking, but slowly, so that the city-bound crowd with its snapping heels and mobile phone chatter flowed around him as if he were an immobile obstruction in its path.

Arriving late, he flashed his pass at the security guards, but didn't give them his usual polite greeting. He shared a lift to the sixth floor with two colleagues to whom he said, 'Hi,' but then pretended to check something on his phone to avoid a conversation. He tried to slip unnoticed through the double swing doors into the open-plan office which housed the complaints department but heads turned as he entered and hung up his overcoat.

Raz appeared in the door of his corner office holding a coffee mug. He was middle-aged but still dark-haired. He liked to talk about how he'd arrived in Britain from Pakistan at the age of three, unable to speak a word of English, though he now had a nasal North London middle-class accent. His shirtsleeves were rolled up and tie loosened, intended to imply that he was hard at work. As Ben approached hesitantly Raz said, acidly, 'Good afternoon.'

It was a favourite joke of his, but exhausted through repetition, and delivered without a smile.

'The trains–' Ben began, but Raz cut him off with a glance at his watch.

'Don't waste any more time,' he said.

Ben took his seat and turned on his computer. None of his colleagues met his gaze.

Ben drifted through the morning at his desk, keeping his head down. The software delivered customer letters and emails ten at a time and, with practised efficiency, despite his state of distraction, he tailored stock responses so that they more or less answered each complaint.

Every now and then, he glanced at the folded newspapers on his desk and felt a surge of frustration.

At the stroke of midday, he checked whether Raz was in his office and, seeing the glass cubicle empty, got up, took the newspapers from his desk, put on his coat and went outside. He headed for a café run by a family of Italian-Londoners on a pedestrianised alleyway behind the Monument. It was expensive, the bread was often stale, the coffee watery, and the staff downright rude, which meant that, even on busy days, there was usually a free stool in the window. Picking at a soggy tuna sandwich on cheap brown bread and sipping from a can of Coke, Ben read the newspaper stories again, but this time paying greater attention to the details.

It was just about possible, he gleaned, that Aaron Greenslade would remain in prison after a review of the evidence but the case had always seemed weak and only Steven Sweetland's sense of certainty had really convinced anyone otherwise. Ben knew that Esther's body had never been found because, from time to time during the preceding decades, he had looked her up on the internet, prompted by the discovery of the remains of other long-lost murder victims on motorway verges or buried on wasteland.

Ben finished his sandwich, drained the Coke can and walked away, leaving the newspapers behind.

On his way back to the office amidst traffic noise, breathing cold, polluted air, he felt the sense of detachment again, and a surge of yearning: he wanted, so wanted, to be walking through Okehampton's quiet town centre on a grey autumn afternoon, past the old coaching inns and dusty shops, heading towards his mother's house.

The thought of Esther Garrett and of his mother reminded him also of Chelsea. He made a mental note to call her, or even to arrange to meet her when he next went home. Through Facebook he knew that she'd just had a second child but had been too busy to send a card though he had clicked 'Like' on the post – the most interaction he could really bear to undertake.

The afternoon was slow and, once he had established that he was on course to meet his target for the day, and that Raz had left the office for a meeting in Guildford, Ben allowed himself a few furtive minutes to look up Esther Garrett online. The same handful of photographs illustrated every news story. When he was eleven, she had looked so grown-up but now he realised how young she had been when she disappeared – certainly still a child, with a child's roundness of features. Now he was thirty-two, and she was forever sixteen, it didn't seem right to acknowledge that he still found her beautiful, so he swallowed the thought before it coalesced.

'Who's that?'

Ben resisted the urge to close the browser window. Instead he turned, hooked his arm over the back of the chair, and looked up at Eddie, the nearest he had to a friend at work. Eddie was from Liverpool, short, dark and pock-marked. He had paused on his way back to his desk with a mug of tea.

Ben cleared his throat. 'She was murdered. Probably.' He gestured at the newspapers on his desk. 'I was just reading about this police corruption case.'

'Oh, yeah,' said Eddie. 'I saw that on TV.' He peered at Ben's screen. 'Devon?'

Ben nodded stiffly.

Nervous, on his first day six years earlier, he had been overcome with the urge to lie just as he'd often done as a child: his colleagues all believed he was born on an army base in Germany and grew up in Scotland and Yorkshire. It was utter nonsense but concocting the story, borrowing details from the biography of a university contemporary, and guessing the rest, had made him feel in control. He socialised so little, and was so quiet when he did, that no more had ever been said about it. He felt another lie coming now, forcing its way up, though he didn't know what form it would take until the words emerged in a low mumble.

'My mum moved there a few years ago, to be near the sea. She's very into sailing.'

He was sure he had never told Eddie or anyone else that his mother was dead but, still, there was a thrilling tension as he waited to see whether the fiction would be accepted.

Eddie nodded. 'Nice part of the world. Whereabouts, exactly?'

'Exmouth,' said Ben. 'It's seaside but not too tacky, if you see what I mean. Lovely estuary.'

'I've never been down that way. We usually go to North Wales because it's easier for—'

'Well, look,' said Ben, cutting awkwardly across Eddie's words. 'I ought to get on with some work.' He closed down the web browser, opened a file with a half-finished draft of a letter and began typing. Eddie shook his head before moving away. He was used to Ben's oddness.

Ben's shoulders slumped. One day, he knew, he would be caught out, and it would be excruciating. Each time he did it, once the brief high had passed, he felt guilty and dirty. It was a habit he ought to have grown out of and perhaps would one day, he thought, if he ever married and had children.

He glanced over his shoulder and then after a moment flipped his display back to Esther Garrett. Looking at her sparkling eyes, captured in time, the old irritation had returned, as insistent as ever it had been: what had happened to her, and where was she now? How could he go through life never knowing? She was out there somewhere, cold and lonely, aching to be found.

That evening, as he often did, he deferred arriving at his one bedroom flat by walking all the way home, across London Bridge and through Bermondsey. The evening was perfect for it, cold enough to prevent him getting hot and uncomfortable, even in his winter coat. His cheeks glowed red in the chill and he felt free and purposeful, striding through evening crowds with a clear destination in mind.

It also gave him time to think.

As a child, so much about Esther Garrett's disappearance had seemed confusing to him. Aaron Greenslade had been in Ben's mind: nothing more than a school bully grown to adulthood and the only motive he had ascribed to his supposed attack on Esther Garrett was violence for the sake of violence. He realised now that she was vulnerable in a different way – she wasn't merely pretty, as he'd thought, but beautiful. She would have attracted attention everywhere she went.

After an hour's walking, he stopped at a pub in Deptford for a pint of lager and a burger, and found a stack of the day's newspapers on the bar. Taking a small table in a dark corner, he worked through articles about Steven Sweetland, looking out for mentions of Esther in particular. Hers was by no means the headline case – Sweetland had gained a reputation for investigating murders, and especially serial murders, and it was those which fascinated the press – but Greenslade did seem to be a prime candidate for release. *The Guardian* had even spoken to Esther's family and quoted her sister, Lucy. 'I was seven years old when Esther disappeared', they quoted her as saying. 'I have always found comfort in the fact that, even though I might not be able to speak to her, or even visit her grave, the man who had taken her away from us was in prison. Mr Sweetland's actions were a betrayal of my family and I can't express my horror at the thought that my sister's murderer has been free to live his life, and perhaps kill again, for these last twenty years.'

When he'd finished his pint and eaten, he went home, walking more slowly the nearer he got until at a little after 9pm he stood outside the no longer new block of flats, Millennium Heights, with his keys in his hand, fixed on the spot. With a sigh he forced himself to turn the locks and step across the threshold.

He had lived there since leaving university. First, he had shared it with a friend from his course – not a close friend, because he didn't have any, but someone similarly shy with whom he was able to get along more or less without incident, avoiding each other at breakfast time and spending occasional evenings together watching TV. The flatmate had moved out when he got a girlfriend and was now married, living somewhere outside London. Ben never heard from him.

For almost two years, Ben had lived there with Fiona, a young woman to whom he had been introduced by her brother at a premature university reunion party somewhere in Docklands.

To fill an uncomfortable silence, he told her a long story about an entirely imaginary trip to Vietnam, where he had never been, stealing details from a Michael Palin documentary that had been repeated on TV that week, and guessing at the rest. It had apparently made him sound interesting, which he wasn't, and she had insisted on a series of painful dates, despite his lack of enthusiasm.

Before long, she announced that she was being evicted by her landlord and, too polite to resist, Ben had let her move in with him. It had continued to be awkward for the duration of the relationship. He had felt conscious of his every movement and at night had been unable to sleep at the thought of the woman lying next to him who was, he kept saying to himself, essentially a stranger.

He was astonished when, after two years she asked if he was ever going to propose marriage. He thought it plainly evident that they were entirely unsuited to each other and couldn't understand how she had coped with him for that long. He summoned the courage and told her as much and she left that night. Though he had not spoken to her for months there were still some of her books on the shelf in the front room and a dust-blackened gap on the wall where one of her favourite art prints had hung. He didn't miss her, not quite that, but the flat did feel emptier with her gone than it had felt before she came, and at night the darkness somehow felt darker.

He dumped his bag by the front door, hung up his coat, and loosened his tie. He walked through to the almost too small kitchen and poured a glass of water that he downed in several gulps. He rinsed the glass and then slumped in the armchair in front of the TV and stared at the blank screen.

'Esther Garrett,' he said, with mild astonishment.

From the lockable mailbox in the foyer he had picked up several letters which he idly sorted with only the light from the hallway. After a moment he dropped the pile on the floor. He was too tired to stay awake but also too tired to go to bed. For a moment, he considered calling his father but the thought of it made him shrink. It would inevitably mean ten minutes of either talking over each other or enduring excruciating silences as if the phone had just been invented and they were learning how to use it. Instead, he reached for the latest issue of *2000 AD* which lay on the coffee table and started reading it from page one.

'I am the law,' he said in something beneath a whisper.

After only a few minutes his eyes drooped and he fell asleep in the armchair, fully dressed.

CHAPTER NINE

To make sure Saturday felt different to any other day of the week Ben always ate breakfast in a cheap café with plastic gingham tablecloths and lurid photographs of menu items tacked to the walls. There were newspapers on the counter and he took two to read with his mug of tea and fried breakfast.

The Mail had a two-page spread on Sweetland under the headline 'HOOKER SHAME OF DISGRACED COP'. The accompanying photograph of the retired detective had been taken with a long lens as he emerged from a convenience store with a cigarette clamped between his thin lips. He looked tired. The story was that, while bribing Darren Napier to testify in several criminal cases, he had also been abusing his position to procure sex with prostitutes, first in Exeter and later in Bristol. 'PERK OF THE JOB' read a sub-headline.

It made Ben feel queasy. Sweetland had seemed so clean and professional, and it was hard to imagine him in some bedsit, on a grubby mattress. Ben couldn't finish his breakfast.

He paid, left the café and walked on. He had reached the bank of the Thames at Greenwich when his phone began to vibrate in his pocket. It rang so rarely that it took him a moment to understand what was happening and he had to rush to answer before it went to voicemail, catching a glimpse of the screen as he did so. It showed a number he didn't recognise.

'Hello?' he said, warily.

'Benjamin Hodge?' said the voice on the other end. It was a woman, well-spoken, with a low, warm tone.

'Who's this?' he asked, suspecting it might be a sales call.

'You don't know me. My name is Lucy Garrett.'

Ben stopped walking and lowered himself onto the low stone wall that ran along the river's edge.

'I think you have the wrong number. Sorry.' He hung up and felt cold air catching in his lungs. The phone rang again. He tried to ignore it, turned down the volume on the ringer, and kept walking. After a minute or two the vibration stopped. Then it buzzed – a text message. He stopped again, sat down on another stretch of concrete wall, and looked at the screen.

Please speak to me. I need your help.

She left it just long enough before calling back.

He answered, speaking before she had the chance. 'I do know who you are and I don't want to talk to you. I can't talk to you.'

'Just listen to me – just for a minute.'

He felt his breath catching. He wanted to swear at her, to ask her if she understood how long he'd spent forgetting Esther. Didn't she understand that thinking about home hurt? But he didn't. 'Fine. Just for a minute.'

'You know why I'm calling?'

'I saw the story in the papers last week.'

'I need your help.'

Ben said nothing but stared out across the churning water of the river, letting his eyes drift to follow a gull that was fixed in place in the sky above, riding the wind. Somewhere inland an ambulance siren pulsed and then began to wail. He felt hot despite the cool breeze.

'I'm trying to get in touch with people who might recall details of her disappearance. You were a witness, right?'

'Yes,' said Ben. 'I guess.'

'Is there any chance we could meet for a coffee some time?' she said.

'No, sorry,' said Ben, more blunt than his usual manner. 'I live in London now and–'

'I'd be happy to pay your train fare.'

'I just can't.' He felt giddy. Sick. How could he ever sit and look at her face with its traces of Esther's? How could he chat about Esther over coffee? It was too long ago but at the same time a too tender wound.

'Why? Because of work? What is it you do?' she asked.

Ben swallowed, almost choking on the lie in his throat, but it forced its way up and out. 'I work at a museum.' Where had that come from? His lies usually had some purpose, answering a need of which his subconscious was aware even if he wasn't. 'I help to organise new acquisitions and organise special exhibitions.'

'Interesting,' said Lucy.

So that was it: for some reason, some need of his own he had yet to realise, he wanted to impress her. He was impressed at himself, in a way – it was a good lie, nothing too glamorous, but more so than his real job, and apparently convincing. He just hoped she didn't ask him any more specific questions, though he didn't doubt his ability to bluff through them if need be. He heard her say something else but couldn't quite make out the words over the growl of a police boat speeding by on the river, chewing up the water behind it. Ben covered his free ear, pressing the phone tighter against his head, and asked her to say it again.

'I don't suppose you'll be in the West Country any time soon?' she said, over-enunciating.

'No. I only come down at Christmas,' he said, truthfully.

'Perhaps if I'm in London at some point–'

'I really don't think it's a good idea.'

There was an uncomfortable, leaden silence.

'I'm sorry you feel this way,' she said eventually, but Ben heard her true meaning: she thought he was a coward and a fool. He was letting Esther down.

'Sorry. I am, really.' He didn't know how to conclude the conversation, but she ignored the signal he was attempting to send.

'At least tell me one thing – what did my sister look like that day?'

Ben bit his lip and squinted with pain. 'I can't really remember,' he said after a moment but closed his eyes and, with no effort at all, was back on the bus, looking right at her, at a moving portrait fashioned from the magic stuff of memory.

'Did she look scared?'

Ben opened his eyes and let them slide to one side, blinking, as his brain worked. He didn't want to encourage her, but felt compelled to answer. 'No, she looked happy, mostly. She was–' He stopped himself from saying 'so full of life', not only because it was a cliché, but also because it wasn't quite true. 'She was laughing when she got on the bus. She smiled at me.'

Lucy Garrett's voice dipped low and took on a strange tightness. 'I see.'

Ben felt as if he had said something wrong. 'Sorry,' he said reflexively, and then, 'What is it?'

'It's just that I'd always thought of her last hours like a black-and-white film.' She sighed. 'I'd always assumed she was sad. I suppose because it was sad, all of this, and it was winter.'

On the riverside path, a couple passed, giggling, arm-in-arm. Ben thought of Esther Garrett in the last few minutes before she stepped off the bus after Aaron Greenslade had started to bother her. She wasn't smiling then – she had looked frightened and angry. Should he tell her? Not then, not on the telephone.

'Well,' said Ben.

'It was nice to speak to you. I hope we'll speak again soon.' She sounded flirtatious – a last attempt to connect with him, keep him hooked, but he resisted.

'Yes, bye.' He hung up quickly and stood for a moment with the phone in his hand. There was a faint tremor there. London, his job, his flat, his very adulthood, again seemed strange and false as if he'd been hypnotised or dreaming. The great river wasn't anything to do with him, or the miles of tower blocks. He felt something grip in his chest and had to close his eyes, but that didn't help: all he saw were the black branches and bare red soil of home.

After dark Ben sat on the sofa in his flat with a bottle of lager in one hand and an iPad on his lap, waiting for a pizza delivery. When he saw an email from Lucy Garrett in his inbox he felt a cold tide wash through his veins. How had she found his email address? What did she want from him?

The subject heading was 'Of Interest?' He opened it and found several links to a private document service with a brief message: 'I hope these will help you understand.'

Part of him wanted to delete the email, perhaps even block her address. There could be nothing good in this except perhaps, he had to acknowledge, that it might be good for *her*, if not for him, and it was sometimes noble to sacrifice one's own needs for those of others. That was a justification, anyway, for doing something he wanted so badly to do.

He clicked the first link.

It opened a video, an extract from a 2005 current affairs programme called *Hard Line*. Ben hit play and set it to fill the screen.

The first shot was of leaves against a sunlit sky, accompanied by the chirping of birds and the opening notes of a Philip Glass solo piano piece. The camera panned down to show Dodd's Wood. Ben felt a flutter at the sight of a place that he had once known so well. An earnest young male presenter in suit, tie and red anorak stepped into shot, his fingers knitted together.

'It's been ten years since sixteen-year-old Esther Garrett was last seen walking into this wood on the edge of the Devon village of Berebroke where she lived and grew up.' He spoke haltingly, inserting pauses between words like a ham actor. 'Aaron Greenslade was convicted of her murder in 1996, but her body–' a glance down, and then up again '–has never been found. As with so many missing people, after a blaze of publicity, with the passing of time, her name has been–' he stopped, frowned, flexed his fingers '– all but forgotten.'

There was a cut to a shot of a red-brick house and the presenter continued in voice-over. 'For her family, though... the wound remains as raw as ever.'

Esther's parents appeared. They were standing in a bedroom decorated with posters and stuffed toys. It was small, mostly pale pink, furnished with plain flat-pack furniture, but clean and neat. Evidently under direction the grey-haired couple moved stiffly around it, pointing at objects on the desk and walls, their comments inaudible.

'Today, Kay and Eddie Garrett have only memories of Esther, and a few of her possessions, which they keep here in her bedroom, preserved just as it was... on the day she disappeared.'

As Eddie Garrett took over the story, there was a close-up on a noticeboard, the camera crawling across hand-scrawled notes with hearts dotting each 'i', the ink pink, purple, orange – any colour but black or blue.

'Esther was my little baby, you know, and I never thought of her any other way than as a little, you know, babe in arms, even when she got older and–'

Ben's finger darted out to pause the video but he was too slow. He dragged the slider backward until he had the image framed as he wanted: there it was – a note in familiar handwriting.

He ran a hand through his fine, pale orange hair, scratching at his scalp as if trying to massage out the memory.

The note in the footage was partially obscured by square artefacts from the process of online video encoding, but he could read it: 'Love you honey and missing you already.' Was it from a friend? In old detective novels, they could always, somehow, tell whether handwriting belonged to a woman or a man but here there was no clue. It was in block capitals and the ink was red. He began to wonder whether the police ever looked into those notes on the board. After all, he knew from first-hand experience that they had a suspect from day one, so why would they have bothered?

Swigging beer from the bottle, he let the video roll on.

'–you know, babe in arms, even when she got older and started to–' Eddie Garrett chuckled. '–become a bit stronger in her opinions, shall we say.'

There was an artful fade into a shot of Eddie and Kay sitting shoulder-to-shoulder at a dining table covered in photograph albums and mementoes.

'The search for Esther won't ever stop while there's breath in my body,' said Kay, her tone almost belligerent, defending herself against an unspoken accusation. 'We just want her to have a proper burial, a proper Christian burial, and to have somewhere we can go and just be–'

'–alone with her,' said Eddie, interrupting. 'Sit with our little girl.'

The journalist's voice came from off-camera, attempting sympathy but unable to muster the necessary sincerity. 'And I understand you haven't had her declared legally dead, though you could have done so as long ago as 2002?'

'Never,' said Eddie firmly. 'Never have, never will.'

'It would be like killing her ourselves,' added Kay.

As the camera fixed on their hands, bunched together in Kay's lap, there was another fade, this time to a panning shot of an empty, wintry field with steep hills behind it.

'Police are certain that, somewhere in the fields, ditches, or forests of the South West, Esther Garrett's body lies concealed. One man, however, could end her parents' ordeal in an instant.'

There was a deliberately startling cut to a pair of eyes captured in a grainy mug shot. The camera pulled out accompanied by a discordant synthesised drone. 'This is Aaron Greenslade. In 1996, he was convicted of the murder of Esther Garrett, but has always refused to admit his guilt, or to disclose how and, crucially, *where*, he disposed of her body. Until he decides to break his silence–'

The camera cut back to the presenter standing in the wood at Berebroke.

'–this beautiful countryside will probably keep its secrets, and her parents will continue to suffer uncertainty.' He looked down at his feet and then straight into the camera. 'And heartache.'

The video ended.

Ben took a sip of beer and then tapped the neck of the bottle against his chin as he stared into space. For all their expressions of parental feeling, they hadn't once mentioned their other daughter – their surviving child. It was as if Lucy Garrett had ceased to exist when Esther disappeared.

The next video was a minute-long clip from an archive news programme. Ben watched it and had the feeling that he'd seen it when it was first shown, or at least one very similar. Another clip was from a *Crimewatch* programme – three minutes cut from a longer round-up piece on missing people. Ben paused that when the Garrett family were shown briefly on screen but a poor-quality VHS source recording meant that the teenage girl lurking beside Eddie Garrett, Lucy herself, was little more than a blob of white for a face and a streak of black for hair.

Finally, there was something apparently filmed on a camcorder with a date displayed in chunky white characters in the bottom left corner: 15:22 01/05/1999. He played it, struggling to discern anything through grain, video compression, and unsteady camera work. There were flashes of light and green foliage and then, in an instant, the picture stabilised as the camera was placed on a flat surface. A teenage girl stepped into shot and Ben started. For a moment he was certain it was Esther Garrett but when she spoke he could tell the differences. She read from a sheet of A4 paper in a stilted, reedy voice with a heavy Devon accent.

'My name is Lucy. I've come here today to make this film to ask you to tell me where my sister is. I know that you had a bad time as a child.' Her cheeks grew red and she tripped over the words. 'And I know that you are a good man, in your heart. It would mean so much to me and to my family if you could only let us know so that we can say goodbye to her and move on with our lives.'

She folded the paper, stepped forward, and looked directly into the camera.

'Please, Mr Greenslade. Please.'

The screen faded to black and a title card appeared.

THIS TAPE WAS RETURNED FROM H.M. PRISON EXETER UNWATCHED. AARON GREENSLADE REFUSED TO WATCH IT OR TO COMMUNICATE WITH ME IN ANY OTHER WAY.

Ben scrolled back and paused the film on the shot of Lucy Garrett, aged sixteen, pleading into the camera, and stared at it for a long time, minutes, until the pizza delivery man buzzed the entryphone.

The next day, after a terrible night's sleep unbalanced by indistinct anxieties and forgotten bad dreams, Ben ate a lunch of cold pizza before setting off to the quietest of his local pubs. It was uphill from Lewisham in Blackheath and he planned to sit there reading newspapers until teatime, surrounded by people and families but not obliged to interact with them in any way.

He strode through streets of yellow-black Victorian houses, a light drizzle falling and frost just at bay, wearing his long work overcoat and a scarf. As he went, he muttered to himself, preparing for an ordeal. When he was halfway there, sniffing and numb, he pulled out his mobile phone and dialled his father's mobile number. After it had rung perhaps ten times it was answered with a fumble, a distant curse, and a long pause.

'Hello?'

Ben cleared his throat. 'Dad? It's me.'

'Everything all right, son?'

'Yeah, fine. I'm—'

'You're okay, are you?'

'Yes,' said Ben, becoming tetchy already. 'I'm calling because I wanted to let you know I might come home at the end of the month.'

'Oh, right.'

There was a silence, hissing on the line.

'Nothing definite yet but would it be all right?' said Ben.

'Yeah, yeah, no problem, course it is, yeah.'

'I've been feeling a bit homesick – missing the countryside.' Even as he spoke, he could see the open green space of Blackheath ahead, and took a deep breath in anticipation.

'Fair enough, son, fair enough. How long will you be about for? I'll be

on my usual shifts, obviously, so we won't see that much of each other.'
For the last fifteen years, Peter had been working at a supermarket
distribution centre, driving a forklift truck.

'Maybe a week,' said Ben.

'I'll get your old room tidied up, then. Make up the bed.'

'There's no hurry. Like I said, it might not happen, with work and
everything. I'm nearly where I'm going, so–'

'Fair enough. Well, bye-bye–'

'–I'd better–'

'–and I'll talk to you later.'

They spoke over each other until both of them paused. Ben said,
'Bye, then,' and hung up.

Talking to Peter always felt that way – clumsy and frustrating, as if
they were strangers. They had lost the knack of expressing affection or
any feeling for each other and the longer they left it, the more uncomfortable the very idea seemed.

Ben entered the pub with a burden of gloom on his shoulders.

CHAPTER TEN

On the following Wednesday morning, sitting at his office desk with a paper cup of lukewarm coffee and a headache, Ben was surprised when his mobile rang in his pocket. He looked at the screen and saw 'number withheld'. Answering, he expected to hear a recorded message telling him he'd won a prize or was eligible for compensation but instead there came a man's voice. It was hesitant, pinched, and with a hint of the north about it.

'Mr Hodge?'

They were only two words but there was something unmistakeably official about the tone with which they were spoken.

'Yes, that's me.'

'I'm Detective Superintendent Ewan Marwick and I need to ask you some questions. I understand you work in the city? Would it be convenient to meet this morning, for thirty minutes or so?'

Ben sat upright with one hand on the arm of his office chair and craned his neck, looking for his supervisor.

'If it helps square it with your boss,' the man on the phone said with a nervous, dry laugh. 'I'm not really asking — it's just that I prefer to express myself politely, when I can.'

'Right, I see.'

'Good. Have you got a pen handy, at all?'

Ben scrambled to find one under the fresh stack of customer complaint letters on his desk.

'Go ahead.'

Marwick gave Ben an address in Waterloo. 'Ask for me at reception. If you could aim to be here before 11am that would be great.'

'Can I ask what it's about?'

'You're not in any trouble,' said Marwick. 'I can't say any more than that at the moment. I'll see you later, then.'

The phone clicked in Ben's ear.

Raz was suspicious, unable to decide if Ben was trying to connive his way into a free day or, worse, was about to be arrested. He made sure Ben knew he disapproved of the whole business, that he would be expected to make up the hours, and insisted on Ben putting his request in an email, before eventually relenting.

Ben put on a coat and took the lift down to the street where a quick glance at his watch told him that he could walk rather than use public transport.

As he crossed London Bridge, he took his phone from his pocket, opened a browser and searched Ewan Marwick's name. The results were all news stories covering cases of police corruption or the prosecution of serving police officers for various serious crimes.

Now he understood. It was about Sweetland.

He negotiated tourists around Borough Market, cutting through the back streets to the busy main road which cut right across from South-wark to Westminster. As he walked, he tried to think about what Marwick might want from him and, under his breath, rehearsed the conversation. Despite the rumbling of lorries and vans along the road the pavement was wide and more or less empty and, anyway, no one in London ever seemed to care when he talked to himself.

'I haven't thought about the Esther Garrett case in years,' he said. Was it a good idea to lie to a police officer? Instinct told him it would look worse otherwise – it would make him seem ghoulish. There was no way he could be cast under suspicion himself but, still, he didn't like the idea of coming across as creepy. 'Esther who, sorry?' he said and then shook his head at the clumsiness of his attempt to dissemble.

The office in Waterloo was a 1960s office building – four storeys of rusting metal framework, faux-marble and dirty glass. There was a sign next to the front door, up a flight of steps, into which several removable strips had been placed, each listing one occupant. Ben scanned the list: there was the Health & Safety Executive (Maritime Div.), something called UKTI Innovation & Science, and several other similarly uninteresting bureaucratic offshoots of central government. One or two private companies also had offices in the building. He found what he was looking for near the bottom: Police Governance Unit.

He walked in out of the cold and into oppressive heat and the smell of dust burning on radiators. The wooden floor creaked under his feet as he approached the reception desk where an elderly security officer in a blue sweater greeted him with a slow blink.

'Yes?'

'I'm here to speak to someone called Ewan Marwick.'

'Name?'

'Ben Hodge.'

The man behind the desk pressed his lips together sourly and ran a thick finger down the clipboard in front of him. When he found Ben's name, he seemed disappointed to be deprived the opportunity to throw him out into the street. He picked up the phone and dialled a three-digit extension.

'Mr Hodge here to see you, sir,' he said, barely enunciating, making 'sir' sound like an insult. He put down the phone and pointed with his pen.

Ben took a seat by the window and leaned his head against it, feeling the glass throb from the vibrations of a bus idling at a traffic light nearby. He let his eyes close for a moment and pictured the interior of his father's bus – the seat coverings in garish orange, the steel bars for people to cling to, unpainted and smeared with fingerprints, and the decaying rubber seals around the windows on which, at the dampest times of year, moss grew. Vibrating engine, foul air, heaters blasting from beneath the seats.

A swing door slammed shut and Ben's eyes snapped open to see a man standing in front of him. In a black suit and dark tie, with neatly trimmed receding black hair, sharp cheekbones and a mournful expression, he resembled an undertaker who had misplaced his top hat. His chalk-white hands hung at his side, bony fingers curled inward. He attempted a smile but managed only a nervy twitch of the mouth, and extended one of his pale claws.

'Mr Hodge? Detective Superintendent Marwick.'

Ben stood up and shook the proffered hand. It felt dry and smooth as if dusted with talcum powder.

'If you'll follow me upstairs,' said Marwick, and set off for the swing door. Ben dithered and Marwick paused halfway. He clapped his hands together and looked at Ben, waiting for him to catch up. There was no lift so they marched up three flights of stairs in silence, past fire extinguishers and double doors, enveloped in the smell of detergent, wood polish and ancient dust.

Through double doors on the third floor they stepped out into a corridor along one side of which ran a temporary plasterboard wall topped with frosted glass. Marwick turned left and, again, waited for Ben, conveying impatience with a slight rise of the eyebrows and pursing of the lips.

'We're almost there.' He gave a small cough and adjusted his tie, fussing rather than preening.

At the end of the corridor, he stopped smartly, almost clicking his heels, and swung open a door, gesturing for Ben to enter first. Inside were a table, two chairs, a jug of water, and a stack of plastic cups. A picture had fallen off the wall and been left where it lay, with shattered glass, leaning against the skirting board. A stack of papers had been dumped on the floor in one corner, grey with dust. Wind whined through gaps in the ancient metal window frames. On the windowsill, caught in the draught, was a small plastic policeman whose oversized, grinning head, faded bone white on one side, bounced on a spring.

'Please, take a seat,' said Marwick, closing the door behind him.

Ben did as he was told. Marwick remained standing, rocking on his heels, hands clasped behind his back. 'I've asked you here today because I have been put in charge of a preliminary review of a case of police corruption.'

'Mr Sweetland?' said Ben.

Marwick cleared his throat and, Ben thought, swallowed a stammer. 'Yes, that's right. I don't need to tell you, then, that the particular reason you are here is because of Esther Garrett.'

After a moment's hesitation, Ben said, 'I guessed it would be that.'

Marwick frowned and barely lifted his hand in a controlling gesture. Ben resolved to keep quiet until he was asked a question.

'What I'd like to do, with your permission, just to keep things above board and properly documented, is call in a colleague of mine as an observer. I'd also like to record our conversation.'

Ben nodded. 'Sure.'

Marwick rewarded him with a brief, restrained smile and stepped over to the door. He opened it and beckoned to someone. A few seconds later, a young woman entered the room, closing the door behind her. She was tall, plainly dressed, with blonde hair cut severely to shoulder-length. She shook Ben's hand and breathed, 'Hi,' before quickly setting about plugging in a small digital recorder. A green light began to blink. 'Okay,' she said after a moment, taking a seat opposite Ben, with Marwick over her shoulder, silhouetted against the window.

'Well, then,' said Marwick. 'Twenty years ago you were a witness in the investigation into the disappearance of Esther Garrett, is that correct?'

'Yes.'

'You were how old, Mr Hodge?'

'Eleven.'

'And you gave a statement to Steven Sweetland, is that correct?'

Ben licked his lips and fidgeted. 'A statement?'

Involuntarily, perhaps, Marwick raised an eyebrow, and almost rolled his eyes. 'Which is to say, you described events to him to the best of your recollection and that was then presented to you as a written document which you confirmed to be an accurate record of your conversation.'

Again, Ben squirmed, leaning forward and holding up his hands in surrender. 'It was a long time ago, but I remember he came to the house and asked some questions.' Ben frowned. 'I didn't see anything written up.'

At this, Marwick closed his eyes and moved his lips silently, grasping for the right words. When he did speak, he got stuck on the first syllable. 'Y-y-ou didn't sign a statement?'

'Not that I can remember.'

The female detective, whose name Ben had not been told, opened a pink folder, removed a sheet of paper, and slid it across the table.

Ben reached for the paper, causing Marwick to lurch forward with a hand extended. Ben froze.

'Actually, don't touch that paper, please.' He leaned to whisper in his colleague's ear, but Ben heard him quite well: 'Fingerprints.'

'Why would you be interested in my fingerprints?' said Ben, feeling heat rising up his neck and into his cheeks.

Marwick raised his hands to placate him and pursed his lips to speak. 'P-p-please don't be concerned.' He sighed and directed a neat fingernail at the bottom of the page. 'If you didn't see this paper during the original investigation then your prints won't be on it, so it would be helpful to keep it that way.'

'Oh, right,' said Ben. 'This is all quite serious?'

'Yes, it is,' said Marwick. 'Now, if you could take a look.' He gestured at the paper.

Ben scanned the sheet. It had been written in block capitals with a biro, the words sliding off to one side as the lines drooped:

THE MAN WITH THE
PRISON BAG WAS
TALKING TO THE LADY ON
THE BUS AND SHE TOLD
HIM TO STOP. SHE RAN
AWAY TO THE FRONT OF
THE BUS AND GOT OFF.
THE MAN GOT ANGRY
AND FOLLOWED HER. I
SAW HIM GO AFTER HER
INTO THE WOOD AND
GRAB HOLD OF HER BY
THE ARM AND THEN THE
BUS PULLED AWAY.

Ben shook his head and looked up, wide-eyed. 'I don't know how to explain this. I never said that.'

Marwick and his colleague locked eyes for a moment.

'Are you absolutely certain?' Marwick got tangled up in the S, hissing through it like a serpent, his stammer betraying his excitement at this news.

'Absolutely, yes, because that's not what I saw.'

'But you do recall talking to Mr Sweetland?'

'Yes. Only for a few minutes, though.' Ben frowned. 'He did perhaps try to put some pressure on me.'

'You were eleven years old,' said the woman. 'Perhaps he just felt intimidating, because of his size and authority?'

'And it was rather a fraught situation,' added Marwick with an awkward, dry laugh.

'Maybe,' said Ben, but he shook his head again. 'I think he wanted me to say exactly this and I couldn't, because it wasn't true.'

'But someone signed it on your behalf,' said Marwick.

Ben craned over the paper and squinted. The signature was unreadable, just a wobbling line, but he recognised it. 'Dad. My father.' He frowned briefly. Should he have said anything at all?

'We were planning to speak to him,' said the woman, reading his concern.

Ben stared at the paper and shook his head in disbelief. He opened his mouth and snapped it shut.

'Is there something you'd like to put on record, Mr Hodge?'

'No, no – nothing,' said Ben. He pushed the chair back and stood up. 'Can I go now?'

Marwick smiled, twitching and thin-lipped. 'I did just have a couple of other questions, actually.' He pressed his hand down through the air as if pacifying an animal and Ben sank back into his seat.

'Do you recall meeting any other police officers?'

Ben nodded. 'I can't remember her name.' He described the female detective who had accompanied Sweetland on his visit to May Hodge's house, and noted another significant glance between the two police officers.

'Christine Kelly,' said Marwick after a moment, and pointed to the countersignature on the statement.

With a sigh Marwick finally pulled a chair out from under the table and sat down to Ben's left, on the end of the table. He put his hands together as if in prayer, lining his fingers up precisely with one another. Once they were correctly arranged he pressed the tips to his mouth. 'This is a big question,' he said, and waited for some sign of assent from Ben, who gave a single sharp nod of his head. 'Given that, as I'm sure you've read in the papers, we can no longer assume that the conclusions reached by Mr Sweetland are, as it were, sound.' He parted his fingertips and then snapped them back together. 'We are forced to consider two possibilities, each arguably as terrible as the other. First, that some of those convicted using evidence gathered by Mr Sweetland were innocent and have therefore been wronged by the justice system.' He looked solemn and pale. 'Secondly, however, we must also consider the p-p-possibility that he convicted exactly the right people but with evidence now so discredited that rapists and murderers walk free, in which case the justice system will have failed victims.' He fixed Ben with a hard gaze. 'So, my question to you is this: do you recall any information whatsoever that might point to a suspect other than Aaron Greenslade?'

As he considered his response, Ben's eyes drifted away from the intense gaze of Marwick's pale blue eyes and towards the female detective who gave a small, sympathetic, encouraging smile.

'I was terrified of him – Aaron Greenslade, I mean. I've never doubted that he did it. Killed her. Who else could there be?'

Marwick grimaced. 'That is a good question,' he said, elaborating no further. He gestured with an open hand and frowned. 'Now, I'm sure I don't need to say this, but the conversation we have had here today is part of an ongoing investigation–'

'Yes, I understand.'

'– which means that you mustn't discuss it with anyone else. You might be approached by people representing, or claiming to represent, Mr Sweetland. If so, I advise you strongly not to talk to them.'

'Right.'

'They m-m-might be lawyers or union representatives or journalists.'

Ben looked troubled. 'And I'm not allowed to talk to them?'

'Allowed is a strong word,' said Marwick. 'Advising, that's all. Strongly advising.'

After a moment Marwick raised both eyebrows and smiled stiffly. 'You can go now – thank you.'

All three stood up and Ben shook their hands, feeling as if he'd failed a job interview.

Outside the building he felt exhilarated, as if his airways were clear for the first time in years. This was the moment when he submitted completely, unable to resist the high.

Ben found it impossible to concentrate on anything but Esther Garrett. London itself seemed barely real and he began to feel detached from his own body, as if he were observing remotely from somewhere far away – from Devon.

Late at night and before work, as he ate dinner or breakfast at his spotless IKEA table, he compulsively searched newspaper websites and forums using slight variations on the same terms. It was a miserable compulsion, a kind of picking at the wound, but he had no appetite, and no attention span, for anything else.

In the office he tried to stick to the targets which gave shape to his day, determined his status on the team, and motivated him to keep picking up the next letter on the pile. Aiming to reply to ten letters a day he found himself managing eight, then seven, and finally six. He gave up trying to catch up on the backlog, instead letting them pile up along with the red flagged reminder emails from the logging system that began to clutter his inbox. He kept drifting back to his web browser, compulsively checking the BBC news website for updates in the Steven Sweetland case, and reading web forums dedicated to unsolved crimes.

There were many of them and most were concerned with serial murderers such as the San Francisco Zodiac Killer of the 1960s and 70s, or 'Bella in the Wych Elm'. They constructed elaborate theories with sketches, photographs and anonymous testimony. Others, however, focused on missing and murdered people who seemed to have been forgotten among the mass of similar such cases. The hostel killer, the babes in the wood, three French tourists shot on a campsite in Cheshire, the murder of Judith Roberts and the wrongful conviction of Andrew Evans. All of this, the mass of sad little deaths that caused brief periods of sensation in the fifties, sixties, seventies, before moss grew over the graves, began to form an additional burden for Ben.

There were a handful of threads dedicated to Esther Garrett's case but they were brief and unhelpful, often simply rehashing facts that Ben knew by heart. He came to dread posts that began, 'Okay, here's my theory', because they were invariably little more than works of fiction whose authors seemed to have forgotten that a real person had died, leaving behind grieving family and friends. For them, it was mere entertainment. Others explored similarities to the habits and locations of serial killers known to be active at the time, and suggested connections to the other well-known missing person cases, but ultimately produced no convincing evidence.

One such thread, much to Ben's surprise, mentioned him, though only as 'the little boy on the bus'. When he had read that, a question crossed his mind: how had Lucy found out about him? His name had never appeared in news coverage, though his father's had on a couple of occasions, and the police papers were confidential. He made a note to ask her next time they spoke.

The more he read and searched and obsessed, the more frustrated he became – there was nothing new to chew on, and without real information, it was all just guesswork. That didn't stop him – it merely turned the process into a grimly repetitive, ever more frustrating grind.

He needed more. He needed, after all, to meet Lucy Garrett.

CHAPTER ELEVEN

A weary-looking intercity train pulled into Exeter St David's station at a little after midday. Ben stepped off onto a platform crowded with students and shoppers. There was a rucksack on his back. He crossed the footbridge and followed Edwardian signage on fired tiles which directed him with pointing fingers to the exit.

Outside the station he sheltered from hammering rain in an awning full of cigarette smoke. He scanned the car park opposite. It took him a moment to notice Peter Hodge waving. He had climbed out of his car and was shielding his head with a newspaper which was already grey and drooping. Ben waved back and jogged across the road, splashing through puddles, drenched by the time he reached the car. Peter had the boot open ready and slung Ben's rucksack in. He slammed the hatch shut and dashed to get into the driver's seat while Ben took the passenger side.

They sat for a moment panting and mopping the worst of the running water from their eyebrows and hair. The light through the steamed-up windows was an Atlantic grey and the rain on the windscreen filled the uncomfortable gap where there ought to have been conversation. Peter switched on the heating to clear the condensation, adding a background hum.

Ben broke the silence. 'How are you then?'

'Me?' said Peter, as if there might be someone else more interesting in the car with them. 'Not too bad, son – mustn't grumble, you know. Going all right. And yourself?'

'I'm fine. The train was busy.'

'Was it, be damned? Busy? Well, there you go.' Peter often carried on like that, filling silence with meaningless filler phrases, clichés and repetition, as a kind of nervous tic.

As the fog on the windows began to fade Peter shuddered with cold. His sodden jacket clung to his torso and his hair was plastered to his head. He started the engine. They pulled out onto the main road and Ben glanced sideways at Peter. Fifteen years since he last drove a bus – he still looked like a professional driver – casual and confident, almost aggressive, his pale eyes moving from mirror to road to mirror as his hands moved smoothly round the wheel and about the gear stick.

'How's work going?'

'Mustn't grumble – it's work, isn't it? Work to live, not live to work, that's what I always say.'

After a pause Ben answered a question which hadn't been asked. 'Mine's going okay but I think I'm going to start looking for something else soon.'

'Yeah?'

Ben gave up and turned his head to look out of the window as they passed out of the city and into the green and red brick of the suburbs. He wiped his hand across the glass with a squeak, clearing a faint film of condensation.

Peter turned the radio on. It was tuned to a local station playing 1980s pop without announcements but with breaks for advertisements.

When they finally hit the A-road to Okehampton, Peter put his foot down, driving above the speed limit despite the wet roads.

Ben saw a sign for an upcoming roundabout and sat upright. 'Dad – do you mind stopping at Berebroke?'

'Why?' said Peter. He looked at the clock on the dusty dashboard. 'We've got to have dinner yet.'

'Just for five minutes,' said Ben.

With a shrug, Peter tapped the indicator switch and changed lanes in one smooth move. He took the left exit at the roundabout.

'Actually, I should say – the reason I've come down – one of the reasons, I mean – is to do with Berebroke.' Ben rubbed at the back of his neck and his cheeks took on a touch of colour. 'Do you remember that Esther Garrett thing?'

Peter looked across at Ben. 'Yeah. You never shut up about it when you were a kid.'

'What?'

When Peter spoke in more than monosyllables and grunts, it always seemed as if he was pushing the words through a barrier. 'Me and your mother, we talked about that, you know. We weren't talking, but we talked about *that*.'

'I didn't know.'

Peter compressed his lips and sniffed. 'God rest her soul, we didn't get on, but she was a good mother to you, and shoot me down if I ever said otherwise. You were a funny kid at the best of times, no offence, but you started reading the paper, watching the news – the news! Eleven years old, and watching the news.' He shook his head in astonishment at the memory.

As the road dipped they followed a tight curve round and down into Berebroke.

'Anyway, that's why I'm here – because her sister wants to meet me.'

Again, Peter looked sideways, but this time he tutted and puffed. 'Bloody hell, son – best not to get involved.'

He slowed at the first speed limit sign, then again as they passed the sign welcoming visitors to the village and imploring them to drive carefully.

It was still raining when Peter pulled over at the bus stop. 'Go on then,' he said. 'I'll stay here.'

Ben got out and then leaned back in to say, 'I'll be five minutes.'

He pulled up the hood of his coat and zipped it, dug his hands into the pockets, and walked into the wood. The path was slick with water and had remained icy in the shade of the trees. The stump that had been used as a shrine twenty years before was still there but there were no flowers or cards this time. He stopped and stared at it for a moment and then took a deep breath of rich, damp air. Looking back towards the car he could see his father's face as an indistinct white circle.

'I'm not sure what I'm doing,' he said aloud.

He waited for a moment, but Esther didn't answer.

With a sigh, he walked back the way he'd come, pausing before he left the wood to take one last look, and to breathe the air again. He climbed into the car.

'What was all that about?'

Ben didn't know how to explain it so, instead, changed the subject. 'Do you ever hear from Auntie Jeanette? Or Chelsea?'

Peter put the car in gear and, with a glance over his shoulder, pulled out into the road and made a U-turn. 'No, not really. Last I heard, Jeanette was getting married and moving to Spain. That girl of hers, what was she called?' He slowed and then revved, forcing himself into a non-existent space in the traffic at the roundabout. 'She works up at the big Tesco now. I've seen her in there sometimes, you know, but not to talk to, not much, anyway.'

Ben wanted to ask how she looked but couldn't find a way to frame the question and his father's brief talkative moment had apparently passed.

After several songs had played on the radio without either of them saying a word, Ben cleared his throat. 'I had to speak to the police last week, by the way.'

'Yeah?'

'You know they're reopening the case – well, sort of – because of that detective, Sweetland.'

'He fucked up royally, son, pardon my French. They called me too. I've got to go into Exeter next week.'

Up ahead, the rooftops of Okehampton came into view under the black clouds.

Ben frowned. 'They showed me a statement I'm supposed to have made, that you signed.'

With a sigh, Peter nodded in resignation and gripped the wheel tighter. 'What can I say, son? What can I tell you?'

Ben's voice took on a hard edge as he replied. 'You could at least try to explain.'

'Look,' said Peter, bristling, sitting upright in the driving seat and hunching forward. 'I'm just a simple bloke, right? I was just trying to do the right thing, by you and by that bloody girl.'

'How do you mean?'

They turned onto a road which led through the estate and Ben saw the doctor's surgery he'd visited as a child, a house where he'd once been to a birthday party – he couldn't remember whose – and a park where he'd played.

Peter rumbled.

'If a policeman tells me to do something, I do it, right? I'm not rebellious, or whatever you want to call it. I trust the police, because I'm a normal, law-abiding type of a bloke, right? Right?'

'Okay, yes,' said Ben.

They passed a row of shops where Ben used to buy sweets and crisps after school, and Peter pulled into a parking space, switching off the engine.

When he spoke next, his tone had become pleading and passive.

'So that copper told me that if we didn't say we'd seen that lad actually, you know, physically touching her, then he'd probably get off.'

The rain tapped on the car window.

'But what *did* you see?'

'What could you see? I couldn't see bloody anything. It was too dark.' Peter slammed his hands down on the steering wheel with a bang. 'That copper believed, in his heart of hearts, son, that the lad had done it. He was a nasty piece of work, no doubting that. He told me, the copper, that whatshisname, he told me that lad had been getting away with all sorts for years – mugging, vandalism, drugs, bothering women, all that.' He shook his head. 'It's always easy with the benefit of hindsight, son, but I thought I was doing the right thing, you see?'

'I guess I might have done the same,' said Ben.

Peter sank in his seat as if he'd been released from a hook.

Ben had arranged to meet Lucy Garrett in a chain coffee shop near her office in Exeter city centre. He arrived twenty minutes early and bought a black coffee. At the back of the shop he found a seat under a large canvas print of a Vespa scooter and bunched himself uncomfortably into a low armchair with high arms. After a minute or so, without realising, he began to drum his fingers on the leather and to bounce his knee. The place filled up with office workers buying grilled cheese sandwiches and muffins; someone tried to take the other seat at the table but Ben rebuffed him. At 12.15, there was still no sign of her. As his coffee went cold, Ben checked his mobile phone repeatedly. He was preparing to give up and walk out when he saw her come through the door.

He recognised her at once, not only from the video she'd sent him, but also from the way she moved and from her smile: for a moment, she was Esther Garrett, and the differences between them were mere superficialities. She was wearing a black trouser suit with a black blouse, under a cherry-red overcoat. He stood up as she approached, and she smiled thinly, extending a small hand to shake his.

'Thank you for agreeing to meet me, Mr Hodge,' she said.

'Ben.' He hadn't meant to sound sullen but couldn't help himself.

'I needn't have worried about recognising you,' she said, gesturing at his red hair.

He winced, defensive and weary.

'Can I get you another coffee?' she asked, pointing at his abandoned cup. He noticed that she had a trace of a local accent.

'Yes – black, thanks.'

It was half past twelve before they were finally sat opposite each other, ready to talk. Now she was still he was able to see that though she might pass for a teenager at a glance there were the beginnings of age lines around her eyes and across her forehead, and that her hands were creased around the knuckles.

'Thanks so much for agreeing to meet me,' she repeated, dabbing at her nose with a tissue. 'I've taken the afternoon off so I'm in no rush.'

'Me neither,' said Ben.

He wanted to say *I shouldn't be doing this*. He wanted to ask *Why did you tempt me?* But he didn't. He simply sat there, blank, and waited for her to lead him. Though she was six years younger than him, she seemed older – a result, perhaps, of an expensive-looking and fashionable hair-cut, her surprisingly deep, mellow voice, and a certain confidence. He felt subordinate.

'First, if you don't mind,' she said, 'can you talk me through that day when you saw her – all of it, from the start?'

Ben rubbed at his throat. 'Sure.' He talked for fifteen minutes, recalling every detail that came to mind, conscious of wanting to please her with the completeness and clarity of his memory. He occasionally closed his eyes to better picture the scene, or to focus his memory on something specific – the badges on Esther's jacket, the other passengers on the bus.

The only facts he omitted were that, in some way he still did not fully understand, he had been attracted to Esther, and that he had collected pictures of her. He knew it would sound sinister and he was ashamed of it, even as he knew he could not be blamed for his pre-adolescent instincts.

Lucy gave no indication of being pleased or otherwise, merely nodding occasionally to urge him on, or tilting her head at certain interesting details.

'And that's it,' he said in conclusion, and then waited, eager to hear whether he had passed what he felt was a test.

'That really was every detail,' she said, and smiled briefly in polite acknowledgement.

Her reaction made him uneasy. He'd been prepared for the conclusion to his account to prompt tears but she seemed barely moved.

'I've thought about it a lot,' said Ben. 'Gone over it in my head so many times. Not so much lately but years ago, I mean. That's why I was reluctant to do this.'

She looked down into the still, black surface of her untouched coffee and gave another tense, joyless smile.

'Tell me about it,' she said. 'For me, it's the day she didn't come home. I remember what was on TV, what I was wearing.' She raised a hand, searching for the right words, picking them out of the air with her fingertips. 'The quality of light in the front room.' She blew through pursed lips. 'The rule was that she had to be home by nine. She was always missing tea but usually because she was having a good time, not because she was being deliberately rebellious or anything. But Dad hated going to bed without having seen her at all. So, at first, he got mad.'

She hesitated and looked at Ben. He met her gaze and waited, sensing that she was judging how much more to tell him.

Half-consciously, he mirrored her cold smile.

Now she had started, he needed more.

'The thing is,' she said, drawing the words out, 'Dad was always very strict with us.' She closed her eyes and waved a hand to downplay what she'd said. 'I don't mean violent. He never touched us.' She sighed. 'That is, he didn't smack us about.'

Ben wondered what she was struggling with.

After an uncomfortable pause, she found some words. 'If Dad said nine, he meant nine. He was the boss.'

Ben observed a small shake of the head, barely a movement at all, and a twitch of the upper lip. His instincts told him there was some bitterness there – contempt, even – but the gesture had been small, and he immediately doubted himself.

'Dad was angry and went straight out, got in the car, and drove off.'

Ben nodded, his face blank, though he felt something spark at the thought of an angry father pursuing a wayward daughter in the dark on the night she disappeared.

'He went to the shopping arcade – that's where she and her friends used to hang out, round the back by the bins.' She shivered. 'Grim, really, but there weren't many other places to go. She had a couple of older friends who used to buy drink and cigarettes at the Spar.'

Ben frowned. He hadn't pictured Esther smoking.

'There were these lads – losers, really – who she and her friends sort of took turns with.' She squirmed and sighed. 'To go out with, I suppose would be the polite way to put it. Not boyfriends, exactly.'

She looked into her coffee cup and swirled the dark liquid with its film of oil. Ben took the opportunity to speak. 'They didn't mention any of this on the news back then.'

Lucy's eyes narrowed and a line appeared between her brows. 'She was just being a normal teenage girl.'

The anger lifted from her look. 'They wanted people to feel sympathy for her and you know what people are like – if you're not a complete saint then it means you were asking for it.'

'Oh, I know,' said Ben. He did know – he felt exactly that instinct to judge but knocked it back.

'Anyway, the kids at the shops told Dad that they hadn't seen her. At first, he didn't believe them, especially not those older boys. I think it got a bit nasty because he came back with a bruised cheek and cuts on his knuckles.'

Ben's skin prickled again.

'She wasn't there and no one could tell him where to find her so next he tried the park – also nothing. He got home at about ten.' She shook her head. 'He was in such a state. Mum was trying to calm him down but getting upset herself. She couldn't help it. I wasn't worried because I assumed she'd gone off with one of those boys, on the back of a moped.' She waved a hand. 'You know.'

Ben felt hot and uncomfortable.

'They went and whispered to each other in the kitchen – angry whispering – then came back in acting as if there was nothing wrong, and sent me to bed. I couldn't sleep. I listened at the door.'

Behind her the coffee shop was beginning to empty, the lunchtime rush coming to an end.

'When she hadn't got home by midnight, I really did start to get upset, and then the doorbell rang.' She gestured with her fingers, mimicking the flowering of fireworks. 'Mum was crying, I started crying, Dad was shouting. I went to sit on the stairs and saw policemen in the hallway.'

She brushed a strand of dark hair away from her face, behind her ear, and Ben felt a prickle of attraction.

'I don't know if you've ever had policemen in your house but there's something so terrifying about it. It ought to be reassuring, right? But they never come with good news. You never call them about anything *nice*. They were both men, big, like policemen used to be, and dressed in black. So intimidating. They made Dad look small and pathetic.'

She spat the last word, giving away more than perhaps she had intended, Ben thought.

'Even from upstairs, I could smell – what was it?' She wrinkled her nose and looked to one side, trying to recall a sense memory from twenty years before. 'Motor oil and aftershave.'

Ben nodded. They looked into each other's eyes for a moment, feeling the weight of the memory together, until Ben blinked and looked down at his bunched hands.

'I don't think anyone slept,' Lucy went on. 'There were cars coming and going all night. No one came to check on me, not even when a policewoman came upstairs to go over Esther's room. Do you know, that's where they find most missing children and teenagers? Hiding under their bed or something.' She frowned and then made a sad, dry sound that was not quite laughter. 'I kept checking her room for years after that, just in case she'd come back, or there was somewhere we'd forgotten to look.'

She moved to sip her coffee, and realised it was cold. 'Shall we?' She gestured towards the door. 'I could do with some fresh air. We can walk while we talk.'

'Okay,' said Ben. 'I like walking.'

As she knew the city better than him, he let her guide their movements. She wasn't short but he stood a full head taller and so had to make an effort to prevent himself striding ahead. That meant he almost stumbled at points. Her heels tapped on the pavement as they picked their way through side streets and alleyways, past pubs and boutiques, towards Cathedral Green.

'When some detectives turned up I knew it was serious,' said Lucy, raising her voice to be heard over an insistent wind twisting its way through the lanes. 'She hadn't shown by morning and Mr Sweetland kept saying not to worry, but then we'd hear him ordering sniffer dogs and frogmen.'

She looked up at Ben briefly. 'What did you think of him? Steven Sweetland, I mean?'

Ben opened and closed his mouth, unsure what to say. 'I was scared of him, I think.'

She nodded – he'd answered correctly. 'Me too,' she said, 'but I...' She stopped herself. 'Oh, nothing.'

He wasn't sure whether it was a good idea to press her but, after a moment's silence, said, 'What?'

'It's a bit weird.' She sighed. 'I had a crush on him, I guess.' She winced. 'It was a strange time. He used to come round every now and then, even after Aaron Greenslade had gone to prison. In the evening, mostly. I think he was drunk sometimes. He said he wanted to check we were doing okay and he'd update us on the search.' She stopped herself and swallowed. 'For Esther. He and a couple of his colleagues kept looking in their spare time. Dad was the same – he'd go out and come back twelve hours later covered in mud, miserable as hell.'

Ben noted that detail – if Eddie Garrett had anything to do with it, why would he waste time looking for her body? Unless, of course, it was all part of his cover.

'Did you ever look for her yourself?'

Lucy shook her head. 'No, although it's hard not to keep glancing into ditches or undergrowth, just in case. I still do it now.'

On the perimeter of the green, over which the scaffolding-clad cathedral stood high and indifferent, the light was already golden and the shadows long. They dropped into the slow amble of a pair of tourists following the pavement alongside the low wall that separated the green from the narrow, cobbled street.

'When they started showing her picture on TV later the same day, Mum lost it. She just wouldn't stop crying.' Lucy stopped, pursing her lips, pulling something back inside herself. '"My baby's dead," she kept saying.' She looked up at Ben and raised her eyebrows. 'Dad hated that. Hated it. He's never really accepted the reality of it, you know? He still thinks she just ran away.'

They stopped to look at the cathedral, cast into shade by the low sun, out of time and looking as if it belonged in another place – Paris, perhaps, or Amsterdam.

Biting her lips, Lucy looked pained. 'I'm going to tell you something that might make me sound bad,' she said.

'Okay,' said Ben, unsure.

'I didn't cry again. Honestly – not once, after that first night.'

Ben thought about this for a moment and then nodded in silent understanding.

'Mum was crying enough for everyone. And Dad. Maybe I thought they didn't need to worry about me too.' She looked away into the distance. 'Sorry, I don't think you need to hear all this.'

'It's fine,' Ben said.

She began walking again. 'I have to be completely honest with you, Ben,' she said, using his first name for the first time. 'There's something I haven't told you, which is the main reason I got in touch.' She looked at him, gauging his reaction. 'I want to investigate the case myself.'

Ben's brow creased. 'Is that a good idea?' he said. 'What with the police reopening the case.'

'What do you mean?'

'They approached me,' he said. 'To ask about Mr Sweetland.'

'Oh, that,' she replied wearily. 'They're not actually reopening Esther's file, not yet anyway. There are too many to look into and ours is low priority, apparently.'

'I see,' said Ben.

'I wanted to talk to you because I was hoping your story might give me something to look into – a lead, I suppose I should call it if I'm going to do this seriously.'

'Right,' he said.

She looked at him, her eyes moving across his face, searching for something. Then she smiled warmly. Ben felt a glow spread through him and swallowed hard.

'I think it's a good idea,' he said.

After a moment's pause, during which she looked away and up at the reddening sky, Ben widened his eyes and, with false hesitancy, said, 'I could even help, if you like. Contribute something practical.'

She looked sideways at him, the smile gone, probing. He made eye contact and held it, trying to convey something in his expression that might reassure her that he was not to be feared and could be trusted.

He sucked in his bottom lip and braced himself.

'Can I be honest?'

'Please do,' she said.

'It's always bugged me that she was never found. I forgot about it for a long time so not always but, recently, since it's been back in the news, I remembered how much I used to think about it.'

'I know what you mean,' said Lucy. She gestured at a bench and they wandered towards it. They sat facing the great doors of the cathedral across a stretch of flagstone paving. It was cold and getting colder and their breath condensed in wisps around their heads. 'At least before I thought the person who had done it had been punished. Now, I don't even have that.'

'Well, I'm not so sure,' said Ben.

She waited for him to elaborate.

'Have you ever met Aaron Greenslade?' he asked.

She shook her head.

'No, he would never see me, and my parents wouldn't let me go to court.'

'I don't think he's exactly what you'd call an innocent victim,' said Ben. 'I was scared of everyone when I was eleven.' He looked down and sighed. 'But he was on another level.' He shook his head. 'A real psycho.'

'That's what he calls himself,' said Lucy. 'That or "Mad Dog".' Her lip curled. 'Ridiculous. And Detective Inspector Sweetland – Mr Sweetland – agreed with you, obviously. At any rate, he'll probably be out soon, won't he?' She shivered and rubbed her upper arms with fingers raw from the cold. 'I'll have to try again to speak to him,' she said. 'I'd like to look him in the eye.' Her eyes met Ben's. 'And if he really is innocent perhaps he saw something that might put us on to the right person.'

Ben noticed her use of the word 'us'. She was reeling him in, but he didn't mind.

'Of course,' said Ben. 'You should try again. Because if not him, then who?'

Lucy raised an eyebrow and gave a small sideways jerk of the head. 'Now that's a good question. The village had its fair share of weirdos and perverts, believe me.' She took a sharp breath and stopped herself, as if she'd said more than intended.

'The police must have looked into all of them, surely?' said Ben.

'I honestly don't think so. Once they had Aaron Greenslade in the frame, thanks to you and your dad, their focus narrowed.'

Ben blew on his hands and rubbed them.

The dull sound of the church bells striking three o'clock echoed across the green and around Cathedral Close. Lucy looked at her watch. 'I'd better be going, I suppose,' she said.

They both stood up.

'How did you get my name, by the way?' said Ben.

'Bribery and emotional blackmail. A couple of hundred pounds and some tears will get you a long way with a retired bus company manager.'

Ben felt momentarily queasy, as if realising the terrain around him had changed and he was suddenly lost.

'I'll call you soon,' she said. 'In the meantime, do have a think about possible leads or clues or whatever you want to call them.'

'Yes, I will, no problem,' said Ben, curious but treading carefully.

'It's really nice to meet someone who understands,' she said, extending a hand.

Ben shook it and, as her skin connected with his, felt a thrill along his spine.

He hadn't touched another person in months, and this wasn't just anyone – it was Esther Garrett's sister. Her hand was soft and dry. He snatched his own away, suddenly terrified that she'd guess what he was thinking.

She didn't seem to notice.

CHAPTER TWELVE

Something Lucy Garrett said played on his mind: if there were oddballs living in and around Berebroke, as she had suggested, it seemed likely to him that there would be some record of similar offences. There were no other missing people but he soon had a list of sexual assaults and abductions, both attempted and realised, between 1985 and 2005, covering almost the whole county.

Looking at them marked on an old Ordnance Survey map, he thought he perceived patterns or connections, and felt moments of elation – the sense that, in an instant, he had found the definitive solution. A cluster around this village, a line passing through that one, a series bunched together in the same town. And then he would restrain himself, remind himself that people better qualified than he were looking into this problem, and also that it was easy to cook up conspiracy theories, forcing evidence to fit the narrative. The cluster disappeared when he removed the earliest instance; the line followed a road, of course; and the series bunched together was the result of a single man, charged and convicted, who died in 1993.

Because there was so little solid information about its circumstances, it was hard to say that any of the individual stories had particular echoes of Esther Garrett's disappearance. He looked for those involving women and girls of around the same age but that barely narrowed the field at all. Then he looked for mentions of woods, forests, and other rural locations, which did help a little because the vast majority had occurred in towns and cities.

What he needed if any progress was to be made was access to paperwork – to original documents or at least contemporary ones. He wondered about going back to Exeter to look at the local newspaper archives, or perhaps approaching Marwick, though he could think of no circumstances under which that grim, officious figure would bend the rules in his favour.

Then, looking at archive photographs of Sweetland for the hundredth time, a thought occurred to him: Sweetland's right-hand woman, the one who had come with him to May Hodge's terraced house, must still be around. He tried to remember her name which had escaped him again. Then when he pictured Marwick speaking and pointing at the statement with his pale hand, he had it.

Ben telephoned Christine Kelly one Saturday morning and got no answer on his first, second or third attempt. On the fourth try, at a little after 11am, she answered with a rasping, bad-tempered croak.

'All right, all right – what is it?'

'Is that Christine Kelly?'

'Whatever you're selling, I don't want it. Whatever I'm entitled to, I don't care. Now fuck off.'

'Wait,' Ben said, raising his voice a touch. 'It's about Esther Garrett.'

'Who?' There was rustling on the line and then, distantly, the sound of lung-wrenching coughing. 'Oh, yeah. I can't talk to journalists so you can do one for starters.'

Panicking, Ben lied. 'Lucy Garrett asked me to talk to you.'

After a short silence Kelly replied, warily, 'Oh yeah?'

'She is, I mean we are...' His voice weakened to nothing.

'What are you, then? Her boyfriend or something?'

Ben gave an awkward laugh. 'Just friends. Well, not even friends. Colleagues, I suppose. We're undertaking some private enquiries into the disappearance of her sister, that's all.'

'Private enquiries – fuck me, that's the last thing anyone needs. Why would I help you with anything like that?'

Ben licked his lips. Something about her voice, about her tone, told him that she was not in a good place. He decided to take a risk. 'I'd be willing to pay.'

This time the pause was longer. He thought he heard Kelly dragging on a cigarette. 'We'd better meet face to face,' she said, cold and cautious.

'Where?'

'My local, The Thatcher's Arms, up West Ealing.'

'When?'

'I'll be there when the doors open,' she said. 'Like most days.'

The Thatcher's Arms was exactly the kind of pub Ben would normally avoid. It was painted, though not freshly, in the gaudy colours of a football team Ben didn't know, and the windows were barred, frosted, and stained with at least twenty years' worth of nicotine.

The entrance was a double door on the corner and as Ben neared he slowed, realising that he was going to have to squeeze between two men smoking shrivelled roll-up cigarettes. The floor was littered with discarded ends. One of the men was short and bent-backed, with jaundice-yellow skin and a shaved head, while the other was taller, though still shorter than Ben, with a dirty grey ponytail and a sagging beer belly.

The stooped man made a double take at the sight of Ben, which made Ben smile nervously and issue an involuntary greeting: 'Good morning.' His Devon accent, which he had all but beaten out of himself, was suddenly quite evident. Neither man replied but they moved just far enough apart to permit him to slip between and into the pub.

He found a single large space with a straight bar at the far end, behind which a bearded man in his fifties, and with tattooed forearms, was eating a bacon sandwich as he read a newspaper. It was a Victorian building but there was little evidence of that in the décor; the walls were painted utilitarian grey, the floor was torn and patched linoleum and the chairs and tables were plastic and chipboard. The handful of drinkers looked up from their glasses as the door banged behind him. Most were old men, or at least men who looked old, with pints of Guinness or tumblers of whisky. As Ben stood, fixed to the spot, they looked away one by one, until only a single pair of eyes remained on him – those of a woman seated on a banquette by the window next to the blinking fruit machine.

Ben gave a meek smile and stepped towards her. 'Mrs Kelly?' The words caught in his throat, barely emerging as a mumble.

'Eh?' she said.

He coughed and tried again, over-enunciating. 'Are you Mrs Kelly?'

As he looked at her face, he realised he recognised her from some-where but it took a moment for his memory to work through the possi-bilities. She had cropped, dyed blonde hair, dark at the roots, and untidy at the edges, and a long nose covered with broken blood vessels. Her eyes were milky and moist.

'That's me,' she growled, and knocked back the clear liquid in the tumbler in front of her and held the glass out. 'Gin and a splash, if you're getting a round in.'

'A splash?'

She rolled her eyes. 'Ted knows what I drink.'

Ben kept his rucksack on, unsure whether it would still be there if he left it at the table, and went to the bar. The landlord put his sandwich down on the newspaper, wiped his hands on his jeans, and stood waiting.

'Whatever Mrs Kelly usually drinks.' He looked up and down the bar. 'And just a Stella for me, please.'

Ted pulled the lager and prepared the gin by pouring in a few drops of water from a jug on the back bar. He rang them through the till and pointed at the price on the electronic display. As he took Ben's ten pound note, he looked him in the eye.

'She ain't *Mrs* nothing,' he muttered.

'Right, thanks,' said Ben, taking his change.

He went back to the table and put the drinks down, took off his rucksack, and sat on a rickety tubular metal chair with a plastic-covered cushion.

'Ta,' said Kelly, picking up her gin and waving it in salute. She placed it back on the table without tasting it.

Ben, who didn't usually drink at lunchtime, took a long draught of his cold beer, which was strangely sour. He resisted the urge to pull a face. 'I'm Ben,' he said.

'Chris,' said Kelly. 'What's your game, then?' she asked.

'How do you mean?' asked Ben.

'Listen, son, this ain't my first time round the track. I don't buy all this private investigation bullshit. You're a journalist, aren't you?'

She read Ben's bemused look.

'Oh, no – you're just one of them internet trolls.' Her nostrils twitched as if at a rank odour.

After a moment's hesitation Ben said, 'You know, we've met before.'

Kelly's eyes narrowed and she pulled her head back. 'Look, sunshine,' she said, her voice all granite and growl, 'if I nicked you, you probably deserved it.'

'No, it's not that,' said Ben. 'Back then you came to my house – my nan's house. I was eleven. My dad drove the bus Esther Garrett was on before she disappeared.'

Kelly pointed at him and clicked her fingers. 'Bloody hell. Of course it is. Should have recognised you with hair that colour.'

Self-conscious, Ben ran a hand over the top of his head.

Then, Kelly's face clouded over. 'What the fuck was your dad thinking, letting her get off the bus with that fucking arsehole after her?'

Ben's cheeks blotched red and he took another swig of lager, which emboldened him sufficiently to reply. 'He's not the one who failed Esther Garrett.' But he swallowed the words and Kelly didn't hear him.

'What?'

He cleared his throat and, with more force than he'd intended, said it again.

Kelly's watery eyes flared and she downed the gin with one jerk of her arm. It dampened her temper and she said quietly, 'No, fair shout.'

Glancing about, Ben became conscious that the other customers in the pub were now watching them as if they were actors on a TV screen, frankly interested and entertained. Kelly raised herself up, leaning on the table, and growled at them. 'Mind your own fucking business.'

Someone grumbled but chairs scraped and every head turned away.

'Listen,' she said, almost whispering, 'I'm sorry about my temper. Blood pressure and one thing and another. I got "encouraged" to retire. Must be ten years ago, now. And, Jesus Christ, I hate it.' She stretched the word 'hate', rolling her eyes in a mockery of woe. 'The worst thing is, my social life went with it, especially when they shut down the social club – I used to go there a lot, the social, but now, this.' She gestured with a jerk of her head, indicating the whole room and the other customers, and tutted.

She held the empty glass in the air and shouted, in a faux-aristocratic voice, 'I say, Edward, old fruit.' The landlord gave a thumbs up and busied himself preparing another drink. When she turned back to Ben she was frowning. 'I've met all sorts,' she said. 'Psychics that say they can help people find their missing nippers, only that's all bollocks, obviously, and they string them along with messages and hints which are *eerily* accurate.' She wiggled her fingers like a magician. 'Of course they fucking are, because they've been nosing around talking to the neighbours for the last fortnight. Then the relatives get upset because we won't dig up a field in fucking Lincolnshire because the psychic says she's seen a tree and a wall and something beginning with the letter P, or is it a B. Meanwhile, this is all costing the bloody family their life savings.'

As she spoke, white spots of spittle flew from her mouth which had become lipless and trap-like. 'Same with private detectives – fucking sharks, the bunch of 'em. They've got a lead – the missing kid's been seen in France or Magaluf or somewhere, and they're willing to investigate for a fee, plus expenses, take the wife and all. Then, when the cash starts running out, they magically come up with another sighting, or an informant, and–' she crashed an open palm down on the table, causing the other customers in the pub to start '–there goes another half a year, second mortgage on the house to cover it.'

She sighed. 'Straight up nutters, too – religious types, people who are in contact with aliens, the ones who say they're the reincarnation of the dead kid.' She gave a throaty chuckle at this, but then waved a dismissive hand. 'They're not so bad, really, because they usually believe what they're saying, though you've got to watch for the ones who drop hints – a donation to fix the church roof might encourage God to pull his fucking finger out, that sort of thing.'

Then she smiled lopsidedly, tilting her head and looking Ben up and down. 'Then, sweetie, there's just sad little people who just get a hard-on from playing at being coppers.'

Ben felt a pang of embarrassment. 'Lucy called me. I didn't want to get involved.'

The landlord approached the table and slammed down the glass of gin. Ben smelled stale sweat and onions. Ted walked away without speaking.

'So,' said Kelly, 'why did you?'

Ben sipped at his lager while he considered his response. 'Honestly?' he said.

'That's how coppers like it, retired or not,' said Kelly.

'I don't want anything to do with this. It messed me up when I was a kid and I spent a long time trying to forget it. I don't know why she's trying to drag me back into it – I can't really see how I'm going to be of any use.'

He swallowed a lump in his throat. 'At the same time, I can't stop now. I know, I just know, I won't be able to sleep until I know who really took Esther. I hate the thought that they might have got away with it.'

Kelly's eyes seemed sharp as she challenged him with a hard stare. 'You'd better be right,' she said, 'because if I hear that you're taking advantage–'

Ben nodded eagerly. 'I understand. I won't. I'm not.'

'What is it you want from me?'

'Papers. Anything. I need information. I've been wondering if there might be similar cases where the connection wasn't made because you thought you had the right man from the start. Or maybe there was something you overlooked for the same reason.'

Kelly nodded. 'I ain't just going to give some stranger my old notebooks.'

Ben looked pained.

'I mean, what's in it for me?'

'What do you mean?'

'What do I get out of it?'

Ben shook his head in puzzlement. 'You don't mean money, do you? Not after that speech you just gave.'

Kelly played with the cigarette packet on the table, turning it round and round, balancing on one side after another. Her face seemed to turn grey and sank in on itself in sadness and self-pity.

'I'm living on my pension.' Her wet eyes narrowed meanly. 'And besides, I didn't come looking for you. All I'm saying is, if I've got something you want, I need a reason to risk letting you have it.'

'Don't you think you owe Lucy Garrett something?' Ben was surprised at his own nerve.

Kelly emptied her glass with a single movement and pushed it away across the table. 'Come back to mine and I'll show you what I've got. If it's any use to you.' She sighed as she began to pull on a black woollen pea coat designed for a man. 'We can talk about nuts and bolts later, all right?'

She waved to the landlord and walked out of the pub.

Ben abandoned his sour lager, quickly put on his rucksack, and followed her out into the street. She had already lit a cigarette, the tip of which glowed bright as she drew on it before emitting a long, gut-deep sigh of appreciation.

'Sorry about the mess,' she said, almost under her breath. 'Well, you know.'

Ben stepped into the short hallway over a pile of unopened letters and recoiled at a background smell of rotting vegetables.

'Straight through,' she said.

As Ben moved towards the sitting room he glanced into the kitchen where dirty dishes full of even dirtier water were piled in the sink. The floor was almost black with filth.

'Cup of tea or coffee or something?' she said. 'I'll put the kettle on.'

'Tea, thanks,' said Ben, then regretted it, wondering how clean the kettle and cup might be.

The sitting room – the only room of any substantial size on the ground floor – was gloomy, in part because a creeping, waxy-leafed plant had grown down over the patio doors like a fringe, giving the feel of some forgotten colonial outpost. There was a single armchair, clear of clutter itself but surrounded by piles of newspapers, magazines, creased paperbacks and stacks of CDs and vinyl records. A small folding table had been set up at one side but was completely covered in empty glasses and tea cups, except for where an overflowing ashtray sat surrounded by fine grey flakes of ash. There was nowhere else to sit – no sofa, no second chair, not even a dining set.

From the kitchen came the sounds of the kettle's hissing and Kelly singing to herself.

Ben dumped his rucksack on the floor and walked over to the cheap stereo system balanced on a plastic beer crate at the foot of the stairs. The record on the turntable was a yellow-labelled 1970s Deutsche Grammophon recording of a Beethoven symphony.

'Like music, do you?' said Kelly, entering the room with two mugs of tea and two cans of lager, dripping with condensation.

'I've never really got into it,' said Ben. 'My dad's never shown any interest and my mum liked jazz.' He wrinkled his nose.

'A woman of taste,' said Kelly. She had been dithering in front of her side table for a few seconds, unable to put down the drinks and finally said, 'Fucking hell – clear a few of them glasses.'

Ben picked up six, sticky and covered in fingerprints, and took them to the kitchen where he just managed to squeeze them into a space on the stained worktop. He returned to find Kelly slumped in her armchair with the can of lager to her lips. She gestured with her free hand.

'Over there,' she said. 'The yellow box.'

He turned and saw a plastic storage container under the stairs in the middle of a stack of nine, all apparently full of paperwork. With some difficulty he wrestled the box free and it crashed onto the carpet with a thud.

'Years of accumulated shite,' said Kelly with a gritty laugh.

He opened the box and peered inside.

Kelly leaned forward in her seat. 'You're looking for two A5 Black n' Reds, spiral bound.'

Ben found them and held them up for her approval.

Kelly nodded.

The books were labelled 1992–1995 and 1995–1999. Ben opened the first volume and began to flip through the pages which were full of notes in black or blue ballpoint ink, some neater than others. On some pages pieces of paper had been pasted in or stapled in place. He stopped to read a random page:

'What?' she said. 'Go on, ask me.'

'What does "SS leading again" mean? Is SS Steven Sweetland?'

'Yeah. Leading, you know.' She sagged in despair at Ben's ignorance. 'When you're questioning members of the public, you're not meant to tell them what to say because it comes back to bite you on the bum in court, but Steve, he'd always be just–' She gestured with a hand, pushing it through the air as if nudging something into place.

Ben frowned. 'Shouldn't you give these to the people investigating the case,' he said, reluctantly.

'What do you know about that?' said Kelly. 'Your tea's getting cold.'

Standing up, Ben stepped over to the table and picked up the mug, wrapping his fingers around it tightly. The house was cold.

'They called me in,' he said. 'To talk about Steven Sweetland "leading".'

Kelly nodded and sighed. 'Yeah, me and all – that fucking stiff Marwick, was it? I told them I'd dig this lot out, so if you want them you'll have to take photos or photocopies or whatever.'

Ben sipped his tea and winced. The milk was sour, floating in nuggets on the surface. He put the cup down.

'I'd better get on with it, then,' he said, and, in the absence of any other option, sat cross-legged on the floor with the books on his lap and smartphone held above the pages. After a minute or so without conversation, broken only by the sound of the artificial camera snap and the hiss of the ring-pull on Kelly's second can of lager, Ben cleared his throat.

'What?' said Kelly, tense and sour.

'I was just wondering if there is anyone else you had doubts about. Any other suspects.'

She weighed his question. 'If we hadn't turned up Greenslade right at the start we'd probably have looked at her boyfriends.'

'She had more than one?'

'That's just how it goes, or used to, anyway – first question: is she a slut, or an angel? If she's a slut, well, what can you do? And if she's an angel, you make sure she bloody well stays one as far as the public's concerned. But it ain't as simple as that, is it? Your so-called sluts, they've got families and friends. They might have made a bad decision or two, depending on your point of view, but that don't make 'em rubbish, does it?' She tutted from the corner of her mouth. 'Fuck sight harder to get the public to give a shit, though. Funny thing is, your angels – well, there aren't any of them either are there? Not that the boss would have that. She was Snow-fucking-White as far as he was concerned.'

She frowned and looked away towards a blank spot on the wall. 'He got a bit funny about her, truth be told. You'd have thought she was his daughter. For years after, he had a photo of her in his desk drawer. He thought none of us knew, oh, but we knew. The way they gossip in offices don't bear thinking about. He was–'

She stopped and blinked, breathing dumbly through her open mouth. 'Anyway, like I say, she was sixteen – she had a new lad every fortnight. Your usual schoolgirl flings, fumble round the bike sheds, but her parents didn't know about them, or at least they didn't know the names. A couple of her friends told us she'd been seeing a lad – another fucking scrote, as it happens, about the same as the one we nicked. A kid called Leslie something.' She jabbed a finger at Ben. 'It's in there,' she said, then clicked her fingers. 'Reeves. Leslie Reeves. Dopey kid.' She waved her finger round her temple. 'Off his nut on weed half the time.'

'Hmm,' said Ben, turning back to the documents. After a moment's brooding he said, 'You should have looked into him, shouldn't you?'

'Yeah, well, hindsight is a wonderful thing, sunshine. We all make mistakes.' She looked around the room as if suddenly confused or lost. When she spoke again, her voice was faint and papery. 'What he did, the boss – Steve – he did because he really believed it was the right thing. We never put anyone away we didn't think was guilty.' She looked at Ben and sneered. 'You wouldn't understand,' she said, waving her fingers to dismiss him. 'Finish that up and then you can walk me back to the pub.'

Ben's camera snapped, and snapped again. He turned the page.

CHAPTER THIRTEEN

When he entered his own flat and turned on the light, Ben stood on the threshold for a moment and his shoulders slumped. It was clean and tidy, and there were seats for guests, but it was just as much the home of a lonely person as Christine Kelly's. He dropped his rucksack, closed the door slowly and slumped against it with his hands behind his back.

After almost five minutes, during which time he stared blankly at the beige carpet, he heaved himself upright and walked to the kitchen, opened the fridge, and took out a bottle of beer. He popped the cap with the opener on his key ring and took a long pull before stopping to look at the bottle and thinking again of Christine Kelly. He reassured himself that he could put it down right then and that if he didn't drink again for another year that would be fine. He nodded, satisfied, and took another swig.

As he transferred the files from the memory card to his computer, he scanned through each one until he found those for the time of Esther's disappearance. They were cryptic but he was able to decipher much of what they said.

12/11/95

SS/CK canvas of bus passengers.
All saw EG board, take last seat.
All saw AG harassing. Bus
driver stalled before letting AG
off. Debate over timings. SS
sceptical — says no delay, which
puts AG in wood with EG.

12/11/95

Canvas residents Coleridge Drive.
Mrs Ellison, 2, think she saw EG
after 16:45 walking CD > Bus Stop,
via woods. Raised with SS: witness
not credible. Cited similar
appearance of most teenage girls
'these days'. After dark. Possible
confusion over times. No
corroboration from others.

13/11/95
AG associates: AG frequently
joked about rough sex, rape,
paedophilia, bestiality. SS
calls it fantasy. Some
evidence that AG abused young
cousin, harmed animals. SS
calls this sociopathic,
evidence of violent tendency,
AG 'escalating'. (SS now
think he is in FBI.)▢

16/11/95
SS has turned up something solid,
viz. an informant. SS has known
him for years, trusts him. Says
AG confessed. Sounds convincing —
jury will love it. 'I want to
catch one, rape it and kill it.'
('It'! Jesus Christ!) Echoes AG's
cousins, aunt.

These and other entries made Ben feel uneasy. Was this how the police always operated? By picking a suspect and building a case around them, rather than by following every lead to its conclusion? He wondered whether the websites he'd looked at, books he'd read, and conversations he'd had with Lucy Garrett, might one day be used to make him sound like a monster: 'He was a loner who kept himself to himself and was obsessed with the murders of young women.'

'Calm down,' he said aloud to himself. 'Just don't murder anyone.' He rubbed at his temples and allowed himself a dry laugh.

Once the files were copied he checked the time – a little after 5pm – and picked up his mobile. He called Lucy Garrett's number.

She answered immediately.

'Hi,' she said. 'I'm so glad you called.'

'I've got some news.'

'Yes?'

For some reason he felt the need to conceal that he'd spoken to Christine Kelly – even though Lucy had wanted his help, he knew it was a step too far to have spoken to Kelly on his own initiative. The news he had was enough, anyway. 'I've handed in my notice and I'm coming back to live in Devon, just for a bit.'

'Oh. Gosh.'

She sounded uncomfortable and he moved quickly to reassure her. 'It's not because of this – because of you and Esther,' he said. 'It's my dad. He's not very well.' He winced, bracing himself for whatever fiction his instincts were about to serve up.

'Oh, I'm sorry – what's the matter?'

'He had pneumonia last year and he's been making a slow recovery. We're not close but I don't want to be too far away. And I've been meaning to research some family history too.'

Family history? He groaned inwardly at this pathetic lie.

'I see,' she said.

'But I just wanted to say that while I'm around if there's anything I can do to help I'd be very happy.' He paused before saying, as coldly as he could manage, 'My own commitments permitting, of course.'

'Oh, of course.'

'So, let me know.'

'That's a deal,' she said with warmth in her voice.

'Deal,' he said.

Ben's father helped him move, arriving in London at the crack of dawn in a rented Transit van, which they parked in the gated courtyard of Millennium Heights and in a little over thirty minutes loaded with the few things Ben hadn't given away or dumped.

Peter had no trouble with London traffic, becoming once again the professional driver, but both of them sighed with contentment once they were on the motorway heading west and there were fewer cars on the road.

'White van men, eh, son?' said Peter, seeming unusually jolly.

Ben laughed and looked sideways at Peter in profile. He had only been eighteen when Ben was born and was not yet 50 years old. His hair remained sandy and thick. His face, though, had sagged, and when he opened his mouth to swear at another driver it revealed a gap where a couple of teeth had been removed.

'So what's all this about, then?' said Peter, his good mood apparently extending to starting conversations. 'Running away from a shotgun wedding or something?' He cackled, revealing the black space in his mouth again.

Ben gave an incredulous laugh. 'I just need a break.'

'Nice to be able to afford it,' said Peter.

'I wouldn't have saved as much if I'd been having any fun. All I've done is work. And, anyway,' he said, his voice growing softer, almost impossible for Peter to hear over the engine, 'I was homesick.'

At this, Peter nodded. 'Fair enough, son,' he said. 'I've never been anywhere, and I wouldn't want to. I know Devon, you know? I'd go spare living in Bristol or London or somewhere like that, where no one knows each other, everyone's speaking different languages, all the crime.'

Ben didn't recall that he'd found Devon much friendlier than London – there was more twitching of curtains and gossip, perhaps, but the estate he'd grown up on was every bit as anonymous, bland and obsessively private as Millennium Heights. Still, he knew what his father meant.

Ben was astonished when, instead of falling into silence as he usually did, Peter continued to speak, each word coming out as being dragged, resisting, from the back of his throat.

'When you were a teenager, I did worry about, you know. I've never been much good at saying it, but I did always, you know, care.' He muttered something to himself – wordless irritation at his inability to express what he was feeling. 'What I'm saying is I'm glad you're going to be nearby.' He puffed air from his cheeks. 'Where I can look out for you a bit, you know? And you can look out for me.'

Peter looked at him and they locked eyes. Ben nodded, a small movement, and Peter nodded back. Then, as if that interlude had never occurred, Peter said, 'What are you going to bloody do with yourself anyway?'

'Mostly just read and do some walking.'

Ben hesitated before going on, knowing Peter would not approve. It sounded crazy now he came to put it in words but he found it difficult to lie to Peter as he would have done to anybody else. 'I'm also hoping to do a bit more looking into that Esther Garrett thing – help her sister out.'

Peter's hands tightened on the steering wheel and he stirred in his seat, grumbling. 'Why? It was twenty years ago, for God's sake, and it's nothing to do with you. Why stick your nose in someone else's business?'

'I don't know,' said Ben. 'I honestly don't know.'

Peter grumbled again, hissing through his teeth. 'Bloody mad you are.'

Ben couldn't imagine living with his father for more than a few days and, despite his urge to be back in the countryside, settled on a one bedroom flat in the centre of Exeter, over an upmarket bakery on Magdalen Road behind the university campus. The front window looked out over the crumbling walls of a Jewish cemetery and across the treetops of a park which sloped down to a row of rusty red brick Victorian houses. In the distance, he could also see open country and high hillsides, looking, thanks to a trick of the light, almost so close that he could walk to them in a matter of minutes. Once all his furniture and belongings had been arranged it still felt sparse and temporary but Ben didn't mind that.

On the first full day in Exeter he got up, showered and dressed, in rainproof coat and inconspicuous walking boots, and went down to the café next door for a full English breakfast and two mugs of tea. He ate and drank at a tiny table in the window, watching rush-hour traffic go by – less intense than in London, but enough to bring home, with a pleasant jolt, the realisation that for the first time in a decade, he wasn't going to work on Monday morning.

Once he was full and the tea had chased away any grogginess he started walking. The cold air made his cheeks turn red and his eyes water, and there seemed, he thought, to be occasional flakes of gritty snow driven in the wind. His intention was to explore his new surroundings because, though he had visited Exeter many times as a child, and ridden through it on his father's bus on so many Saturday or Sunday shifts, he did not know it well. Somehow, though, his feet took him to places he hadn't quite intended.

First, he skirted the city centre, walking alongside busy B-roads which carried traffic away from the pedestrianised shopping district. Young trees and scrappy grass ran along either side, while new buildings housing chain restaurants and cinemas clustered around every junction and roundabout. The noise and fumes began to give him a headache until he turned a corner and realised that he had walked almost directly to, of all places, the bus station.

It was in an especially ugly part of town – a victim of German bombers, post-war planning, and 1980s speculative building projects. Ben jogged across several lanes of traffic and, almost involuntarily, with a swimming sensation, entered the concourse. It had not changed in two decades, except in superficial ways. There were still people sitting glumly on benches and ledges, shopping bags around their feet, and tourists in anoraks baffled by the layout and timetables. The concrete pillars were as grim as ever, and the institutional sans-serif signage remained, though it had become simultaneously blackened by fumes and faded by the sun.

He wandered to the bay from which he was quite certain his father's bus had departed on the day Esther Garrett disappeared. There was a single-decker bus parked there, behind steel railings, idling with the doors closed as the driver performed checks and set the destination indicator.

Ben frowned. He knew, at that moment, that he would have to board the bus. It was a compulsion – a physical need.

A shuffling mob had begun to gather around the gate, none of them wishing to push, exactly, but all manoeuvring for position in the absence of an orderly queue. When the door finally popped open with a hiss, contactless barging began. Ben hung back and waited until the elderly passengers in their beige and brown had boarded, followed by teenagers in black and red, and a pair of Germans in matching waterproof jackets. There was plenty of room, even on a small bus like this.

He stepped on board and bought a single ticket to the end of the line, but intended to get off after a few stops. He was surprised to find that what he thought of as his seat was still free – the single berth facing out into the aisle with the window behind it, against the driver's cabin. As he lowered himself onto the garishly patterned cushion he felt his breath catch, just briefly.

The bus jolted with the release of the handbrake, the doors rattled together, and Ben's head whirled. It was almost, but not quite, like travelling through time. The angle was wrong because he was so much taller now than then, and the details were jarringly incorrect – the seat covers, the strange colour of the metalwork, even the flooring, which was no longer cork marked by cigarette burns and blackened chewing gum. But still there was enough there that, as his eyes misted, he could see the past before him like a hazy film.

He was sure his fellow passengers could see the state he was in – his jaw felt slack and his eyes unfocused – but, to them, he was just a young man slumped in his seat with a vacant expression. They didn't notice his eyes tracking along the aisle, coming to rest on a seat in front of the space set aside for pushchairs – following the path Esther Garrett had taken.

The seat – Esther's seat – was occupied by a middle-aged man, but Ben could barely see him. Esther's slender body seemed to materialise before him, indistinct but recognisable. He willed her to stabilise, to take material form. There was something she had done, something that wasn't right. If only–

'What are you fucking looking at?'

Ben shook his head and wiped his eyes.

The middle-aged man had risen to his feet and was standing with his hands bunched at his sides, more anxious than truly aggressive.

Ben reddened from his neck to his scalp. Showing his palms and widening his eyes, he said, 'Oh, I'm sorry. I was miles away.' He sprang up to ring the bell and stop the bus. The driver put the brakes on even though they were between stops and Ben jumped out onto the pavement, the door closing behind him almost before he'd touched the ground. As the bus pulled away Ben saw disapproving faces directed at him from the dirty windows and he flushed with shame, wondering if this might be how Aaron Greenslade had sometimes felt.

Then another thought crossed his mind: after she had disembarked, had Esther Garrett looked back? What had she seen? His face, perhaps, in the light of the bus, and Greenslade demanding to be unleashed. He shuddered. If he had been in her position, he'd have run. Did she run, in fact? He didn't think so.

CHAPTER FOURTEEN

More than two weeks later, Ben was still in bed at 10am, rain rattling against the window as a near gale blew across the open land of the park opposite his flat. He was awake but hadn't moved. His eyes were fixed glassily on the white far wall, turned a cool grey by the weak, cloud-filtered daylight.

He had imagined that moving away from London and leaving his job would lift the gloom but it had grown deeper than ever. Days passed without him noticing, lost in hours of TV or re-reading old comics. He had eaten mostly sandwiches, unable to find the enthusiasm to cook, and the stack of books on his bedside table was untouched. He had found himself going to bed later, sitting in the dark aimlessly watching TV and drinking bottled lager, and then sleeping in to compensate. Just for the first few days, he had told himself – just to unwind, before the serious work begins. But the wasted days piled up and seemed to slow him yet further with their gathering weight.

Half asleep and with headache, at first, he did not hear his mobile phone vibrating over the sound of the weather but, blinking, came out of his reverie, folded back the duvet and in three strides was at the phone.

'Ben? Lucy Garrett.'

His throat was dry and he had not spoken to anyone else for almost two days and so he managed only a soft grunt of acknowledgement.

'Did you move home after all?' she asked.

Ben noted, with pleasure, that her accent became momentarily stronger as she stretched the A in 'after'.

'Yes,' he said.

'How's your dad doing?'

He cleared his throat. 'Pretty well, thanks.'

Fortunately, Lucy didn't seem to be especially interested beyond pleasantries, which saved him having to elaborate.

'Dare I ask if you're busy tomorrow?'

Ben looked around the almost bare, almost dark flat, and scratched the back of his head. 'No, nothing that can't wait till another time.'

'I did as you suggested and wrote to Aaron Greenslade again and, guess what?'

Ben didn't say anything at first and then, reluctantly, played along. 'He said yes, I suppose.'

'I've arranged to visit him tomorrow afternoon.'

'Great,' said Ben without conviction.

'And I wondered, would you come with me? I'll be taking notes but it would be good to have someone else there to listen.' She gave a short, frustrated sigh. 'Also, frankly, I'm scared – of him, I mean, and of being in a prison. I need someone to lean on. Moral support.'

Ben was astonished at the idea of himself in such a role, and they barely knew each other, after all. 'What about your dad?' he asked.

'I can't take him,' she said, vehemently. 'He spent so long hating that boy – that man, now, I suppose – that I don't think I could control him.' She took a breath which sounded almost percussive over the phone. 'No, I certainly can't take Dad.'

'If you're sure, then of course I'll come.'

'Thank you. Meet me outside the prison at two? Bring a passport or driving licence and two recent bills to verify your address.'

'Okay.'

'And wear a suit and tie, I think. I want to look professional, credible.'

'Right. I'll be there,' he said.

Once he'd hung up, he rubbed his chin, and decided to shower and shave.

HM Prison Exeter is in the centre of the city – a citadel of grey Cornish granite and soft purple-red brick which might suit just as well as a lunatic asylum or army barracks. Carved across the lintel of its great stone gatehouse are the words DEVON COUNTY PRISON. Behind the old building are newer structures of modern red brick, with a high wall presenting a blank, severe face to the street.

Ben arrived at 1350 and was standing on the pavement at the foot of a ramp which curved up to the visitors' entrance. For the first time since leaving London he was dressed in his favourite three-button jacket and trousers, in plain dark grey. His tie was also plain, in dark brown wool. Over the top he wore a black overcoat which hung almost to his knees. Because the weather was balanced on the cusp between spring warmth and winter chill he felt hot when he moved, but, after ten minutes standing in the shade, even with his hands in his pockets, he was shivering.

When he heard the sound of brakes squeaking, he turned to see a worn-out red minicab mounted on the kerb. Lucy stepped out of the back seat and the cab pulled away at once into the sparse traffic. She was dressed in a dark blue suit with a grey overcoat and low heels. She carried no handbag. She waved and walked towards him and, as she got close, he noted her pallor and the grimness of her expression. Having not seen her in person for some months, he was reminded afresh, and with a jolt, of just how closely she resembled her sister despite being almost twice as old as Esther when she disappeared.

'All right?' said Ben.

'Terrified,' she said. 'Shall we?'

They walked up the steep curving slope which led from the street to the prison forecourt which was covered with chevrons and arrows. Lucy stopped in front of the blue double doors for a moment and looked up at the barbed wire which topped the gate house. A sign on the door warned them of the consequences of bringing mobile phones, cameras, cigarettes, drugs, weapons or anything that might be used to effect an escape. Lucy rang the bell and, after a moment, there was a buzz and clunk as the door unlocked. She pushed the door open and they stepped through, Ben bending his shoulders to avoid banging his head.

They were greeted by a middle-aged, white-haired man in a blue sweater who looked at the paperwork Lucy presented and directed them to the visitors' centre in an old stable block across the yard.

There they found another middle-aged, white-haired man in a blue sweater, sitting at a desk, tapping the keys on a chunky old computer. There was a bank of red lockers with glass doors and a coffee table around which sat several women, one with two children on her knees. The prison officer checked them in, gave them a visitors' card, colour coded and dated, and pointed them to the lockers. 'Leave your coats and remember not to take anything into the visiting hall other than small change.'

'Okay,' said Lucy.

'And if you have any property to give the prisoner please leave it here with me now.'

'No, nothing,' said Lucy.

'Then wait here,' said the prison officer, his voice dull and flat, but betraying suppressed hostility. He pointed to the coffee table and the women who were already sitting there. 'Your number will be called.' He gave an automatic, dismissive smile.

They folded their coats and put them in the same locker, Ben taking the key. There were no seats left so Ben and Lucy stood by the wall. As more visitors arrived, and especially more children, the area became almost crowded. No one spoke, except to mutter the occasional muted, breathy 'Excuse me', or 'Hi'. Ben sensed Lucy's suppressed agitation and saw from the corner of his eye that she couldn't stop nibbling and picking at a damaged thumbnail. The clock ticked and the room grew uncomfortably warm, filling with the smell of perfume, washing powder, deodorant and human bodies.

After fifteen minutes, a prison officer entered through the door of the waiting room, and the warm air rushed out of the room in one go, along with the tension. She stood holding the door open as she called out numbers: 'Fifty-eight – five eight – to seventy-two – seven two – follow me, please.' Everyone moved at once, yanking children from the floor, smoothing skirts and sweaters as they went. Ben watched as one young woman, like a heroine from a Victorian novel, pinched her cheeks to redden them.

As they marched in a column across the yard, feet clattering on tarmac, Lucy said, 'We'll have to be sensitive to his reactions.'

'How do you mean?' said Ben.

'I've got a suspicion he'll talk to you more than he'll talk to me. I could be wrong,' she said, speaking tentatively, 'but I think your background was more like his.'

Ben bristled. 'What do you mean by that?'

'And he'll be more used to dealing with men.'

A prison guard interrupted them as they began to file into the visitors' hall. 'Prepare to be searched, madam, sir.'

They stepped into another institutionally-decorated room, only this one was yet more sparse, uncarpeted, and smelled strongly of neat disinfectant, like a doctor's surgery. The other visitors, evidently used to the process, were moving through the electronic scanner without a murmur, raising their arms before they were asked. Most had dressed in easy-to-search clothing with few pockets or folds. The guards asked Ben to remove his suit jacket and turned it inside out, feeling the seams and inspecting under the lapels.

'Very formal attire, sir,' said one of the officers, a thin black woman in her forties.

Ben didn't know how to respond.

'I'm afraid that's my fault,' said Lucy. 'This is rather an important meeting for me and I wanted us to look–'

'Okay, move through the barrier, please,' said the officer, her face falling slack.

They passed through the metal detector without incident and, at last, found themselves in a room which resembled a canteen or school assembly hall with rows of simple tables and chairs bolted to the ground. The more experienced visitors had taken what they knew to be the best seats, away from the flapping door of the toilet and the persistent draught that sliced through the room below knee height. Ben and Lucy picked one of the remaining tables and took a seat. Ben looked around, reading all of the posters and the notices. The one by the door they had just come through read NO PRISONERS BEYOND THIS POINT, as if a sign might make the difference.

After another minute or so, there were a series of buzzes and clanking sounds before two prison officers entered through a door on the far side of the room, taking up position on either side of it. A line of men in red high-visibility bibs followed them. From around the room came sounds of recognition, muted but, in most cases, joyful. A child called out before being shushed by her mother. As per the guidance they all knew by heart, most of them embraced and kissed briefly under the eyes of the guards, before separating.

One man stood alone in the doorway, hovering and hesitant. He was thin, like an anatomic study, with his head shaved to the skin. His eyes were deep beneath his brows and ringed with darkness, and his cheekbones jutted out over tight skin. He made eye contact with Ben and gave a thumbs up as he began to walk towards them with a twitching, rolling gait.

'Oh my God,' said Lucy, grabbing Ben's hand under the table. 'It's him.' She transmitted waves of panic as he came near, as if she had seen a snake. Her hand was restless, tightening and loosening, almost vibrating with shivers, all in the space of a second or two. Ben was pleased to be distracted from the feeling in his own gut which urged him to stand and run: it was him, the boy, only further eaten away by his own rottenness.

Greenslade reached the table bringing with him the smell of sweat and carbolic soap. He paused to look down at Lucy with a lopsided grin, his head bobbing slightly like a boxer's. She stared back at him. Her face had become bloodless, and even her usually dark lips were almost blue, pressed tightly together.

A guard intervened, 'Sit down, please.'

Greenslade smirked and took his time sliding onto the plastic chair. He immediately passed one hand over to grab the other elbow, making a barrier of the arm that twisted across his chest. His face was that of an old man, though he was not yet forty years old, but his bony, elastic body and posture were those of a teenager. His eyes were marble-blue and shone with excitement. He leaned forward and addressed Lucy only. 'I don't get many visitors.'

Lucy swallowed hard, unable to speak, and blinking compulsively.

'Thank you for agreeing to see us,' said Ben, filling the silence.

Greenslade briefly let the corners of his mouth turn upward in acknowledgement but continued to look at Lucy. 'Please,' he said, and suddenly the swagger that seemed to manifest in his every move and gesture dropped away. He placed his hands flat on the table and extended his bony fingers. 'Don't be scared. If I was dangerous, they'd have me behind glass.' He lifted his hands from the table to show his palms. 'Fifteen years and I haven't laid a hand on anyone.' His Devon accent was strong but shaded with inflections of a hybrid cockney-Jamaican-Indian accent he'd picked up inside.

'What about the first five years?' said Lucy.

Greenslade scratched furiously at his elbow and blinked with his whole face – some kind of tic.

'I was a right little cunt back then,' he said and gave a wheezing laugh through clenched teeth. His expression flattened. 'I won't say I'm a changed man but I'm not angry anymore.' He winked. 'I've spent a lot of time sitting in circles talking about my feelings and do you know what – it fucking works, if you keep at it for twenty years.'

He looked at Ben for the first time, casting his eyes over the suit jacket and tie, before returning his gaze to Lucy. 'Is he your boyfriend?'

'We don't have very long, Mr Greenslade,' said Lucy. There was a tightness in her voice which gave it a high, grating overtone that wasn't normally there. She breathed out slowly, trying to calm herself and then flashed a wide open, manic smile. 'I'm sorry,' she said. 'It's just I don't know for sure whether you did or didn't kill my sister.'

Greenslade scratched his face, digging yellowed nails into the flesh of his hollow cheek. 'I get that, I get that,' he said. 'I can tell you I didn't, which is what I've always said, and you might not believe me.' He pinched the end of his nose and sniffed. 'But why don't you listen to my version of the story – because that's the only one I'm telling – and assume it's true?'

'Okay,' said Lucy. She crossed her legs, brushed a strand of hair from her face, and, with her chin up, said, 'As I mentioned in my letter, I'm trying to come to terms with the loss of my sister, and I'd like to know as much as possible about Esther's last day. Assuming you didn't touch her – I have to believe you didn't or I couldn't sit here talking to you – then you were one of the last people to *speak* to her.'

'That's true, yeah,' said Greenslade.

Ben was mesmerised by him, not least because, at certain angles, and with certain expressions, the same face that had spat and snarled on the bus twenty years before could be discerned in the worn features of the man in front of him.

'I'm not going to say anything to you I didn't say to the filth back then. It should all be on record somewhere.' He rubbed a finger under his nose and sniffed. 'I'd just got out of here, that same day. My first stretch – two months, that was all.' He rolled his eyes and sighed. 'Fucking stupid – I dodged a train fare and then decked the ticket inspector. I was pissed, obviously.' His hand tugged at the loose skin around his Adam's apple. 'I was fucking near always pissed from about twelve onwards, because my mum and dad was both pissheads, and my brother and all, so–'

Lucy interrupted him. 'My sister, Mr Greenslade, please.'

Greenslade gave another of his twitching, nervous nods. 'I was on the bus because I didn't have anywhere to go and my cousin, Jay, he lived out Berebroke. She come and sat next to me.' He sniffed and his eyes wandered over Lucy's body. 'I hadn't touched a girl for two months.'

Lucy closed her eyes in disgust.

'I'm telling you,' Greenslade hissed, 'how it was.' He scratched at his arm again and, as if he'd released a valve, his momentary irritation seemed to pass. 'Sorry,' he said. 'I'd had a drink and I couldn't help myself. But when I spoke to her, she just looked like she was going to be sick. I don't remember it well – it's hazy – but I think that pissed me off.'

Lucy raised her fingertips to cover her mouth and gave a shivering sigh.

The prison officer standing to attention by the wall had detected the tension and was watching them closely. Ben gave him what he hoped was a reassuring smile.

'Then she got off at Berebroke, and I forgot to – I hadn't been there for years, to be honest. When the bus driver let me off, she was out of sight, but I know she was there on the path ahead of me.' He smiled with one side of his mouth, showing a few yellow teeth. 'She was singing.'

'Singing?' said Lucy. 'Singing what?'

'I dunno, man,' said Greenslade. 'It didn't have any words – la la la – but she was really fucking happy about *something*.'

Lucy blinked and looked at Ben. 'You said she was happy.'

'Yes,' said Ben.

Greenslade's eyes drifted in Ben's direction and his face creased. 'Oh my God – you're that little ginger cunt off the bus, aren't you?' He slapped his thigh, his eyes gleaming slits, and let out a pealing laugh which caused other visitors to turn and look. Ben's fingers gripped the chair, ready to push himself up and away.

'You stitched me right up,' said Greenslade, still laughing, but slowly coming down until his face was blank. 'They read your statement in court. What a load of shit that was.'

'I know,' said Ben. 'I didn't say any of that. They made it up.'

Greenslade tossed his head back and dug his knuckles into his temples. 'I fucking knew it,' he almost shouted.

'Quiet down, please,' said the prison officer, stepping forward with a hand on a panic button attached to his belt.

Lucy leaned across the table and reached out a hand. 'Mr Greenslade, please, we only have a couple of minutes – tell me about the wood.'

Greenslade clicked his fingers. 'I fucking knew it.'

'Please,' said Lucy, glancing at the white plastic clock on the wall.

'Okay,' said Greenslade, sitting forward and folding his arms. His leg bounced up and down, sending vibrations through the entire table and both benches. 'I got off the bus. It was pitch dark except for that light by the bus stop. I didn't want to take that path because it was unlit but I could hear her up ahead, singing at the top of her voice, so I thought, *Right, if it's good enough for a little girl like that, then it's okay for a hard nut like me* – like I was, I mean. I was wearing these poxy trainers and it was muddy so I kept slipping, but once we were in the wood, it got easier to see, funnily enough. I followed her all the way through, down the hill, and out the other side. She didn't look back.' He closed his eyes and put the tip of his tongue on his lips, summoning the memory. 'The last thing I remember is watching her unlock the door of that house–' he mimicked the action of a key turning in the air '–and go in.'

'Our house,' said Lucy. 'She went home?'

'That's what I've been saying since nineteen-ninety-fucking-five,' said Greenslade, 'but I got told so many times that I done her in that I started to believe it for a while. That bloke who said I'd confessed to him? I'd never spoken to him in my life, but he stood there and said I said this, or I said that, and I thought–' He gave an exaggerated shrug, widened his eyes. 'Maybe I did?'

He ran a hand over the stubble on his head and puffed air from his cheeks.

'Do you know what gaslighting is? It's where you convince someone they're going mad. You move the furniture round and swear blind you didn't, or change the clocks, that kind of thing. Well, that's what this was like. That Sweetland, he was a psycho, worse than what I am. He kept saying I was imagining things, I'd forgotten stuff, or he'd show me statements I didn't remember making.' He raised a finger and wagged it in admonition. 'But I know for sure now.' He put his hand on the table, almost touching Lucy's. 'I didn't kill your sister. I was a little cunt, and I did a lot of bad things, but I didn't touch her.'

Lucy didn't say anything.

He smirked, but seemed forlorn with it. 'I was hoping you'd say "I know you didn't," or something,' said Greenslade.

'We'll see,' she replied.

'I ain't got all that much faith in the system, to be honest, but, yeah, we'll see.' He grabbed the tip of his nose between finger and thumb and rubbed it hard. 'I'm 99 per cent sure I'll get out of here by the summer but I don't want it.' He sniffed. 'I don't want it to be *he got out* – I want it to be *he's innocent*. Know what I mean?'

Lucy nodded and said, again, 'We'll see.'

'I need a drink,' said Lucy as the blue door slammed shut behind them and they began their walk down the slope and away from the prison.

'Me too,' said Ben. 'Do you know somewhere?'

'Yes,' she managed to say before her entire body shook and she covered her mouth with her palm. They walked faster and Ben glanced sideways to look with concern at her pale profile, partially covered by her dark hair blown forward by the wind.

Once they were on the street below, she surprised him by taking his arm. She shivered against him but not, he thought, because of the cold.

'Did you believe him?' she asked eventually, raising her voice over the idling engines of the queuing early rush-hour traffic.

Ben paused for a long time as he considered the question. Assuming Christine Kelly was right, it was a belief in gut instinct that had led Steven Sweetland to falsify evidence, but Ben had no such faith. People were so easily fooled by sales people or conmen, after all. Greenslade, though, was no charmer, and hadn't made any real effort to win them over.

'I think so,' said Ben, haltingly.

'I don't know – I just don't know,' Lucy replied. Her eyes were moist with tears but Ben wasn't sure whether that was a result of emotion or the harsh wind that had blown up.

As the sun had already dipped beneath the skyline, the streets were cast into blue shade and the hint of warmth that Ben had earlier felt was now entirely gone. They hurried into the fringes of the central shopping district – the down-at-heel end of town around the bus station where there were empty buildings and kebab shops – and Lucy pointed out a pub set into a modern building behind a department store.

'This place is usually quiet and it has lots of corners.'

They dashed across the road and in through the front door. Inside was a narrow space so intimately lit as to be almost dark with several small rooms branching off it. There were only one or two other customers and loud folk music was playing over the stereo system. Lucy ordered a large glass of red wine for herself and a pint of lager for Ben, which they took into a back room lined with paperback science fiction books and old copies of the *National Geographic*. The moment she had sat down, Lucy lifted the bowl-like glass to her lips and knocked a third of it back. With her eyes closed, she breathed a sigh of contented relief. 'That's better.'

She held her left hand out in front of her and watched it shake. 'Well, that's steadier than it was,' she said, noticing Ben's concern.

'Let's assume he's telling the truth,' said Ben. 'If so, that probably ties in.'

'Ties in? With what?'

Ben hesitated for a moment, wondering if it was too soon to mention Christine Kelly. Things were still delicate between he and Lucy but he was sure the connection was stronger now. 'With something I dug up.'

Lucy cocked her head to one side. 'What do you mean?'

'I found Christine Kelly. The other detective. She gave me some papers.'

Her eyes darkened. 'Why didn't you tell me before?'

He sighed and sipped at his beer, buying a moment to compose his response. 'It just didn't seem right, not until I knew you a little better.'

She stared at him, assessing and judging. 'Ties in how?'

He leaned forward, fidgeting with the beer glass, turning it in circles on its drip mat with his fingertips. 'One of the notes mentioned a witness who claimed to have seen Esther after 5pm walking from Coleridge Drive back towards the bus stop, by which time the police argued – well, Steven Sweetland, that is – that she was already dead.'

Lucy shook her head in bewilderment. 'I've never heard that before.'

'There's also something else that's always bothered me,' said Ben.

'Always?' said Lucy. There was something almost cruel in her tone.

'Like I said, this has played on my mind for a long time, which is exactly why I don't want to be here.'

'I know. I'm sorry.'

Ben stared into his beer, swirling the liquid. 'Do you remember when they found her handbag in that skip in Exeter?'

'Of course I do,' said Lucy. 'I was braced for them to find her body somewhere nearby, but they never did.'

'When I saw her the day she disappeared she didn't have a handbag. I was looking right at her and she was wearing her duffel coat, trousers, top, but her hands were free.'

Lucy nodded emphatically. 'You're right – she never took one to work, and we told them that, but we assumed she must have done that day for some reason. She went out before anyone else was up.' She sighed. 'Well, you know, she didn't come home.'

'But the one they found – it was definitely hers?'

'Yes, we all identified it, and it had some of her things in the inside pocket – library cards, friends' phone numbers, that kind of stuff.'

'So she must have gone home and changed. It's undeniable.'

Lucy finished her wine and licked her lips with a blackened tongue.

'She can't have changed,' she said. 'Or we'd have found her work clothes at home.'

'Well, she picked up a handbag, at least.' Ben frowned. 'Do you know if any of her other clothes were missing?'

'No,' said Lucy. 'She had a lot, and she did her own washing.' She raised her eyebrows momentarily. 'My mother wasn't too hot on household chores.'

'I wonder if she grabbed a change of clothes, a handbag, and then put them on somewhere else – a friend's house, perhaps?' He paused, softening the landing. 'Or in the back seat of a car or something.'

Lucy waved her hand. 'There's no point in guessing.' She blinked and a dark look passed over her face. 'She was my sister, you know, not yours.'

Ben said nothing but averted his eyes, hoping the moment would pass.

'Who would she have been meeting?' said Lucy.

Sensing that the question was not for him but for herself, Ben remained silent. When, after a few seconds of staring at the far wall, Lucy had still not answered it, Ben cleared his throat. 'Christine Kelly told me Esther had a boyfriend.'

'Who?'

'Leslie Reeves,' said Ben.

Lucy shook her head slowly, drawing a blank. 'I never met him. He wasn't from Berebroke – not one of the village kids we grew up with.' She glanced at her empty glass and then towards the bar. 'You didn't grow up in a village, did you? You have kids of all different ages in a small school, everyone knows everyone else.' She laughed brightly. 'Almost everyone is a cousin.'

Ben reached out for the wine glass. 'Let me get you a drink – same again?'

'Please.'

When he returned from the bar, which was beginning to get busier, he found Lucy using her smartphone.

'Thanks,' she said. 'I'm just looking up Leslie Reeves – it's an unusual name so I figured that, if he's still around, he won't be hard to find.'

'You want to talk to him, then?'

'Yes, but maybe in a couple of days.' She held up her hand again. The shaking had stopped. 'When you don't know who is to blame, it feels as if everyone is.' She looked at Ben and gave a slight smile, conveying an apology and her gratitude without words.

'I'm free tomorrow,' he said, 'if you want to track down this neighbour of yours.'

Lucy took a deep breath. 'Yes, why not?' she said. 'Why not?'

It struck Ben as a curious reaction – there was, he thought, probably a good answer to her rhetorical question, if only she'd share it.

'And I'd like a set of those papers you keep talking about.'

'Sure, I can email them now.'

CHAPTER FIFTEEN

The next afternoon, Lucy picked him up in her hatchback. It was a new model but littered with sandwich packets, fast-food cartons and discarded clothing. She drove them to Berebroke in bright sunlight which suggested the approach of spring.

She was quiet and, when she did speak, her voice had a croak in it. 'I stayed up late last night going through those notebooks of Christine Kelly's. I printed some pages out.' She gestured at the dashboard where Ben found a plastic wallet containing several sheets of A4 paper.

'Are you sure Mrs Ellison still lives at number two?' asked Ben as Lucy slowed to turn onto a single-track lane almost overgrown with budding bramble bushes.

She switched up gear and accelerated despite the blind curves in the lane.

'Yes, and I telephoned this morning to let her know we're coming. She said she'd stay in all afternoon.'

The lane led past several farmyards, thick with mud and surrounded by flimsy-looking, gloomy buildings with corrugated roofs. At one, a dog barked through the gate as they sped past. Heading ever downward the road eventually widened to two lanes before bringing them out on the lower road into Berebroke.

Ben hadn't seen the village itself since he was eleven and was astonished to realise how small it really was. Twenty years before it had seemed difficult to navigate with wide roads and endless rows of blank-windowed cottages and houses. Now, he could see that it was really no more than a few cul-de-sacs branching off a main road. Even the church, which he recalled as looming and gothic, was barely taller than a house, its stunted tower barely deserving the description.

Lucy parked the car on the main street near the arcade of shops. Ben wondered why she didn't use her parents' driveway on Coleridge Close. She sat for a moment with her hands on the wheel staring out through the windscreen and along the main road. Ben looked sideways and down, studying her expression. He saw a bare flicker of a smile followed by a brief, sad dip of the eyes.

'Let's go, then,' she said, and popped her door open.

As they walked, Ben realised they were retracing the route he had taken with Chelsea when they had visited the woods and he felt a jolt of emotion. Now he was in the West Country, there was really no excuse for failing to get in touch with her – the nearest he had to a sister. It would be nice to talk to someone who remembered his mother and who understood what it had been like to grow up there and then, surrounded by those people.

'Number two,' said Lucy, nudging him with her elbow.

The close had become more run down since Ben was last there, paintwork peeling and PVC window frames stained yellow. Number two was just like every other house except perhaps a touch tidier. An effort had even been made to brighten the garden with plants in urns and tubs. The car parked on the driveway was a silver Rover at least two decades old but so clean and well cared for that it looked practically brand new. There were net curtains in the windows, one of which also bore a poster advertising a concert at the church. As they walked up the path to the front door, Ben saw several stickers on display in its frosted glass panel: 'No junkmail please', 'Polite notice: no canvassers, cold callers or salesmen, please', 'This is a Neighbourhood Watch Area'.

Lucy pressed the doorbell button, triggering a piercing, insistent buzz.

The door opened almost immediately, as if Mrs Ellison had been sitting just inside waiting for them, though at first it was only a crack enforced by a short length of chain. The face that looked out at them was round and creased, topped with straight, dry-looking, grey hair, and expressed sour disapproval.

'Yes?'

'It's me, Mrs Ellison – Kay Garrett's daughter, Lucy, from across the road.'

Mrs Ellison's blue eyes widened ever so slightly and a hand rose to the top button of her tan-coloured cardigan as she tightened her already compressed lips. 'I don't recognise you – can you show me some identification?'

Ben felt a sinking sensation. How could she fail to recognise someone who had grown up within a thirty-second walk of her home? And who, Ben knew from his own experience, looked so similar to her sister and mother? Steven Sweetland's diagnosis of this woman's unreliability as a witness was perhaps sound after all.

Lucy rummaged in her handbag and found her driver's licence which she passed through the crack in the door.

Glancing around the close, Ben saw a face at the window of number eight – that of a middle-aged man in a checked shirt observing them openly – keen, Ben thought – to convey the message that he would not stand for any trouble.

Apparently satisfied, Mrs Ellison slammed the door shut, released the chain, and swung it wide open. 'Come in, come in, make yourselves comfortable.'

The stepped into the hallway, wiping their feet on a piece of spare beige carpet, the same as the one beneath, laid out for that purpose, and followed her to the kitchen.

'I'm sorry about all that,' said Mrs Ellison over her shoulder, 'only I was rather badly stung a year or two ago.'

'Stung?'

'Conned. Robbed.' She pointed at her cheekbone. 'Assaulted.'

The kitchen was colourless, too, with old but well-maintained pine furniture, sandy-coloured cupboard doors, and brown tiles on the walls, every tenth one of which was decorated with flowers rendered in shades of umber so that they looked dry and dead. It was also perfectly clean, the oatmeal-coloured linoleum reflecting sunlight like a pool of still water. Mrs Ellison headed straight to the kettle by which she had already laid out three brown mugs that looked as if they might have been given as wedding presents around 1974.

'Take a seat, take a seat,' she said, and Ben and Lucy found places at the dining table. 'Tea for everyone, I assume?' she said. 'Yes, last summer, it was. I was still working then, three days a week, but I was at home with the flu when someone knocked on the door.' She looked over at them as she poured hot water over the teabags. 'Forty years I've lived here and never had any trouble, so I didn't think twice. Nice young man, or so I thought, came to "check the boiler", so-called.' She replaced the kettle and began to stir the teabags and prod at them with a spoon. 'He looked the part − boiler suit, clipboard, and so on, but when I went up there with a cup of tea, I found him going through David's office desk.' She fished out the teabags and gave each a squeeze against the spoon with the tips of her fingers. 'The next thing I knew, he was kneeling on top of me punching me in the face.' She pointed. 'Broke my nose.'

'That's awful,' said Lucy.

'Here! In Berebroke!' said Mrs Ellison, carrying two cups of tea towards the table. 'Nothing like this ever happens in Berebroke.' She stopped dead, still holding the brown mugs. 'Oh, well, sorry − there's me forgetting about your poor sister.'

Lucy smiled coldly and reached out to take the mug. 'It's okay.'

Mrs Ellison sat down herself, almost collapsing into the seat so that her feet momentarily left the ground. She sighed with relief. Though the house was unnervingly clean she herself smelled musty, almost mousey. Her teeth were bad, too, stained brown by too much tea and not enough cleaning over the years.

'As I mentioned on the phone,' Lucy said, 'I'm trying to find out more about my sister's disappearance, and Mr Hodge is helping me with my research. We have reason to believe…' Lucy stopped herself and gave a brief self-deprecating laugh at the lapse into officialese. 'I understand that you told the police that you'd seen my sister on the day she disappeared and–'

Mrs Ellison cut in, sounding panicked and defensive. 'Now, I'm not sure I'm allowed to talk about this kind of thing. Isn't it confidential or something? I mean, shouldn't I ask permission?' She gestured vaguely.

'I don't think there's anything to stop you speaking to whoever you like,' said Ben softly.

'I don't want you to do anything that makes you uncomfortable,' added Lucy, 'but Ben – I mean, Mr Hodge – is right, I'm sure.'

Mrs Ellison eyed them sideways, working her jaw as if grinding her teeth, her lips pursed with disapproval. 'It doesn't seem right,' she said.

Ben leaned forward. 'They ignored you back then,' he said. 'They thought you were – sorry to be blunt – but they thought you were too stupid to know what you'd seen, or that you were making it up.'

The elderly woman seemed to rear up in her seat. 'You're just trying to provoke me.'

'No,' said Ben. 'I'm just being honest.' His voice quavered – he was used to backing down and this confrontation, small as it was, made him forget to breathe. 'Steven Sweetland ignored you and because he ignored you, the wrong man went to prison, and nobody can say for sure what happened to Esther Garrett.'

Mrs Ellison nodded. 'I suppose you're right.' Her eyes narrowed and she looked at Lucy. Her jaw jutted out. 'I'm very busy,' she said. She blushed. 'And, well, time is money they say, don't they?'

It occurred to Ben that the twenty-year-old car, 1970s crockery, fraying cardigan and reused teabags were signs of genteel poverty.

Lucy's eyes closed in weary dismay. 'How much?'

Mrs Ellison's eyes shone briefly. 'Fifty pounds,' she said, clamping her mouth shut as her cheeks flushed pink.

'Okay,' said Lucy, and reached for her handbag.

When she handed over the notes, fresh from a cash machine, Mrs

Ellison beamed and said, as if it was an unsolicited gift rather than having been extorted, 'Oh, very kind of you, thank you, thanks.'

Ben felt a surge of annoyance as he recalled Christine Kelly's warning about those who would take advantage of the grieving relatives of the dead or missing.

'That November,' he said sternly.

'Yes, yes, of course,' said Mrs Ellison, but she hesitated still. The money in her hand hadn't settled her anxiety over breaking what she was certain must be a rule and, as far as she was concerned, she was being paid to do something immoral. At last, she forced the words from her mouth. 'I was getting in from work, walking up the Drive from the One Stop–'

'That's the shop in the village,' said Lucy for Ben's benefit.

'It was a horrible evening – that really penetrating rain, you know? And cold with it.' She gestured in the air above her head. 'I had my hood up and I was sort of pulling it down to protect my face, because it was no use trying to use an umbrella, believe me. The wind got hold of me when I came round the corner and pulled it back, and that's how I saw her.' She rocked back in her seat and squinted. 'She was outside number six, just before the path into Dodd's Wood.'

'What time was it?'

'I know for certain it was just after five because I finished work at 4.30 and my friend who gave me a lift always managed the drive down from Exeter in twenty-five minutes.' She held up a hand, anticipating a challenge. 'And I remember that Sarah was putting down her shutters as I walked past, so that would have been bang on five o'clock.'

'Sarah's is the bakery,' said Lucy, again for Ben's benefit.

'She was always coming and going, your sister,' said Mrs Ellison. 'Always being picked up by boys on mopeds or in cars.' Something about the set of her lips and a slight raising of the eyebrows betrayed a combination of disapproval and relish.

Lucy twitched but she let it pass. 'But about that evening?'

'It was a matter of seconds. She was just there, ahead of me, walking, the way she used to, you know.' She stopped and swallowed. 'All girlish.'

She smiled briefly, congratulating herself on finding a word that wouldn't offend Lucy. 'She was wearing that black coat of hers.'

'The black duffel coat?' said Ben. 'How can you be sure it was her, if she was in a big coat like that?'

'Oh, I'm sure,' said Mrs Ellison, bridling at even this slight challenge. 'When my hood blew down, so did hers, and she stopped, you see, and turned round to put her back to the wind while she got it up and fastened it. She was right under the street light, plain as day.'

'Did you tell the police that?' asked Ben. 'Only they seemed to think it was too dark for you to see.'

'I can't remember,' she said, her eyes darting away from his gaze. 'I must have done, yes, because that detective–'

'Detective Sergeant Kelly?' offered Ben.

'Yes, that's right – rude woman. She was just the same as you, she didn't believe me. I said to her, "She was right under the light, in her black coat, carrying a white bag."'

Ben turned immediately to exchange a look with Lucy, who seemed almost to be alight with satisfaction, suppressing a smile, and breathing a little too deeply.

'Did you get a sense of what might have been in the bag?' he asked.

'How should I know? It was twenty years ago.' But then Mrs Ellison paused and held up a finger. 'Now, don't hold me to it, but it was something soft, because she dropped it on the ground–' she mimicked the action, holding her hand out to form a claw and then snapping her fingertips apart '–while she fastened her hood. Very casual, very careless.'

'Could it have been clothes?' asked Ben.

'Oh, yes, I'd have thought so.'

'Then what?' asked Lucy.

'Then she picked it up, turned around, and walked on.' She rubbed her temple and took a sip of tea. 'Do you know, I have half a fancy that she was singing out loud.'

As Mrs Ellison's front door closed behind them, Lucy turned to Ben and grabbed his arm with one hand.

'We're going to do it,' she said. 'We're going to find her – I know it.'

Ben gave a faint smile of acknowledgement but was distracted by his desire to take a proper look at the Drive and its layout with Mrs Ellison's account in mind. Yes, there was a street light directly opposite, outside number six. He pointed towards it without speaking and began to walk in its direction. Lucy tugged on his sleeve, stopping his progress. 'No, come on, let's go back to the car.'

'I just want to take a look.' As he spoke, Ben saw Lucy's eyes drift to number ten as her brow furrowed.

'What's wrong?' he asked.

'I'd like to go, please, as soon as possible.'

Ben followed her gaze and saw a curtain in the front room of her parents' house swing back into place.

She started walking without him, in a hurry. He caught up in a couple of steps.

The door of number ten opened and a grey-haired man in a heavy cotton shirt and V-neck sweater stepped out with his hand raised. 'Lucy? Is that you, love?' he called out across the street. It was Eddie Garrett, fatter and with less hair than he had appeared in the 2005 TV appearance Lucy had sent Ben.

Lucy stopped and waited for him to cross the road.

He stopped a short distance away as if up against a glass barrier. 'Hello, love,' he said.

Lucy said nothing.

He jerked a thumb back towards the house. 'Come in for a bit? Mum'd love to see you.'

Lucy shook her head. 'No, I can't – I'm busy with something.'

Her father looked at Ben and stuck out a hand. 'Eddie Garrett.'

Instinctively, Ben introduced himself and shook Eddie's hand. When he glanced at Lucy, he saw that her eyes had become as hard as granite.

'What are you doing here, then?' asked Eddie. He looked, puzzled, in the direction from which they'd come. One of the houses was for sale.

'Not moving in, are you?' he said, and laughed. He stopped at once when Lucy responded with nothing but a frown.

'Well, we need to go,' said Lucy, and began to walk slowly backwards away from her father. Ben followed her.

'Please,' Eddie said, 'just come in, for a few minutes?' He was trying to sound calm but there was something frantic in his tone. He began to follow them.

Lucy ignored him.

'Please!' Eddie shouted, loud enough that it echoed around the close.

Ben flinched and stopped, torn between Lucy and Eddie. He noticed curtains moving at number eight.

Lucy kept walking but, after a few more steps, realising that Ben wasn't coming with her, turned with a sigh. She glanced briefly at Ben, conveying disdain with the slightest of changes in her expression, before facing Eddie with her lips pressed together.

In the silence, Ben heard crows calling and distant chugging of a tractor.

Eddie smiled encouragingly, gesturing towards the house with a sideways nod and a tentative move of his hand.

Reluctantly, Lucy nodded and, folding her arms, began to walk towards the house. She passed Ben and fell into step next to her father, keeping him at arm's length. Something about the slump of her shoulders made her look as if she had reverted to adolescence.

The front door was ajar and Eddie pushed it open before standing aside to direct them in. Ben felt a thrill on crossing the threshold: he was in Esther Garrett's house, where she had grown up and lived. Pictures of her in gilded frames covered the wall. Most of them he'd seen before in one news story or another but one or two were new to him. He wanted desperately to stop and look but could feel Eddie behind him urging him forward into the sitting room, his hand hovering around Ben's back.

Lucy had headed straight for a corner of the sitting room where she stood with her arms still folded, leaning against the wall. She looked sulky and adolescent and therefore more like her sister than ever.

Ben stepped to one side and took the room in at a glance. There was an expensive carpet and three-piece suite, but both were well-worn. The wallpaper was flowery and stained beige by nicotine. There was another photograph of Esther in a silver frame on the mantelpiece but otherwise there were no ornaments or pictures. The air was thick with the candy-sweet aroma of a concealed air freshener. It looked much as it had a decade before when the BBC had filmed here – bland, and not quite homely.

'Sit down, take a seat,' said Eddie eagerly, but Lucy met Ben's eye and gave a brief, insistent shake of her head. They both remained standing. Eddie frowned and winced. Hovering in the doorway he said, 'I'll get your mother.' He stepped into the hall and shouted upstairs, 'Kay, love – we've got visitors.' He came back into the sitting room and looked at Lucy intently. His breathing was uneven and he kept opening and closing his mouth as he sought words that would convey his meaning without driving her away.

'I tried to call,' he said, at last.

Lucy shrugged. 'I've been busy.'

'It's been difficult for us with all this new business.' Eddie swallowed and rubbed his hands together. 'How have you been?'

Lucy's smile was cruel and sarcastic. 'I'm coping.'

The stairs creaked and a moment later Kay Garrett appeared in the doorway. She was wearing a light cotton dressing gown tied off with a belt and her hair, now white, was disarranged. Her eyes were puffy and raw. When she saw Lucy, she clamped her mouth shut and recoiled.

'Hello, Mum,' said Lucy. There was barely any inflection in her voice but Ben sensed a hint of sarcasm.

'What's she doing here?' Kay asked Eddie. Her voice was hoarse and low, deadened by sleep and perhaps also by a hangover.

Lucy continued to smile sourly but said nothing.

Eddie jangled the change in his pockets.

'She's here with her friend.' He swallowed drily and gestured at Ben. 'I saw them outside and–'

Kay waved a hand at him as she shuffled past in slippers and lowered herself into an armchair, arranging the dressing gown around her legs and then resting her head on her palm. She didn't look at Lucy.

'So,' said Eddie with false jollity, 'what *are* you doing in Berebroke?'

After a moment's thought, Lucy said, 'Something no one else can be bothered with–' She breathed in sharply. 'Trying to find my sister.'

At this, Kay rolled her eyes.

'What?' Lucy said, challenging.

Kay shook her head slowly, her eyes closed. 'We don't need your drama,' she said softly.

'Now, look, love,' said Eddie, 'let's not start all that.'

Ben felt hot with embarrassment and didn't know where to look. If Eddie hadn't been blocking the door he might have been able to slip out but, as it was, he was trapped.

Lucy rubbed at her temple. 'I shouldn't have come in,' she said. 'I knew this would happen.' She made a move towards the door but Eddie stayed put, barring her path. As she approached, he reached out and placed his hands on her upper arms, squeezing, kneading with his thumbs. Neither moved or said anything but something palpable sparked between them.

Trying to look away, squirming at his invasion of this intimate moment, Ben couldn't stop his eyes drifting back to the weird tableau – Kay in her armchair looking at the carpet, no longer defiant but crushed; Eddie and his daughter, communicating wordlessly, their faces inches apart. Lucy's hands were clenched into fists and her chest was rising and falling with the effort of controlling her breathing. Eddie looked desperate, sad, but also angry.

After a moment, defeated, Eddie's hands dropped away. 'I'm sorry,' he said, the words surely carrying more weight than the small misplaced gesture required.

Lucy stared into his face until he shied away, fixing his gaze on her neck. He stepped back, showing his palms in surrender, and Lucy pushed past him. Ben, still trapped, heard the front door open and slam.

'I'd better leave.' He gestured towards the door.

Eddie fixed him with a fierce glare which suddenly faded and was replaced with a smile in a conscious manoeuvre. 'Sorry about all that, mate,' he said. 'Family – you know how it is.'

Ben nodded and began to edge out of the room.

'Does she mean it?' said Eddie. 'About finding our Esther?'

Kay snorted.

For a moment, Ben stood in the doorway looking into the room, not sure how to answer. 'Yes, she's very serious about it.' He licked his dry lips. 'And I think she can do it, if she gets the right help.'

'If there's anything we can do,' said Eddie, letting the sentence tail off.

'Right,' said Ben absently. There was something about Eddie's insistence that struck him as false, perhaps even with a background note of fear.

On the way out, Ben took one last look over his shoulder at the pictures on the wall – multiple Esthers with the same luminous smile at every age, the same creased and gleaming eyes, her laughter almost audible in the dreary hallway.

By the time Ben caught up with Lucy she was already sitting in the driver's seat, drumming on the wheel without any rhythm. Before he had his seatbelt on, and almost before he had closed the door, she pulled away and began to speed through the village wilfully ignoring admonitions to 'Please drive carefully'. They passed down the hill and out of the other side of Berebroke on the lower road. When they reached a lay-by, she pulled in and took her hands off the steering wheel. There, she raised a hand to her mouth, which was already contorted, and let out a sob.

Ben had no idea what to do or say, so he did nothing. The longer he sat silent and unmoving the less possible any action became. Accompanied by the swish of car tires on tarmac and the rumbling of lorries, she continued to weep and he felt blood rise in his face. Finally, he pushed himself to speak. 'What is it?'

She leaned towards him and after a split-second's hesitation he hugged her, uncomfortably, over the gear stick and handbrake, unsure where to put his hands. One settled lightly on her shoulder blade, the other on her lower back.

Her crying intensified – not stage tears to be dabbed at with a lace handkerchief, but howls from the gut. When she finally looked up and pulled away from him, her eyes were pink and swollen, her face covered in tears and snot. He felt some of what she felt and the feeling pushed up behind his eyes. It hurt him to see her hurt, and the depth of his own feeling surprised him.

'It's nothing,' she said, congested and snivelling.

He reached for a packet of tissues on the dashboard and handed them to her.

'I must look a state,' she said, and blew her nose.

Ben hesitated. Should he say something reassuring? She did look a state, but he didn't care. When he finally spoke, it was to say, 'This can't be nothing. I want to understand.'

She leaned back in her seat, rubbing at her cheeks with a tissue. 'Dad and I don't get on because he crossed a line,' she said. 'Just once.'

Ben felt frozen – what should he say? If he asked the wrong question, or said the wrong thing, he felt sure she would close off again.

They both started when someone tapped on the car window. Lucy looked over her shoulder to see a police officer gesturing for her to wind the window down. He was tall and lean with grey cheeks visible between the turned-up collar of his high-visibility winter coat and the peaked cap pulled down low over his eyes. Ben glanced at the rear-view mirror and saw that a police car was parked behind them, another officer in the driver's seat. Lucy pressed the button and the window slid down, admitting a gust of chill air.

'Yes?' she said.

'Everything all right?' asked the policeman flatly, his eyes flitting over Lucy, Ben and the car.

'Fine, thank you,' she said, but her swollen eyes and hoarse voice made it sound unconvincing.

'This lay-by isn't intended as a car park,' said the policeman. 'If you've finished whatever you're doing, please move along.'

'Okay,' said Lucy. 'Is that it?'

The officer paused to take one more look around the car before saying, reluctantly, 'Yes, that's all. Drive carefully.' He stood upright but stayed where he was, waiting for them to move away.

Lucy wound up the window, started the engine and, taking extra care, pulled out onto the road and hit the accelerator.

'When I was riding the buses with my dad, we always used to see police cars patrolling up here, especially near Christmas,' said Ben, the emotional fugue forgotten. 'Drink drivers and boy racers. I wonder if they've got records of cars stopped and checked on the evening Esther went missing?'

Lucy sighed and sniffed, her eyes still red. 'It's all too much. I can see why the police are always in such a hurry to narrow the list of suspects.'

Ben smiled. She sounded almost herself again. 'What next, boss?' he said, hoping that she would appreciate the joke.

'I need to go home and do some thinking,' she said. She glanced away from the road for half a second, catching Ben's pale profile. 'Why don't you come round for something to eat first, though? It won't be anything special.'

Ben thought of his flat and its bareness, of its permanent twilight, and of yet another kebab dinner. 'That would be nice, thanks.'

Lucy Garrett lived in a suburb of Exeter, on the wrong side of the river, traversed by dual carriageways and broken up by vast retail parks. It was busy with traffic and full of light but at the same time lacking in life with few pedestrians and little green space. She turned off the main road and down a side street lined on both sides with Victorian terraces. They were small houses but neat, most with newly-installed driveways and the kinds of exterior fixtures which betray middle-class occupants – French shutters, calico blinds, tidy shrubs in steel planters, and recycling bins full of broadsheet newspapers and wine bottles. She stopped the car at the very end of the road, on the crest of a gentle hill, facing the high red-brick wall of a looming Edwardian school building. Her house was like all the others except less well cared for, the paintwork of the front door black with city smut and peeling, while the front yard – it was not a garden – was covered with cracked paving slabs between which grew weeds and moss.

'It's a bit untidy,' she said, opening the door and stepping inside, over a pile of mail and several weeks' worth of free newspapers. She turned on a light, hung up her coat, and walked through to the kitchen. Ben slowly closed the door behind him and looked around. There were several pairs of men's shoes in a heap, with a light layer of dust, and, on the ledge by the door, a stack of mail. Ben glanced down and saw that it was addressed to Mr D H Arthur.

'Come on through,' shouted Lucy.

He walked slowly down the hall, glancing through an open door into the sitting room where he saw full bookshelves and piles of paper. In the kitchen, he found Lucy opening two bottles of lager. She held one up and he took it. As he took a swig, he looked around the room, noting that it was clean, but only just, and that the small breakfast table by the window was covered with documents, books and unwashed coffee mugs. On the door of the fridge was a picture of Lucy with a man – older and balding but handsome nonetheless with trimmed grey stubble and a broad, perfect smile.

Seeing his eyes rest on the picture, after an uneasy pause, Lucy said, 'That's David, my partner. He travels a lot. He's been in Hong Kong since October last year.' She leaned back against the work surface with a small sigh, turning to face the window. In profile, in the dim light, she looked tense and tired, her nose pink from crying, and from her perpetual cold. He looked at the photograph again, where she was enfolded in her partner's arms, tanned and laughing.

Ben didn't know what to say. 'That must be difficult,' he mumbled after a few seconds.

'Not really,' she said. 'We find ways of making it, you know, work.' Her voice tailed away into another sigh.

Ben took a swig of beer and then spoke softly. 'You were going to tell me something about your dad.'

She shook her head. 'It's not important.'

With a frown Ben looked down at his own left hand, flexing it to ease a sudden soreness from the joints. After a second he spoke, softer again. 'It might be.'

Lucy lowered herself onto a chair and gave the barest nod of her head. Her eyes looked small and seemed to have shadows beneath them. A tension came over her whole body. 'It was just a small thing, just once. It was after Esther had gone, years after, and he was drunk.'

She swallowed, struggling.

'He and Mum were out with friends but he came home early. When I saw he was drunk I mean really legless. He'd ignored me, or so I thought, for all that time, but suddenly he was all affectionate. He kept calling me "his girl".'

Her hands came together on the table and she began to pick hard at the nail on her forefinger, digging audibly at the rough skin on either side.

'I sometimes think I imagined it or read too much into it but, no, the way he touched me and looked at me was wrong. He kissed me and it wasn't the way a father ought to kiss his daughter.'

Her eyes came up to meet Ben's, bright with anger. 'Mum didn't believe me, of course, because it wasn't convenient for her. Thought I was acting up for attention.'

'I'm sorry,' said Ben weakly, and thinking fondly of his own parents who, for all their flaws, never treated him so reprehensibly. Then he pictured Eddie Garrett behaving the same with Esther and his flesh chilled. He wasn't sure whether to put it into words but something made him hold back – a sense that Lucy had somehow failed to extrapolate from this incident to imagine a scenario in which her father had something to do with the disappearance of her sister, and in which her mother might be complicit.

Lucy stared, dead-eyed.

Awkwardly, eager for an escape from the crushing silence, Ben pointed at the telephone mounted on the wall by the back door. A red light was blinking. 'You've got a message,' he said.

Lucy looked and pulled a face, puzzled. 'I always forget I've got a landline – I never use it.' She walked to the phone and pressed the button to playback messages over the loudspeaker.

'One... new... message. Message. One. Today... at... Fourteen... Twenty-two.'

There was a hiss and then the sound of a hesitant voice with the ghost of a stammer. 'This is Detective Superintendent Marwick – Ewan Marwick. I tried to ring your mobile but couldn't get through.'

'That's country living,' said Lucy.

'I'm calling about a couple of things. F-first, please don't read too much into this, but I need to speak to you about certain developments in my investigation which might appear in the press in the next day or two. Please call me at the earliest opportunity.'

He hesitated, apparently riffling through a notebook. 'Oh, yes, so, I understand from various s-s-s-sources that you might be looking into – or rather interfering in, that is to say – the ongoing investigation into your sister's disappearance.'

Lucy looked at Ben and gave a sulky roll of her eyes. 'That old cow must have phoned him.' She meant Mrs Ellison.

Ben stepped nearer to the phone and clenched his free hand to stop it shaking. He wasn't sure if he was scared or excited to find himself at odds with the avatar of authority.

'I would obviously be happy to d-discuss this with you in person at the soonest possible opportunity but, um, in the meantime, please do not approach anyone or discuss the case.' Marwick cleared his throat which translated, on tape, into a harsh buzz. When he spoke again, there was a hard edge to his voice. 'I need you to back off and trust us to investigate properly, in a measured way, following due process, or you run the risk of compromising whatever chance we might have of reaching a satisfactory conclusion.' The energy drained from his rebuke.

'In, as it were, the long term. As I say, do give me a call.' He rattled off his number, repeated it more slowly, and then concluded with a jarringly meek, 'Bye, then.'

Lucy drank from her bottle and wrapped her arms, shaking her head.

'I don't trust them, that's the problem. They had their chance and this Marwick, he doesn't care about Esther – only about putting Steven Sweetland away.' She looked sideways and smiled slyly. 'Did you notice that he didn't actually tell us we must stop – he was asking. We're not actually doing anything illegal.'

'So you want to keep going?'

She took a sip of lager and then held the bottle to her mouth, tapping it against her lower lip as she considered. 'If you do,' she said, at last.

'Of course,' he said, surprised at his own certainty.

She took his hand and squeezed it briefly before dropping her arms to her side. 'Thanks.'

Ben looked at the clock on his phone. 'You'd better call Mr Marwick,' he said.

'He can call me back if he wants to talk.'

CHAPTER SIXTEEN

When Ben checked his own voicemail that evening on arriving back at his flat on Magdalen Street, he also found messages waiting. The first was from Christine Kelly warning him that Marwick knew he had copies of her notebooks and wasn't happy about it.

The second was from his father. After a long pause and a grunt of frustration, Peter spoke with excruciating awkwardness: 'Uh, hello, son. Are you going to come round and see me this weekend or what? Give me a ring. Okay, then.'

Sitting on the edge of his bed with one walking boot off and the other unlaced, dangling from his foot, Ben sat for a moment looking at the phone's screen. He couldn't recall Peter ever calling him out of the blue or expressing a desire to spend time together though he knew that his parents had argued grimly over custody when he was a child. He was pleased, and even a touch moved. Checking the time, he decided that it wasn't too late to call back, especially as he knew Peter was in the habit of sitting up late watching films on TV – westerns, old horror films – after he'd been to the pub on a Friday night.

Peter answered at once.

'Dad? It's Ben. I can come round tomorrow morning for brunch, if you like, and then we can go for a drink at lunchtime.'

'Brunch?' said Peter, slightly mocking.

'A fry-up, then,' replied Ben wearily. 'I won't get there until after ten o'clock, because of the trains.'

'Fair enough, son. I'll pop out early and get some shopping in, and I'll see you when I see you.'

They both hesitated, hanging on the line, knowing that there was something else they ought to say, but unable to put it in words.

'Night, then,' said Ben.

'Night, son. See you tomorrow.'

When Ben arrived at the house in Okehampton and let himself in with the worn old Yale key he had been carrying for almost twenty years, he found Peter in his usual place, in front of the TV. It was showing a repeat of a football match from the 1970s on an obscure cable channel but Peter was concentrating on a tabloid newspaper from which he did not look up when Ben entered.

'All right, mate,' he said.

'All right,' said Ben. He slouched into the other armchair, the one which had for so long been his grandmother's, and felt it sag beneath him, the springs creaking. The house hadn't changed much since his grandmother's death: her knitting bag still sat at the side of the chair, and her odour suffused the furniture, curtains and carpets, providing a background hum of lavender perfume, cigarettes, antiseptic and talcum powder.

He glanced across at his father who was absorbed in the sports pages, chewing on a hangnail with his nose wrinkled in concentration. Ben sighed quietly and looked around, wondering what to do while he waited for Peter to come out of his morning reverie. There were stacks of old newspapers and copies of the *TV Times* under the coffee table. He bent to rummage through them, looking for the most recent. He found one only a few weeks old and began to turn its pages, not stopping to read anything.

He was relieved when his phone rang in his pocket and rushed to answer.

'Ben? It's Lucy. Put the TV on.' She sounded triumphant, elated, and a little wild.

'Okay,' said Ben. 'Which channel?'

'Three,' she said.

Peter looked up, finally, as Ben beckoned to him for the remote control.

'What's on, son?' he asked dully, and blinking, as if he'd just come round from a deep sleep.

'Hurry up,' Lucy said in Ben's ear.

'The remote,' said Ben, reaching. 'I need to change channels.'

Peter put down his newspaper and passed the control to Ben who immediately switched to ITV where a national news bulletin was underway. The screen was filled by a slow zoom on the round face of a young man with thick black hair and scars indicating the remains of a cleft lip. '...in 2004. Police are now investigating his movements in relation to several murder cases investigated by disgraced detective Steven Sweetland which are set to be overturned by the High Court next month. Marlon Wakefield is known to have targeted young women and police have long said that, as well as the four murders for which he was convicted, he may well have been involved in many more from 1989 onwards.'

'Are you watching this?' said Lucy down the phone.

'Yes,' Ben replied.

There was a library shot of the revolving sign outside New Scotland Yard and then DSI Marwick appeared, standing against a louvered blind in a plain office, with his hands behind his back. He spoke more precisely and fluently than usual, as if performing the part of an authority figure on stage and thus more conscious of his diction.

'At this stage my team is working closely with police services up and down the country to ensure that evidence reviews are undertaken with a view to securing new convictions, where that is appropriate. There have been significant advances in process and forensic technology in even the last few years.'

A carousel of the faces of young women against a swirling blue background began to scroll across the screen accompanied by the news reporter's voice-over. Esther Garrett was among them, in that smiling school photograph Ben knew so well. As the reporter uttered a melodramatic summing up, Ben muted the TV and spoke into the phone.

'What did he say to you?'

'He told me not to get excited. He said he was only letting me know so that the news wouldn't come as a shock and that these things very rarely come to anything.'

'That's true,' said Ben. 'They're always announcing stuff like this, or arresting people. It doesn't necessarily mean a lot.'

There was a moment's silence on the line.

'I've got a positive feeling,' Lucy said. Ben read the coolness in her voice – she wanted reassurance, not argument.

'It's definitely good news that they're doing something,' said Ben hastily. 'He's right, though, Mr Marwick – don't invest all your hope in this. We should keep working.'

'No, we should wait and see,' said Lucy. 'I don't want to do anything that could make it harder for the police to get a conviction now.'

Ben felt his gut sink. 'As long as it is the right person this time,' he said. 'Otherwise, we'll never find her.'

'Don't lecture me about that. You didn't have to live through that the first time.'

'Okay, sorry,' he said, his voice leaden. He sensed it was too late as the line fell silent again. 'Perhaps we can talk later? Or tomorrow?'

'Maybe,' she said, and hung up.

Ben took the phone away from his ear and weighed it in his hand for a moment, lips pursed.

Peter stirred in his seat and gave a rumbling cough. 'All right, son?' He had been listening to Ben's side of the conversation intently and his face was creased with concern.

'Yes, fine,' said Ben dismissively, unsure of his father's capacity to understand the situation and unwilling to expend energy explaining.

'That was your friend, was it?' He snapped his fingers at the TV. 'The sister.'

'Yes,' said Ben.

'What is it you two have been up to then? I mean, I ain't hardly seen you, and you looked knackered, so you must have been busy.'

Ben gave an adolescent groan and dismissed the question. 'Do you want this fry-up, then?'

'I'm not hungry,' Peter replied, his face betraying the worries that he couldn't put into words. He looked at his watch. 'Let's just go straight down the pub, eh?'

There were several pubs near the house but Peter's favourite had always been the Waterloo. It was an unremarkable building on the corner of two back streets, gloomy all year round, with sticky carpets. Ben remembered spending summer afternoons sitting in the yard drinking fizzy pop and, later, drinking lager there as a nervous teenager. That morning, he and Peter were the first to arrive and found the land-lord, Martin, wiping away the previous night's spilled beer and folded crisp packets. He was a small man with wispy white hair who looked permanently worried and whose jeans and polo shirt hung loosely about him.

'Peter,' he said in greeting, pronouncing it 'Peeder', accenting the final syllable as in a song.

'Mart,' said Peter. 'You know my boy, don't you?'

Ben could tell from Martin's expression that he was surprised to be reminded that Peter had a son, and certainly didn't know him, but said anyway, 'Certainly do, certainly do – how's you, young man?'

'Good, thanks,' Ben mumbled, feeling like a nervous child again – an alien in his father's world.

The three of them stood for a moment saying nothing as the pub dog, a limping and elderly spaniel, sloped across the floor yawning and smacking its lips.

'Usual is it, then?' Martin said eventually, putting down his yellow rag and moving towards the bar. Peter nodded and Martin began to pull a pint of cider. 'And for you, young man?' Ben asked for a pint of the weakest lager on the bar and got out his wallet. Peter extended a hand. 'I'll get this one, son,' he said, pulling a brand new folded ten-pound note from his shirt pocket.

Once he had his drink and had paid, Peter leaned against the bar and began to roll a cigarette with deft movements of his calloused fingers. Ben stood away from the bar with his pint, waiting for his father to move towards a table. He realised, after a short while, that Peter had no such intention and always stood at the bar to drink, where the conversation happened. Tables were for snobs. He leaned next to Peter and tried to make himself comfortable.

Martin turned on the radio, tuned to 'Sounds of the Sixties' on Radio 2, and continued cleaning.

Staring at his nearly-completed cigarette as he formed the seam, Peter spoke softly. 'What do you want to get caught up in all this for?'

'It's hard to explain,' said Ben, already regretting coming out with his father.

'What's it all about?' Peter said. 'Just for fun or what?'

Ben sighed. 'Not fun, exactly, no.'

'They never did find her, did they?' said Peter. 'How do you know she's not in...' He waved the perfectly formed roll-up cigarette for emphasis. 'I don't know, bloody Thailand or somewhere.'

Ben laughed involuntarily. 'Where did you get Thailand from?'

Peter smiled shyly, embarrassed. 'Some of the lads in here, they spend six months of the year out in Thailand.' His smile broadened a touch. 'Friendly girls, so they say.'

Ben curled his lip. 'Jesus, Dad.'

Peter's face fell at the broken connection between them and he looked down at his fingertips. 'Anyway, looks as if they've got someone in the frame now,' he said.

Ben nodded reluctantly. 'Yes,' he said. He hesitated, wondering why he was bothering to explain to his father, who wouldn't understand. 'That's why Lucy wants to stop for a bit, just wait and see.'

'Well, there you go,' said Peter, and took a long swig from his glass, downing a third of a pint in one go. It seemed to go immediately to his head, causing his sallow cheeks to flush and his eyes to become distant and milky.

'I think she's desperate for a solution even if it's the wrong one because some of the other possibilities are too much for her to think about.'

Peter frowned and stuck out his bottom lip, expressing his puzzlement at the complexities of human behaviour and motivation.

'I think it might be to do with someone in her own family.'

'Jesus wept,' said Peter, shaking his head. 'Bloody awful.'

'But she isn't ready to consider that.'

'Fair play, son – who would be?'

Ben gave an exaggerated shrug, adopting the body language of the pub discussions he'd watched so many times as a teenager.

The door opened and another man entered the pub, a football shirt stretched over a ball-like gut, red-faced and bleary-eyed. 'Peeder, Mart,' he said gruffly, and then gave Ben a brief, wary nod.

'Davey,' said Peter.

Davey ordered a beer and set himself up at the other end of the bar with a newspaper.

Peter gave Davey one last look to check he was settled and then turned back to Ben. He jabbed a nicotine-stained finger. 'I'm not being funny, Ben, but how long are you going to hang about down here, wasting your time?'

Ben tried to make light of it. 'Trying to get rid of me already?'

'Don't be daft, son,' said Peter. He downed another third of his cider and twirled the cigarette between his fingers. He seemed to be searching for the right words to express something more but gave up and, instead, patted Ben on the arm, rubbing his sleeve. 'All I'm saying is, you got away, didn't you? Even though me and your mum didn't do such a good job. That rests on my conscience, it really does.'

Ben opened his mouth to speak but Peter held up a hand to silence him. 'We fucked it up, but you turned out all right. Clever lad, got it together, career and a good salary.' He let out something like a growl. 'It's breaking my heart that you gave that up to come back down here. What's here for you? Nothing. The point was for you to go somewhere better, not end up stuck here like me.'

Ben blinked, picked up his glass and took a long draught, overcome and unable to look his father in the eye.

The door opened and a couple entered – a man and woman in late middle age, both wearing sheepskin coats, she with a tie-dyed headscarf tied around her head and he with an Australian bush hat pressed down over long grey hair. A small dirty-looking dog on a lead walked between them. They waved at Peter, greeted Davey by name, and ordered two pints of bitter and chasers of Bell's whisky before retiring to a corner table by the grimy window where they sat staring and silent.

'You didn't fuck up,' said Ben, a rising tone in his voice signalling a 'but' to come. He shifted positions, his elbow numb from leaning. 'I wasn't happy in London. I'm not happy now.'

Peter looked down at his boots. 'I've got to ask, son – you're not thinking of doing anything stupid, are you?'

'Christ, no,' said Ben. 'Nothing like that.'

'I wouldn't forgive myself, son, if you did.'

'I just need to work a few things out, and helping Lucy is part of that. And being here.' His hand came up to echo the word. 'Home.'

Peter nodded firmly and said, 'Fair enough,' though he wore a sceptical expression. He finished his pint of cider and held the empty glass in his hand. 'Your round, son.'

Ben downed his own drink faster than he would have liked and ordered two more which were pulled into the same glasses. When Martin had moved away, Ben, his tongue loosened by the first pint, said, 'I wish I hadn't been on the bus that day, and that I'd never seen Esther Garrett, but I was and I did. I can't just drop it.' He frowned and gave a grunting sigh of frustration. 'I've got this weird feeling – I've had it for years – that whatever happened to her, it all started on the bus.'

'What, that Greenslade, you mean?' said Peter, his face contorted with confusion.

Ben shook his head furiously, the drink beginning to make his movements broader and clumsier. 'No, no, not that.' He grappled with his memory. 'As if something she did or said was significant.' He waved a hand and scowled. 'It sounds stupid.'

'A bit far-fetched,' said Peter.

Ben tried again. 'You know how when the police say that they want people to come forward with any information, however unimportant it might seem?'

Peter turned down the corners of his mouth and gave one nod to the side, conceding the point.

'Well, that's what I mean – that I worry that maybe something I saw, like one of the other passengers, or something she said or did, might be the bit of information they needed to find her, if they hadn't been so fixated on Aaron Greenslade.'

Peter looked into the amber liquid in his pint glass and swirled it. 'I see what you mean.' He looked up and rubbed the grey stubble on his chin with the tips of his fingers, making a rasping sound loud enough to be heard over the burbling radio. 'Can you actually remember any of the other passengers?'

'No, that's the problem,' said Ben. 'I can picture her perfectly.' He gave an exaggerated shrug. 'But everyone else – they're just grey blobs.'

Peter put his roll-up in his mouth and began to search his pockets for a lighter.

'I don't suppose you can remember who was on the bus that day, can you?' Ben asked him.

At first, his eyes widened, and then Peter let loose a throaty guffaw when he realised Ben's question was in earnest. 'Do you know how many times I drove up and down that road? I can't hardly tell one day from another.' He sighed. 'I did have a few regular passengers, though. I'll have a think,' he said, resigned and weary. 'I'm going to have a fag outside – coming, or do you want to stay here in the warm?'

PART THREE

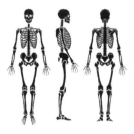

CHAPTER SEVENTEEN

Ben didn't remember going back to his flat or how he got there but woke up early in the morning with a dry throat and a sense that he was viewing the world through a slowly rotating, distorted lens. He grasped for a glass of stale water on the bedside table and downed it with his eyes closed and then collapsed back onto his bed, covering his face with an open palm.

Apart from a sense of regret at having drunk too much he felt fearful at what might have happened or been said during long stretches of the afternoon which had disappeared from his memory, like demagnetised portions of the cassette tapes he'd listened to as a child.

After another hour of drifting in and out of sleep while a headache came on, he forced himself to get up and drink more water and then picked up his mobile phone from the coffee table where he'd dumped it. It was almost out of charge but there was enough for him to see that there were no missed calls or voice messages, which meant Lucy had not tried to get in touch. He groaned quietly and rubbed at his temples.

After eating a breakfast of toast and bacon, and managing to keep it down despite his churning stomach, he had a shower and got dressed. Then, still feeling woolly-headed and unsteady, he sat himself at the dining table and dialled Lucy's number.

She answered, eventually.

'It's Ben,' he said.

'I know.'

He heard a great deal in those two words: the heat of their shared obsession was gone, for now at least. He felt his mind grow foggy – he didn't know what to say or do. The silence between them was long and heavy.

'This isn't a great time,' she said at last, as if he was a complete stranger, a cold caller.

'Okay, sorry,' said Ben. 'Just ring me whenever, all right?'

'Right,' she said, and Ben felt both her pity and her irritation. For now he had been dismissed. She had no use for him.

For two days Ben did nothing. It didn't seem right to go on without Lucy Garrett who had legitimised what he knew was a strange interest. He also hoped that she might change her mind and call him. He spent his days walking the streets, getting to know odd corners of the city, drinking coffee after coffee, and as the very last dregs of his hangover passed after a few days, a few pints of beer.

He tried to distract himself by planning a holiday – a tour of somewhere hot and exotic which would take his mind off Dodd's Wood and the lonely road into Berebroke – but kept circling back to the dark undergrowth. In idle moments in cafés and pubs some nagging thought made him keep searching online for information about Eddie Garrett.

Crouched over his phone or laptop, he crawled through newspaper archives but found nothing other than mentions in relation to Esther's disappearance. There was certainly nothing more about Eddie's conviction for dealing pornography that had come up during Aaron Greenslade's trial. It had either gone unreported or was for some other reason missing from the records. He tried searching obliquely, omitting Eddie Garrett's name, and succeeded in finding a local memories Facebook page which made reference to the 'famous Berebroke swingers' and bookmarked it for future reference.

Leslie Reeves, Esther's ex-boyfriend, was easier to track down online. In his Facebook profile picture he appeared to be on the deck of a yacht and looked tanned, healthy and expensively dressed, with Ray-Bans and a perfect white smile. His wife was blonde and photogenic and there were also three children; two boys and a girl, aged between five and ten as far as Ben could tell. Reeves worked for an international power company as an engineer with specialist technical expertise which took him around the world. Ben wished he believed in gut instinct but, stare as he might into the eyes of this stranger, no mystic voice spoke to him to confirm Reeves's guilt or innocence. What Ben did know was that people can change a lot in twenty years.

Marlon Wakefield, Marwick's new chief suspect, was inescapable. The old mugshot taken when he was arrested a decade before appeared on the front page of at least one newspaper every day. There was a sigh of relief implicit in the coverage – a certain delight in the neatness of the solution – which was echoed, Ben thought, in statements from the police. The scarred, scowling face in the picture looked as that of a murderer ought to, which people seemed to find reassuring, or at least less terrifying than the idea of a killer who looked and acted like the men they lived and worked beside.

There was no doubt he was a dangerous man but it seemed obvious to Ben that he had nothing to do with Esther's disappearance. His victims had all been older, had all lived in towns and cities, and all had either worked as prostitutes or were otherwise vulnerable. None of them lived at home with their families in quiet villages. They had also all been found within weeks of being abducted – Louise Brennan in the basement of a squat in Bristol, Kelly Cooper wrapped in a sleeping bag on wasteland in Gloucester, and Chantal Holmes in a disused shed on railway sidings in Reading. It made Ben feel queasy to read about decomposing bodies and to think of Esther Garrett in that context but he couldn't resist looking into the foul details of each death, just in case there was a resonance or hint he had previously missed.

Perhaps Wakefield had said something to the police, or maybe they had found something they had not yet made public, but Ben doubted it: Wakefield, he thought, was the perfect replacement for Aaron Greenslade in the frame – conveniently unsympathetic, with nobody interested in taking his side.

On Wednesday morning, Ben called Christine Kelly, hoping to catch her in the hour between her rising and the pub on the corner of her street opening for business. She answered promptly and sounded businesslike and lucid – like a police officer, as if she had never retired.

'I could do with some advice,' he said.

'Go on,' she growled.

'Lucy Garrett wants to leave it alone for a bit, wait and see what happens.'

'Because of this Marlon whatshisname.'

'But I can't.'

'Well, you should,' said Kelly.

'I don't think he did it. It's neat for the police, of course, but I think it suits Lucy because it's more palatable than the truth might be.'

Kelly sighed, the sound pinched and made harsh by the narrow bandwidth of the phone line. 'Like I say, understandable.'

There was a hard edge in her voice which told Ben he ought to get to the point.

'I can't let it go,' he said. 'Otherwise, what's all this been for?'

'We used to hate coppers like you on the force. The crusading thing.' She tutted. 'Up to a point, it's all very laudable, but you have to learn to live with loose ends. You can go mental trying to wrap up every case.'

'But I'm not a policeman,' said Ben, 'and this is my only case. It's been my case since I was twelve, against my choice.'

She sighed again and it turned into a horribly liquid cough. 'Have you got a pen handy?'

'Yes.'

She recited a phone number with an 0117 Bristol area code.

'Whose is that?' said Ben.

'Steve's.'

It took Ben a moment to process what she meant.

'You mean Mr Sweetland's?'

'Tell him I told you to call.'

Ben had to work up to making the call, clearing his desk and sitting down with a pen, a notebook and a cup of coffee. Twice he dialled the number only to hang up in panic when he heard the first ringing tone. On the third attempt, it rang and rang and rang but no one answered. He was relieved, in a way, and could feel his heart thumping in his chest. He waited an hour and then forced himself to try again.

'Yes?' said a woman's voice, warily.

'Can I speak to Mr Sweetland, please?'

'I'm afraid he isn't available.'

'Christine Kelly told me to call.'

'Who?'

'She used to work with him.' He spoke quickly, fearing that she might hang up, but trying to sound calm and unthreatening at the same time. 'Please, if he's there, just tell him it's Ben Hodge and that Christine Kelly told me to ring.'

'Hold on a moment.'

After almost a minute, the line crackled into life.

'Mr Hodge?'

'Mr Sweetland?'

'Steve, please. Why do I know your name?'

'We met when I was twelve. My dad was driving the bus that Esther Garrett took before she disappeared.'

'Good lord.'

'I know.'

'And Christine told you to call me?'

'Yes. I met her a few weeks ago.'

'You'll forgive me being cagey, but I've had a lot of journalists on the line trying to dig dirt. I'm not supposed to talk to anybody.'

'I'm not a journalist, but I would like to see you.'

'Why?'

'I'll explain when we meet,' said Ben. He knew this wasn't persuasive and furrowed his brow, trying to think of something to say. 'I'm a friend to Esther Garrett and I think you are too.'

Sweetland grunted. 'I'm not sure this is a good idea.'

'Please, just meet me. You can walk away once you've heard me out.'

'I'm under investigation, you know.'

'You're not under arrest, though, are you?'

'I'm under strict instructions from my lawyers not to say anything to anyone.'

'Just meet me and listen.'

Sweetland fell silent for a moment before saying, 'Where are you now?'

'Exeter,' said Ben, 'but I can be in Bristol in an hour.'

'Do you know the city?'

'Not at all.'

'There's a pub near Temple Meads station called the Admiral Hawke. Meet me there at, say, six?'

'Okay.'

'And bring some ID. I need to know you're who you say you are.'

Ben caught one of the back-and-forth shuttle trains at Exeter and was in Bristol well before six o'clock. After a short walk in the rain, he found the pub easily enough, on one of the streets that ran off opposite the station. It was a 1960s red-brick bunker with a flat roof and frosted windows that looked more like a community centre than a pub. Taking a breath, he went in.

Pink Floyd was playing over speakers mounted on the wall and the air was warm and dry. There were plenty of drinkers, mostly men in small groups wearing ties and suits. Ben bought a pint of lager and took a seat near the jukebox from where he could see the door.

At five to six, when Ben had nearly finished his first beer, the door
was flung open and Sweetland entered. Ben stood up and gave a tentative wave. Sweetland didn't respond, not even with a nod. He
unwrapped a black scarf from his neck and shook the lightweight black
raincoat from his shoulders. He hung them on a hook by the door and
approached, brushing water from his short white hair. Sweetland did not
dress with the same flair he had shown as a young man. He was now
wearing the sagging corduroys and plain woollen sweater of a middle-
aged man. The haughty, domineering jut of his chin had gone, too, as his
face had sagged and neck bent.

'Mr Hodge?'

'Yes.'

There was a moment of tension until Ben realised that Sweetland
was waiting to see his ID. Not wanting to be too conspicuous he took
his passport from his pocket and handed it over. Sweetland took a pair
of wire-framed glasses from his pocket and put them on to peer at the
photo. He looked up and down and then handed it back.

'Okay.' He put his glasses away and then extended a prematurely
bony hand. Ben took it and shook. Ben remembered how he had once
smelled of aftershave but now there was only the faint aroma of cigarettes, coffee and cheap deodorant.

Gesturing at the bar, Sweetland said, 'Do you want something to
drink?'

'Lager, please.'

Sweetland caught the eye of the dark-haired woman behind
the bar.

'The usual for me and a lager for my friend here, when you're ready,
Rosie, love.'

He lowered himself into a chair with a groan. 'How exactly do you
think I can help you?'

Ben felt the moment of decision – lie, or not? – but made the calcu-
lation quickly. 'I was helping Lucy Garrett until recently. She wants to
know what happened to her sister and now I've realised I won't be able
to move on until we've found her.'

The barmaid put their drinks on the table. Sweetland's usual was a glass of white wine.

'Until recently?' said Sweetland, curling his lip to reveal the glint of a canine tooth.

'She believes Marlon Wakefield did it.'

Sweetland's face brightened and he tipped his head back to emit a sudden shout of laughter. No one else in the pub paid any attention. 'It's nothing to do with him, I can tell you that.'

'You still think Aaron Greenslade did it?'

Taking a sip of wine, Sweetland wrinkled his eyes in thought. 'Yes, I stand by that conviction. No pun intended.'

Ben's shoulders sank and he gave a sigh that sounded more exasperated than he had intended.

Sweetland went on. 'I'll say to you what I've said to everybody else–'

'To Mr Marwick?'

'To everyone.' He leaned forward and spoke as if into a microphone at a press conference. 'I only ever acted in good faith. I never sent down anyone I didn't sincerely believe was guilty, using evidence I personally believed to be sound.' Colour came into his cheeks and his voice gained a ragged edge. 'I could not have sat down with the families of those victims, or my own family, and looked them in the eye if I'd ever once massaged evidence or fudged a line-up. I got into police work to help people, not hurt them. Even criminals, I wanted to help – to get them on the straight and narrow. If I sometimes leaned hard on people, and I'm not saying I did, then it was only with the best of intentions.'

He finished his speech and downed the wine in his glass with one throw of his wrist.

'Got it?'

Ben tried to speak but the words caught in his throat. He swallowed and tried again. 'What about Darren Napier?'

Sweetland's grey features took on a look of disappointed resignation. 'It comes to something when the word of a police officer with twenty-five years on the force counts for less than that of a known drug user and petty criminal. My only dealings with Mr Napier are on record, by the book, just how I always liked it, and I've got no doubt I'll be cleared if the investigation is thorough and proper.'

Sweetland looked at his watch. 'I've got nothing else to say so I'm going to leave. I suggest you stay here, finish your beer, and then go home and leave this to the professionals.'

Sweetland stood up, gave a brief nod and walked away.

Ben watched him put on his coat and step out into the rain.

It had seemed so convincing and yet Ben knew that Sweetland was not the objective player he pretended to be. He knew from Lucy and from Christine Kelly that Sweetland had been emotionally involved. After a few seconds processing Ben darted towards the door and out into the rain.

He looked both ways and saw Sweetland just in view approaching the corner at the bottom of the road. In the low evening light, made lower yet by dense cloud, he was able to follow Sweetland quite easily. He didn't know why exactly he was doing so other than an urgent instinct – a memory, perhaps, of the day in the wood when he and Chelsea had spied on the detective as they crouched in the undergrowth.

With his height and confident stride, Sweetland cut through the crowds, moving towards the station. Ben nearly lost him crossing four lanes of traffic at a roundabout but saw Sweetland stop and duck into another pub. When Ben caught up, he glanced through the window and saw Sweetland leaning at the bar with a glass in hand but, this time, it was whisky, not wine.

'All right, pal?' said a middle-aged red-haired woman who was standing in the doorway smoking.

'Just looking to see if my friends are here,' said Ben brightly. 'They're not.'

He walked on until the pub was almost out of sight and then found shelter in a shop doorway.

Sweetland stayed in the pub for nearly twenty minutes. When he emerged he had a newspaper folded under his arm which he used to protect his head from the rain. He dashed across the road and up a side street. Ben hurried and then ran. When he turned up the road, which ran between two blocks of converted Victorian warehouses, there was no sign of Sweetland. There were two pubs on the street and Ben guessed Sweetland had entered one or the other. The first had its curtains drawn and a bouncer on the door. Ben slipped inside and found it crowded, brown and lit low. He glanced around, dripping on the floor. He couldn't see Sweetland but perhaps he was sitting down or in the back bar. Ben looked back at the door then moved on into the pub. He checked the alcoves and booths, the back room, and the hidden corner beyond the end of the bar, squeezing between groups of people in business suits and party dresses. His ears rang with shouted conversation and the repetitive thudding of the background music.

There was no sign of Sweetland and, anxious that he might have now lost him, Ben headed for the door as fast as possible.

'Cheers,' said the bouncer as Ben passed him.

He stopped and turned right at once to avoid Sweetland who was emerging from the pub opposite, now looking quite unsteady. Ben had his hood up, there was a crowd of students passing between them, and Sweetland was misty-eyed from what must be his fourth or fifth drink, and so he didn't notice Ben. As Sweetland walked on he fell into step thirty metres or so behind, keeping his head dipped. As his feet slapped into potholes and puddles on the uneven pathway, Ben felt water penetrating his boots. His jeans were drenched and his black hiking jacket had begun to leak at the wrists and neck. He shivered.

Up ahead, Sweetland was heading towards a pub on the waterside when a shaven-headed young man in a stained anorak and torn trainers accosted him. He had the look of a drug addict − dark-eyed, pale, thin and in need of a shower. Ben heard most of his words, though indistinctly, '...my return ticket... couple of quid... hate to bother you but... get back to Cheltenham tonight−'

Sweetland shook him off and growled.

Ben slowed, not wanting to get too close.

Sweetland and the young man exchanged more words which Ben

couldn't hear but he could see the young man winding himself up, putting his weight on his back foot ready to launch forward.

Pedestrians swerved around the confrontation, avoiding eye contact.

After a final growled warning, Sweetland turned to walk away. At this, the young man leapt forward and pushed Sweetland in the back, causing him to fall into the cobbled gutter, tangled up in his own limbs. The young man pounded a boot into Sweetland's gut which made him curl. As he writhed, the young man took the wallet from Sweetland's trouser pocket. Ben dashed forward, shouting.

The young man saw Ben, a tall figure dressed in black, and ran before he'd finished picking through Sweetland's pockets.

Ben stopped running after a metre or so and returned to Sweetland, around whom a small crowd had begun to gather.

'Is he all right?' asked someone, excited by the drama rather than really concerned, Ben thought. He ignored the voice.

'Mr Sweetland? It's Ben Hodge again.'

'I thought I told you to fuck off.' His voice was slurred.

'You did. Do you need an ambulance?'

'No I bloody don't.' He laughed sourly.

'I can call one,' said someone else.

'Go on, clear off,' shouted Sweetland, raising himself onto his elbows and then using the kerb to heave himself onto his feet. 'Clear out of the way, all of you – there's nothing to see.'

To Ben he said quietly, 'Help me out.'

Ben took his arm. 'Hospital?' he said.

Sweetland shook his head. 'Get me home – there's a cab office this way.' He waved his free hand weakly and began to limp in the same direction.

They found the cab office and Sweetland got a price from the operator. 'Got £15 on you?' he asked Ben.

'Sure.'

'I'll pay you back when we get there.'

While they waited for the cab to pull up at the kerb, Sweetland tried to keep the weight off his rapidly swelling ankle, grunting occasionally at the pain.

'Were you following me?'

'Yes.'

'I ought to knock your bloody teeth out.'

Ben's instinct was to say sorry, but he wasn't.

The cab pulled up and Ben helped Sweetland into the back seat, taking the front passenger seat himself. The driver was a middle-aged Afghan with a neat moustache who said nothing after his initial greeting. As the car crawled out of the city centre and found the main road out to Henleaze, Sweetland sank low in his seat and brooded, while Ben watched people on the pavements rush through the rain.

Sweetland's house was clean, modern and tastefully decorated. Crashing in through the front door and limping across the whitewashed floorboards, Sweetland left a trail of muddy water behind him and collapsed, still in his wet overcoat, onto an antique upholstered chair.

'The missus is out,' said Sweetland between gritted teeth. 'Can you go into the bathroom and get me some painkillers from the cabinet? And then find me a bottle of whisky from the cabinet in the sitting room?'

Ben did as he was told and watched, fixed in his own muddy footprints, as Sweetland took four pills and washed them down with a generous measure of single malt.

'Ah.' He sank into the chair and rested the glass on his stomach.

A clock ticked, deep and resonant, speaking to the quality of its manufacture.

'Are you sure you don't need to see a doctor?' asked Ben.

'Certain,' said Sweetland. 'When I was a beat copper, I used to end up like this at least once a week. Nothing a good night's sleep won't sort. Toughens a bloke up.'

He poured another two inches of whisky and took something more than a sip.

'Why were you following me?'

Ben put a hand behind his head and looked away, lost. 'I'm not really sure. I don't know why I do half of what I do these days. Esther Garrett's disappearance is the most important thing that ever happened to me. My life isn't important.' He gave an exasperated grunting sigh. 'That's not quite what I mean. Can I sit down?'

Sweetland nodded and held up the whisky bottle.

'No, thanks.'

Ben lowered himself onto a white-painted bench across the hallway. It creaked beneath his weight.

'I feel like everything changed for me that day, is what I'm trying to say. I feel like if I can find Esther, and help Lucy–' he looked down at his fingertips '– even if she doesn't want my help – then I might be able to start living an actual life.'

Sweetland drank more whisky, smacking his lips as it warmed him through. When he spoke, his voice was low and cracking. 'I shouldn't say this – I shouldn't say anything – but I really did think I was a clean copper, compared to the generation I learned under. I was never racist, I didn't hate gays, if someone murdered an Asian shopkeeper, that was the same to me as killing anyone else. I didn't take bungs from anyone – never, not a penny. My mentor when I joined CID was a bloke called Docherty. A fat, lazy bastard who thought he was entitled to whatever he liked, whenever he liked.'

Sweetland drank more, poured more, closed his eyes. 'If we found cash at a crime scene, he took it. And women.' He shook his head in disgust. 'We were meant to protect them – people who'd been abandoned, exploited, treated like animals – but he used them in every way you can think of, then depending how he felt, he'd either kick them out into the street without anything, or have 'em banged up.'

He shifted stiffly in his seat, emitting a weak moan as he momentarily put weight on his injured leg. 'And I never did any of that stuff – never. God knows Mr Docherty tried his best to corrupt me. At first I didn't understand why it mattered to him what I did, but then I realised. You see, me keeping clean was like a judgement on him.' He raised his eyebrows and sighed. 'That and me being clean meant he had nothing on me, and he didn't like that. If I'd had the nerve or the inclination, I could have him put away in a heartbeat, but I was pure as the driven.'

He leaned forward and rested an elbow on his knee, waving the glass from side to side so the remaining whisky made waves.

'He sussed me, though – he worked out that where he could get me to bend the rules was if I thought I was doing the right thing. He gave me a case, straightforward bit of business – a bloke called Eric Pringle got stabbed in a pub cark park, and his mate from work...' He snapped his fingers softly several times, trying to summon the name. 'Barry Hill, they'd just had a row in the pub about Eric's missus, who Barry had been seeing to while poor old Eric was on nights. The thing is, no one would swear to it, and we couldn't find the knife. Barry's missus was a doormat – he used to knock her about – and she swore blind he'd come straight home from the pub, right as rain, no blood on his hands or clothing. He was smug about it, too – he had this smirk, thought he was clever, was round at Eric's seeing to his widow two days later, bold as you like.'

He tried to shrug but his aches were worsening and he growled with pain, the sound turning into a cough as he shivered. He swirled the whisky and drank the glass dry, baring his teeth as it hit home.

'Mr Docherty, he says to me, "You know he did it, I know he did it, so what are you gonna do about it?" And I didn't know what he meant at first but then I thought, if someone saw Barry disposing of the weapon, and then it turns up when we search, that would be pretty hard to argue with.'

There was a long silence and Sweetland looked almost as if he might have gone to sleep. The clock seemed louder.

'So you found a witness?' said Ben softly.

'I found a witness – a bloke who wasn't too popular on the estate on account of his habit of flashing at little kids, bloody stank, rotten teeth.' He shuddered. 'I was friendly to him, slipped him fifty quid, and told him to come into the local station the next day and tell the desk sergeant that he'd seen Barry Hill drop something into the canal, up by the old Customs office. Then I went out and bought a flick knife, well-used, wrapped it in a couple of carrier bags, and went out there at two in the morning, just me and the frogs. I slung it in. Ten hours later, a diver comes up with it in his hand and I act surprised.'

'What if this Barry Hill didn't do it?'

'That's the beauty, you see – he did, and he confessed, stupid bastard. "That's not my knife – the one I used was blah blah blah". No one believed him and, my God, it was sweet to send him down. Wiped the smile right off his face. Mr Docherty told me I was a good lad, very promising. And that's how it went on.'

'But the papers said you slept with prostitutes.'

'That's a bloody lie,' said Sweetland through his teeth. 'I mean, it wasn't like that.' He slumped and dropped the glass which shattered on the floor between his awkwardly splayed feet.

'What should I do next?' said Ben, sensing that Sweetland was about to pass out.

'Aaron Greenslade did it.' He puffed air between his lips, almost snoring. 'Then again, that dad of hers was a funny bugger.' He shook his head.

'How do you mean?'

'The defence were right about one thing: he was the biggest fucking pervert in town.'

Ben blinked, stunned. 'I remember they brought up something about pornography during the trial.'

Sweetland coughed out a laugh, recalling the past triumph. 'That didn't do them any favours. It made them look like bullies – desperate.' He opened his eyes and peered at Ben. 'We downplayed it, obviously, but it was all true. Him and his brother ran a video shop, back before the big chains came in. You won't remember them, video shops, but it was a poxy little place with a couple of bookshelves and, say–' he waved a hand, grasping for a number '–fifteen videos or something like that, Betamax and VHS, in those great big black plastic boxes. Word got round eventually that these stupid bastards were renting adult stuff under the counter, shipped in from Amsterdam. All right, so no big deal, bigger fish to fry.' His face twisted in disgust. 'They weren't happy with that, though – they had to go too far, and started dishing out stuff with boys, horses, dogs.'

He shuddered.

'Officially, they managed to convince the magistrate that they didn't know what was on the tapes – they'd never watched them, and, anyway, they thought it was all staged, faked up. Load of old rubbish, but, first time offence, they got fined and that was that. Unofficially, I reckon it doesn't hurt if one of your customers is the chief constable, another one's the head of the local Masonic lodge, another one's the mayor, and so on.' Sweetland went on, slurring and slowing as he went.

'And that wasn't all, but the defence never got wind, thank God. He had form, Eddie, from back in the early seventies. He used to drive a van for work, old Eddie, and round about 1975, he picked up a hitchhiker – a student on her way back to Exeter from a music festival somewhere or other. He pulled over into a lay-by and tried it on; she said no; so he punched her in the face, knocked her half silly, and tried again. Fortunately, she stuck her boot in his nuts and had it on her toes.'

'Was he charged?' asked Ben.

Sweetland shook his head.

'They said she shouldn't have got into the van in the first place. They said she was provoking him by wearing a tight T-shirt, short skirt, no bra, all that. And she was a hippy – a few blokes on the go, free love, handbag full of johnnies. He said she'd been up for it and then tried to rob him, which of course my esteemed colleagues bought, being sceptical altogether about women's lib.' Sweetland laughed grimly.

'So, a few years later, same thing, only this time, he's picked up a couple of girls outside a secondary school. Angels, they were – good girls, through and through, but by that time, he knew people who knew people, know what I mean?'

Ben thought of Eddie Garrett and his drunken advance on Lucy and felt anger on her behalf. 'Why the hell didn't you investigate him twenty years ago?'

'We had our man,' said Sweetland firmly, and then grimaced. He sighed the pain away. 'Like I said, everyone was at it.'

There was a long uncomfortable pause during which Sweetland's head rolled on his chest and he groaned in discomfort.

'When will your wife be home?'

'Who knows,' said Sweetland.

With some effort, Ben got Sweetland into the sitting room and laid him on the sofa in the recovery position. He swept up the broken glass in the hall and then looked in on Sweetland who was snoring deeply. Ben left, closing the front door behind himself without a sound.

CHAPTER EIGHTEEN

It took Ben a short while to build up the nerve to call Kenny Curtis, a school contemporary of Leslie Reeves, who now lived in New York. That, Ben thought, would minimise the chances of them bumping into each other or otherwise being in touch. He calculated the time difference and phoned at 1am UK time, hoping to catch Curtis after work but before bed.

'What do you want?' said the voice on the fizzy transatlantic line. 'I'm eating dinner with my family.' Curtis's West Country accent had taken on a slurring hint of the American.

'I'm sorry to disturb you,' said Ben, playing up his own Devon twang. 'I'm calling from Exeter in the UK.'

Curtis gave a delighted laugh. 'Are you? Bloody hell,' he said, then, anxiously, 'Hang on, what's up? Is it Mum?'

'No, God, nothing like that.' Ben hadn't considered until that moment whether to give a false name but decided to tell the truth after a pause which made it sound as if he was lying anyway. 'My name is Ben Hodge.' Then he did lie. 'I'm a journalist—'

'For who?'

'Freelance. I'm working on an article about people from Devon who've been successful in life.'

'Oh,' said Curtis, his voice brightening. 'Well, that's very flattering. Blimey. I mean, my business isn't all that glamorous.'

'I think people will be really interested,' said Ben. 'You have to remember, to most of us bumpkins–' Curtis laughed at that '–New York is as exciting as it comes.'

'Yeah, of course. Where do you want me to start? How long have you got?'

'Perhaps you can begin by telling me briefly about your early life in Devon, and then say a few words about how you went about training to be an actuary?'

Ben looked at his watch and rolled his eyes as Curtis began, contributing the occasional 'Yes', 'No' or 'Uh-huh' to keep the monologue coming.

Once Curtis had run out of steam, which took twenty minutes or so, Ben asked a few questions for the sake of the subterfuge, and then said, 'There are also a couple of your contemporaries from school I'm planning to write about. What are your memories of Leslie Reeves, for example?'

There was a moment's uncomfortable silence.

'What's he done with his life, exactly?'

'He's rather a well-respected engineer.'

'Is he?' said Curtis. 'Hmm.'

'What is it?' asked Ben.

'No, nothing. We weren't especially good friends, that's all. I was into sport and the academic side of things, he was – how should I say this? He was with a different crowd.'

'Oh, right,' said Ben, feeling a fluttering thrill in his chest. 'How do you mean?'

'I don't want to gossip about other people,' said Curtis before giving an insincere, almost aggressive laugh. 'Anyway, I was enjoying talking about myself.'

'It's all useful background even if I don't include it in my article. I won't quote you, but–'

'No,' said Curtis. 'I don't want to get sued.'

Sensing that the conversation was winding to an end Ben quickly changed the course of his questioning.

'Can you tell me one thing – who were his friends? And his girl-friends?'

There was a pause and then Curtis sniffed. 'What is this?'

Ben's instinct was to slam down the phone and end it there but he managed to say, calmly, 'This would really help me with my article.'

'I suppose you could talk to old... what was his name? Robert Clegg. And I'll tell you who he used to go out with.'

He let it hang, seemingly waiting for Ben to play along.

'Who?'

'That girl that got murdered – Esther whatshername.'

When he called Robert Clegg, he had learned his lesson and decided to tell the truth, or something close to it.

Clegg wasn't listed in the phone book but Ben found a local newspaper story about the opening of his shop in Exeter city centre, and decided also to visit in person. Ben didn't know Exeter well but he knew the medieval street it was on, leading to a long gone city gate, and home to kebab restaurants, and to shops selling vinyl records, skateboards, legal highs and other drug paraphernalia. On a cool, grey, weekday morning, he walked almost its entire length, finding Clegg's shop at the cheapest end, surrounded by shuttered industrial units, in a two-storey Victorian building with weeds growing between its bricks. It was called Ink'n'Strings and, behind a fine metal cage, the window displayed both tattoo designs and a range of colourful electric guitars on stands.

Ben hovered outside for a moment. There were no lights on inside and the dusty window made it impossible to see who or what might be waiting for him. He jumped and swore when a white Staffordshire terrier, pink around the eyes and mouth, leapt against the window, barking. The door of the shop opened and Ben stepped back, fearing that the dog was being released to chase him away. Instead, a man stepped out and shut it behind him.

'Sorry about that, mate,' he said with a strong, sleepy Devon accent.

He was dressed in the clothes of a young man – skating trainers, beanie hat, baggy jeans and a black sweatshirt with the logo of an American alternative rock band – but his long beard was grey, as were the wisps of hair around his ears and neck. He was holding a coffee cup, half empty and chipped.

'Robert Clegg?' said Ben.

Ben's eyes followed the mug through the air and into the gutter as Clegg tossed it away and by the time he had raised them again he saw only the back of Clegg's sweatshirt receding into the distance. He was running away towards the park at the bottom of the road.

Ben gave an exasperated shrug and groaned.

The dog continued to bark, slavering over the window pane, flinging itself against the glass.

Clegg, unfit and already slowing down, looked back over his shoulder and saw Ben's gesture. He stopped and stared warily back. 'Who are you?' he shouted between cupped hands.

'A journalist,' Ben shouted back, and shrugged again, hoping to convey that he was essentially harmless.

After a moment's pause, Clegg began to lope back up the hill, panting and pale-faced. As he neared Ben, he glanced up and down with his lip curled in disgust, before stopping and looking at his shattered coffee mug at the side of the road. 'That was my favourite mug, that one. My daughter gave it to me.' He stooped to pick up the largest section with the handle attached. 'Badass Dad, it said.' He sighed, coughed harshly, and then gestured at the dog which stopped barking at once and retreated from the window, licking its lips.

'I'm writing an article about Esther Garrett and I'm trying to talk to people who were at school with her.'

Clegg reacted with astonishment but, this time, did not run. 'Come on in, then,' he said. Glancing sadly at the fragment in his hand. 'I've got some more mugs. We'll have a brew.'

Ben followed Clegg into the shop, hanging back until he was certain the dog was subdued. It had retreated to a basket in the corner where it lay yawning and stretching. The showroom was unlit and smelled of animal musk, weed and creeping mould. One wall was covered with hooks for guitars but most were empty. An amplifier rig was set up below but a misspelled sign across its front read TEMPORALY OUT OF ORDER. Behind the counter Ben could see a chair and equipment underneath a poster which read, 'Ink-Friendly Zone: Leave Your Bullshit at the Door'. Clegg pulled a fold-up chair from behind the counter and flipped it open before passing it to Ben.

'I'll get the kettle on. Coffee?'

'Yes, thanks,' said Ben, rubbing his hands. It was actually colder inside the shop than on the street. He followed Clegg into the back-room tattoo parlour and leaned against the door post. While Clegg went about making the drinks, Ben retrieved a small notebook and pen from his coat pocket.

'What do you want to know, then?' he asked over the rattling hiss of the kettle.

'I'm just trying to get some background detail and a sense of her personality,' he lied. 'Just to fill out the piece I'm working on.'

Clegg processed Ben's statement and pronounced it credible with a nod. As he poured boiling water over instant coffee granules, he said, 'I don't know how to put this.' He sighed. 'Business ain't exactly storming, if you know what I mean.'

Ben took a mug from Clegg who looked at his feet, shuffling his trainers from side to side on the concrete floor.

'What I'm saying is, does it pay? Talking to you.'

Ben reached for his wallet.

'How much?'

'You're the professional. How much do you usually pay?'

'Nothing,' said Ben.

'Oh,' replied Clegg, and then slurped his coffee.

Ben offered a £20 note which Clegg scissored between the forefingers of his left hand.

'What I'd really like to know is about her friends and boyfriends,' said Ben, deciding to get to the point before Clegg asked for more.

'First,' said Clegg, 'I've got to say one thing: she was really nice. I mean, just a really cool girl. I didn't know her well, but she was always a good laugh, no hassle, and interesting too – do you know what I mean? Like, you could talk to her for hours about music or films and shit like that. I had this one chat with her at a party for, like, forty-five minutes, just about, like, *Dracula*, because we'd both read it after that film came out with Keanu Reeves.'

Ben blinked. No one had ever mentioned that Esther liked to read and it felt as if a new spotlight had been shone upon her.

'Yeah, she was a smart girl all right.' Clegg smiled bashfully. 'I probably had a bit of a crush on her, to be honest. Like, I didn't just want to bone her – I actually liked her.' He looked around the desolate, empty workshop. 'I don't get like that with girls very often either.'

His head turned back sharply and he fixed Ben with a wide-eyed stare. 'Oh, I mean, I never done nothing about it, obviously. Like I say, we hardly knew each other.'

'What about Leslie Reeves?' asked Ben.

Clegg adjusted his stance, shifting his weight onto the other hip and wincing as he did so. 'Lezzer?'

'Is that what you called him?'

'It's what everyone called him.'

'He went out with Esther, didn't he?'

A troubled look passed across Clegg's face but the thought behind it couldn't break through the fog. 'Yeah.' He laughed and shook his head. 'But then Lezzer went out with a lot of girls. Not being gay or nothing, but he wasn't much to look at – fucking spotty as fuck for starters.' He laughed again and then whistled. 'But he had the gift of the gab. I couldn't hardly look a girl in the eye at fifteen, but Lezzer never had that problem. He'd chat anyone up. He'd chat up your mum if you left them alone too long, know what I mean?'

'Where did he and Esther meet? At school?'

Clegg wrinkled his face, trying to remember. 'Well, yeah, in the first place, but I think they actually got talking at the end of summer, in the park up town.' He gestured towards the door and the world outside. 'We used to come in on the bus, hang out there with a radio and a guitar, puffing and getting wrecked.' He took a gulp of coffee and narrowed his eyes, peering off to one side as he tried to remember. 'I think Les called her and her mate over one day when she was walking past in her work uniform, so it must have been a Saturday. It was hot, anyway – I remember that.'

'And they came?'

'Yeah – like I say, he had the gift of the gab. He had a way of doing it that wasn't creepy. He made them laugh, the sun was out.'

'Who was her friend?'

Clegg kissed his teeth.

'Fuck. It was a long time ago. She was quite fit. Blonde.' He outlined a woman's curves in the air with his hands. 'I got off with her once so I should know her name.' He clicked his fingers. 'Rebecca something.' He waved his hand frantically. 'Don't talk about it. If I don't think about it, it'll come to me. But she worked at Our Price too.'

Ben took a sip of his coffee which was already almost cold and tasted weak.

'Creech,' said Clegg. 'Rebecca Creech. I remember it now, because I've got a load of cousins called Creech down Dorset way.'

Ben scribbled down the name. He closed his notebook and put the mug down on top of a nearby cabinet full of tattoo catalogues. 'Can I ask you something? I don't want you to take it the wrong way,' said Ben, pre-emptively wincing.

Clegg nodded.

'Do you think there's any chance Leslie had anything to do with Esther Garrett's disappearance?'

Though his eyes widened momentarily, Clegg didn't react angrily. 'No, no way,' he said. 'The thing is, right, me and my mates – we were permanently loved up, man.'

Ben tilted his head. 'I don't understand.'

Clegg sighed. 'When we wasn't smoking weed, we was doing pills.

We used to turn up to school assembly fucking high as fuck. We didn't get angry, we didn't fight anyone, we just laughed all the time.' He gave a sheepish look. 'You saw what happened outside – any sign of trouble and I'm out of there, and Lezzer was the same. I never saw him lose his temper, cuss anyone out, and he definitely wouldn't ever have hurt a girl, however gutted he was that they split up.'

'And was he? Gutted, I mean?'

Clegg said, 'No, not really.' It sounded shifty and unconvincing.

Ben stared and waited.

'He was more serious about her than he was about his other birds, I suppose,' Clegg said, 'and I suppose he was used to doing the dumping, not being dumped, like.'

'Did he take it badly?'

'No,' said Clegg, shaking his head vigorously. 'Not at all. Definitely not.' He could not conceal a troubled expression and his brow was creased with doubt.

'That's been really helpful, thanks,' said Ben, sensing that Clegg's defences were up. Ben stood up and half-turned to face the door. He paused. 'Are you in touch with Leslie?'

'No,' said Clegg with a sad shake of his head. 'Not even on Facebook or anything like that. Last thing I heard, he went to uni somewhere up north.'

'I see. Well, thanks again.'

He walked to the door and, as he opened it, causing the bell to ring, Clegg spoke in a murmur, half-distracted. 'I was talking to Esther this one time, in some caff where they let us hang around so long as we bought a few drinks, and I started telling her about my uncle.' He frowned. 'He's dead now, but he was only a couple of years older than me, more like a cousin, really. He had leukaemia and I was saying to her that I didn't like visiting him up at the hospital. She says, "Are you close to him, then?" And I said, "Yeah," and then she said, "Tell me about him." So I did.' He raised a hand to his face, waving it near his eyes. 'I almost cried – not quite – and she says, "There's nothing wrong with loving someone." And afterwards, I thought, you know what? None of my so-called mates had said anything, asked me how I was feeling, nothing.'

Ben waited.

'Oh, sorry, that's it,' Clegg said with a grin. 'Funny the little details you remember about people, innit?'

Ben was sure, then, that Robert Clegg had more than liked Esther.

CHAPTER NINETEEN

Men were easier to track down than women, Ben learned, because men rarely changed their names and were less careful about their privacy. He pursued Rebecca Creech through wedding announcements – three in twenty years – and eventually found her, he thought, listed on Facebook as Becky Marlowe-Smith. He could not be entirely certain because the handful of publicly available photos did not match the description given by Robert Clegg: even in carefully posed shots taken at arms-length, it was clear that her face was plump, and her hair was certainly no longer blonde but dark, and close-cropped.

When Ben called her that evening, sat in the armchair in his flat, the phone was answered by a teenage boy whose voice was in the process of breaking. 'Mum – there's some guy on the phone for you.'

'Hello?' she said a moment later. Her voice was loud and seemed to suggest a laugh waiting to erupt.

'You don't know me,' Ben said, 'but I'm writing an article and would like to talk to you about Esther Garrett.'

'Oh my God!'

Ben moved the phone away from his ear and frowned. He had expected a note of quiet regret or perhaps even tears at the mention of her childhood friend but, instead, the laugh in her voice had broken free.

'What's it for?'

'I'm freelance and I haven't sold it yet.'

She hesitated and then said, warily, 'What did you say your name was?'

'It's Ben,' he said, withholding his surname unless she asked explicitly, but she didn't.

The line hummed. 'I don't want to get in any trouble.'

'I understand. It's just a chat.'

'But I do want to talk to someone. She don't get enough attention if you ask me, compared to some of them others.' She was still laughing – a low background chuckle – and Ben realised it was a nervous habit rather than an expression of amusement.

'I agree,' he said, more vehemently than intended. Once again, he repeated the outline of his purpose, aware that the words flowed rather mechanically now, but sounding no less passionate.

'I don't want to do this on the phone,' she said.

'That's fine by me. I'm in Exeter and happy to meet whenever is best for you.'

'What time is it now? Just gone six? Can you come round here tonight, maybe? After we've got the youngest to bed? I'd like my husband to be around.'

His energy was low – he felt bruised and spent – and he cringed at the awkwardness of visiting someone's home under false pretences, but his desperate desire for more and better information overrode those concerns.

'Sure.'

The evening air was cuttingly cold and he thought he could discern occasional flakes of snow in the beams of car headlights and street lamps. He pulled his scarf up over his chin and mouth and the warmth of his trapped breath only emphasised the burning sensation on his exposed cheeks and forehead.

As he walked, he felt a darkness settling over him – his exhaustion gathering new weight, and a sense of complete loneliness sucking the marrow from his bones. He liked to be alone most of the time but this was different. It was a sense of absence and a corresponding yearning: he missed Lucy Garrett. Not in some intellectual sense, as a colleague in their amateur investigation, but at a purely emotional level. He wanted to see her, to hear her, and perhaps even to touch her – to feel her hand brush his as it had so often as she sought to emphasise some point or other.

'I should phone her,' he muttered to himself, confident that no one would overhear him on a wide city street crammed with stationary, fogged-up cars, but with few other pedestrians willing to brave the cold, and patches of ice reforming on the pavements.

'No, you shouldn't,' he replied, this second voice mocking and scornful. He took his mobile phone from his pocket and weighed it in his hand for a moment before hitting the icon to make a call. Lucy Garrett's name and number was listed as 'frequently called', third only behind his father and the local takeaway. His thumb hovered over the screen, and then, holding his breath, he forced himself to press the button. She didn't answer for a long time and he imagined her weighing up whether to answer, or perhaps cursing at his name on the screen. He was about to hang up, ashamed and embarrassed, when she answered.

'Hello?'

'Hi,' Ben tried to say but the word stuck in his throat.

'Hello?' she said again and then grunted in irritation.

'Hello,' Ben said decisively, forcing the sound out of the tightness of his throat with a shove.

She sighed, barely. 'What is it?'

'I thought I ought to let you know, I've been speaking to some people.'

'Oh, Ben,' she said, imploring and despairing, like a mother to a persistently naughty child. 'Please, leave Esther alone. Leave my sister alone. Leave me alone.'

'Sorry,' said Ben, his voice shaking, his grip tightening on the phone, 'but you can't just drop this now – not now you've brought it all back and got me involved.'

'It's not about you, or even me. It's about Esther, and you don't know anything about her. She snored – did you know that? I know because we shared a room until she was eleven and then I could hear it through the wall. Because she was *my* sister. Sometimes she would come into my room, curl up on my bed and put her head on my lap. She didn't say anything. I used to stroke her hair. It was so soft, Ben, and it smelled of strawberries.

'Then other times, she would be mean to me all day from the minute we got up – she used to pinch me until I screamed. But then, when I was seven years old, a girl on the close bent my fingers back until I cried, and Esther went to her house, called her out into the front garden and punched her in the eye. Because she was *my* big sister – that's why she did that. Once, when she was twelve and I was six she bought me a present with her pocket money for no reason – it wasn't my birthday or anything. It was a scrunchie for my hair. I've still got it.

'When she got a bit older, she used to yell at me to stop following her everywhere and stop copying everything she did. Do you know why I followed her and copied everything she did? Because she was my big sister and I thought she was the coolest person on earth.

'I once caught her stealing £20 from Dad's wallet but I didn't tell him. She was good at school but she hated it because she thought she was stupid – of course she wasn't. She loved art lessons, though, and she used to draw all the time at home. She never let anyone see the pictures, except me that is. Because I was her sister and sisters are almost part of one another.'

She paused momentarily.

'Okay, I get it,' said Ben.

'Don't you want to know all about what Esther was really like from someone who actually knew her?' Lucy replied, acid in her voice. 'Or are you more interested in your fantasy?'

'I'm sorry,' said Ben, panicking, urgently wishing to defuse the rant.

'I looked at her face for hours every day. At breakfast she always had sleep in her eyes – little yellow nuggets in her tear ducts – and her breath smelled bad until she'd eaten something. She used to chew the dead skin of her lips – she didn't know she was doing it. She chewed her nails – really tore chunks off them, so they were like horrible little half-moons, hardly anything left sometimes. She only stopped because some boy told her it was disgusting.'

'Lucy–'

'There were two different ways she laughed – one was controlled and sort of low-pitched – that was her sexy, sophisticated laugh. She used that when she was flirting. But the other was a sort of honking sound she used when she thought something was *really* funny. When she started laughing, I couldn't help myself – we used to just roll around crying, which made us laugh even harder. We had our own little collective hysteria.'

'I said I'm sorry,' said Ben, but she ignored him.

'Do you know what her favourite food was?'

'No.'

'Of course not – she wasn't *your* sister. It wasn't anything fancy: just boring old tomato soup, with two slices of bread. When Mum was out, she used to eat it in front of the TV with her legs crossed. Bare footed, with black soles. She used to lick the bowl clean at the end because it was just us two and she could do anything in front of me.

'Do you know what her favourite record was? Of course not. When she was with her friends, she used to listen to bloody awful dance music but at home, in her room, she had this cassette of the soundtrack to *Labyrinth*. She'd had it since she was little and it was almost worn out. She used to know all the words. She tried to learn the guitar once but it was too difficult, or the teacher told her she was no good – I can't remember exactly – and she smashed it to pieces in the garden. Dad was furious.'

She stopped, out of breath. The last few words had been spoken with an unsteady voice only a breath away from a sob.

'I really am sorry,' said Ben quietly.

'She was my sister, Ben, and I'm telling you to leave her alone. Leave her alone and leave *me* alone.'

Ben looked at the screen of his phone as it went blank. He slipped it away and rubbed his now painfully cold, sore red hand. She was right, of course, and he wanted to stop, but it wasn't as easy as that. The fact was, there was nothing else in his life that mattered.

Becky Marlowe-Smith lived in Exwick, a village on the other side of the main railway line into Exeter, beyond the river. It had almost been sucked in by the city and the occasional old half-timbered buildings were surrounded by weathered red-brick housing estates and shopping arcades.

Her house was not one of the cheaper dwellings on a newly-formed 'close', nor one of the old village buildings clustered around the church, but a between-the-wars semi-detached house separated from the busy main road by only a small, paved front yard. A white van was parked on the drive – 'No tools are left in this vehicle overnight' – alongside a hatchback, one wing of which was a different colour to the rest of the car.

Standing for a moment on the pavement outside, Ben noticed the steady thump of music from an upstairs bedroom where curtains were open, affording a glimpse of walls covered in boy band posters, while the downstairs window was blue with light from a television flickering in darkness. Approaching the front door, he noticed plastic buckets and spades, wellington boots, water pistols and a tiny BMX bike with stabilisers piled up on one side of the porch, beneath a rack filled with children's coats in various sizes.

He rang the doorbell and almost at once, the hallway light came on behind the leaded glass in the white PVC inner door. A face peered out and then the door opened. A skinny teenage boy with long hair hanging over his face, bright yellow jeans and striped socks stepped out and opened the outer door. He didn't say anything but stood to one side so that Ben could enter, making it clear that he resented being obliged to do so.

'Thanks,' said Ben.

'She's in the front room,' said the boy, slamming both doors behind them.

The hall would have been spacious if it were not so cluttered with skateboards, folded pushchairs, toolboxes, more wellington boots, a couple of racing bikes and a step ladder lying folded on its side. The teenager pointed lazily through the open door and, arms swinging, bounded upstairs two at a time. Ben followed his direction and stepped into a room lit only by the screen of the TV.

'Hello?' he said, taking a moment to discern two figures on the sofa. One was a broad-shouldered, tall man with a vast, taut gut, dressed in paint-stained combat trousers and work shirt. He had close-cropped hair and a drooping face. He glanced at Ben very briefly before standing up and, without saying a word, leaving the room.

'Hi,' said Becky Marlowe-Smith casually, almost as if Ben was a friend who had let himself in with a front door key. She was double-chinned and thick-featured, dressed in a shapeless, sack-like T-shirt and tracksuit bottoms. 'Turn the light on, will you?' she said, lurching forward from the sofa to find the remote and switch off the TV. 'Gary'll finish watching this in his den,' she said.

A door slammed somewhere else in the house.

Ben found the switch on the wall by the door and flipped it, and the bulbs slowly came to life, revealing another large space with high ceilings that had somehow been rendered cramped by the accumulation of furniture – a computer desk, several buckling bookshelves – along with scattered toys and tools.

In the light, he saw that her short hair was black but dyed red at the tips, and that she was deeply tanned – a real tan, Ben thought, not painted on.

'Have a seat,' she said, almost shouting with that background giggle, and pointed towards a sagging armchair. Ben moved a pile of cookery magazines off the cushion and sat down.

'Thanks for making time for me,' he said, unwrapping his scarf and reaching into a pocket for his notebook.

'S'alright,' she said, chuckling. 'Not as if I was doing anything special this evening.' Despite her bubbling laughter, there was sadness in the way she looked around the room. Her gaze returned to Ben and she asked, 'What's your story, then?' Her mouth was turned up in a smile and Ben had a sense that she was flirting with him – like the constant laughter, a habit rather than a conscious action. It was disarming and, face to face, he found himself being more honest than had been his intention.

'I've got a confession – I'm not really a journalist.'

She was still listening, not shocked or annoyed, so he went on.

'I grew up round here and I remember Esther going missing. It's always been on my mind.'

'Yeah?'

'So I'm just trying do something.' He sighed and frowned, frustrated at the difficulty of finding words that didn't sound self-important. 'I just want it resolved.' His cheeks reddened but Becky Marlowe-Smith nodded appreciatively.

'Bloody good on you,' she said softly.

She, at least, understood. Ben was pleased to have read her correctly.

'I don't know how long I'll keep going, or if I'll ever get anywhere, but I'm taking one lead at a time. And, right now, I'm looking into someone in particular.' He hesitated, adjusting his position so that he was sat on the very lip of the armchair, his long arms folded over his pointed knees. What if she was a friend of Leslie Reeves? 'There's an ex-boyfriend of hers I'm trying to rule out as a suspect in her disappearance.'

'Which one?' She laughed and covered her mouth, flirting again. 'Oh, no, I'm not saying anything bad about her. It's just that all we ever thought about was boys, not that we knew what to do with them when we had them. Hormones, I suppose it was.'

Ben smiled nervously. 'Leslie Reeves was her boyfriend at the time she disappeared, or so I understand.'

She frowned and waved a hand in denial. 'No, not quite right – they split up a bit before.'

'I know,' said Ben, 'but not long before, right? And was that friendly?'

'They got off, they, well, you know, shagged a few times, I think, and then school started up again. As far as I know, it wasn't anything heavy, you know? Just a fling, really.' She drew her brows together. 'I think he was more into her than she was into him, though.' The chuckle bubbled over again. 'He was a lovely lad, though – really. That's why we liked hanging around with him and his mates – because they were chilled out, talked to us like we were human beings. Almost like girls, if you know what I mean.'

She lowered her voice and glanced around as if checking for eavesdroppers. 'No dick swinging. He wasn't my type, but Les was just a nice-looking, nice lad.' She sighed and looked upward. 'That was the problem though – he was a lad, just like I was a silly girl. But Esther was a woman, right? We were best friends, but it started to feel, near the end, like she was bored of everyone, including me – like I was a little kid hanging on her coat tails. You know when you're talking to someone and you can tell they're not really listening? She got like that. She stopped telling me stuff.'

Ben felt a prickling sensation. This was important.

'She had things on her mind, I know that – not that anyone was interested back then, because they had that Greenslade kid, didn't they? But, yeah, she had things on her mind all right.'

'Such as?' said Ben sharply.

'Family stuff. She wouldn't ever let me come to her house, for starters. I did go once and I wasn't allowed upstairs – her mum's rules, apparently. Est always wanted a dog – used to go soppy over one if we saw one out on the street – but they never let her have one because of the furniture.' She shook her head, pursing her lips, disapproving in hindsight of Kay Garrett's refusal to indulge her children. 'It was weird round there anyway.' She looked at Ben with what was intended to be a smouldering glance. 'Back then I wasn't bad-looking, believe it or not. Esther was pretty and all that but I was the sex bomb and you should have seen how her dad looked at me.' She laughed. 'Poor randy old sod.'

Involuntarily, Ben's hand rose to his face, at first covering his mouth but then sliding down to rub at his jaw. He hoped she hadn't noticed his reaction.

'She was a clever girl – cleverer than me, anyway – and she was working it all out.' There was a note of pride in her voice as she recalled her friend. Then she blinked and her face fell. She fixed her eyes on a spot on the crumb-covered carpet. When she continued, her voice had become distant and uncharacteristically hesitant. 'I never really thought about it,' she said, each word falling like a stone. 'I never really thought about it till now, because of that Aaron Greenslade, but she told me she'd met someone.'

Ben held his breath for a moment and then asked, 'Who?'

Becky Marlowe-Smith closed her eyes for a moment. When she opened them, they were shimmering. 'She said he wasn't from our school and he wasn't from work.' She waved and then bunched her plump fingers. 'I mean, I asked if he went to our school, and she said no, and I knew all the boys at work.' She tutted. 'I wish I'd been nosier.'

There was a bump on the floor above and then, after a moment's delay, the sharp wailing of a child, followed by the teenager's unsteady shout.

'Mum – Taylor's crying.'

'I'd better be going,' said Ben. He scribbled down his number, ripped the page from his notebook, stood up, and handed it to Becky.

'If I think of anything, I'll let you know,' she said, and then, muttering under her breath, began to heave herself to her feet.

At the front door, she grabbed Ben's arm. 'I just want to say that I don't think it was just a sex thing, this new bloke,' she said, mouthing the word 'sex' without sound. 'Not for Esther, anyway. It was something more than that.'

'She was in love?'

'I don't know about that. But it was important to her.'

Ben did not want to go back to the rented flat with its bare walls and rattling windowpanes. Instead, he wandered slowly back towards the river on the Exwick side, passing the low stone wall of the cemetery. In the distance across rooftops he could see the floodlit spire of the cathedral. The steady trudge of one aching foot after the other seemed to help with his increasing sense of anxiety at the overwhelming number of possible leads.

Though he disdained the idea of gut instinct, nothing he had heard made Leslie Reeves seem a likely culprit: he had been a mere boy, a gentle one, with no means of abducting a young woman or disposing of a body. At that thought, Ben berated himself: didn't all murderers seem harmless, keep themselves to themselves, and so on? He could not quite rule Leslie Reeves out.

Eddie Garrett had come to seem almost too obvious a suspect. Didn't they always say to look close to home? Ben thought about the brief time he had spent in Eddie's company, looking into his eyes, and tried to read his own feelings. His gut told him that whatever kind of creep Eddie might be, or had been, he couldn't have done this. But his gut was as inexperienced and naïve as any other part of him – it wasn't trained or practised in the art of divining human behaviour. He needed to know more about Eddie, or to rule him out, or to have a compelling reason to suspect someone else above him. No, Eddie remained in play.

As an aside, Ben also wondered about Esther's uncle, the partner in Eddie Garrett's early grey-area criminal enterprise – where was he these days? And where had he been when Esther disappeared? It wouldn't be the first time a young woman had been seduced or exploited by an older male relative. For that matter, were there cousins, or family friends? And who else lived in Berebroke? He'd barely considered who or what might lay behind those bland front doors, or buried in the black earth of back gardens.

With all that to chew through, the mysterious boyfriend mentioned by Becky Marlowe-Smith seemed almost inconsequential – a man about whom he knew nothing, who might not exist. In the first instance, though, he knew he could look through the goldmine of Kelly's notebooks. Perhaps there would be some hint there, in euphemism or abbreviated code, to put a name to the shadow.

After almost an hour, by which time the streets were growing emptier and the suburban houses were dimming their lights, he reached the concrete bridge that flew over the river near St Thomas station, where the water was walled in. It had been widened, and so resembled the main tributary of a city in Eastern Europe, or perhaps a pinched stretch of the Rhine. He walked halfway across and then stopped to look down into the slow-flowing black water, his hands on the municipal-blue railing. The cold air blowing down the cut felt good, sharpening his wits, keeping him awake despite the time.

'I need someone to talk to,' Ben muttered.

Pushing himself backwards with a jolt, he kept walking. On the other side of the river he paused at the head of a flight of steps leading down to the path alongside the water. It was late and dark and the path was shadowy – in London he would never have dreamed of taking that route but there in Exeter the night held no threat for him. At the bottom he found the water lapping over the edge of the embankment, thick with dead leaves, plastic bottles and other floating scum. His footsteps echoed from the sloping wall as he walked until, with a jolt, he stopped.

Up ahead, he saw something move in the shadows and heard a frantic pattering: rats, twenty or more, gathered on the grass verge, scattered and dispersed. One ran along the path towards him before slipping over the edge and into the water.

Ben jerked his head as if trying to shake something free.

CHAPTER TWENTY

Ben slept poorly but somehow, drifting around the borders of consciousness in the dreadful, quiet darkness, his thoughts organised themselves. By dawn, awake and vibrating with high tension, he had formed a clear plan. He got up, showered, shaved and drank a mug of instant coffee. Then, more or less awake, he found Leslie Reeves's work address online. He wrote it down in his notebook, put on a waterproof coat, and headed out into the blue morning light and the drizzle.

For the first time since leaving London, Ben felt a moment's anxiety about his dwindling savings as he paid for a peak-time train ticket to Birmingham at Exeter St David's ten minutes before the train was due to depart. He found the platform without any trouble and settled into a seat with a window view and, almost at once, fell asleep with his head resting against the greasy glass. He awoke to the sight of canals, wasteland and scrapyards far below, and the gleaming mirror panels of Birmingham's skyline beyond.

The weather was fine and bright. Ben walked through the city centre, downhill past the marketplace, stopping once or twice to check a map on his phone. Twenty-first century gloss gave way to twentieth-century concrete and soot-blackened Victorian red brick. The roads widened and, soon, he was surrounded by graffiti-covered industrial buildings over which flew railway viaducts.

JC Kenner occupied a converted warehouse on the corner of the main road. Glass doors had been fitted into an old stable entranceway and chromed letters bearing the company's name were mounted above art nouveau tiling advertising the building's original occupants, 'Albert French & Sons'. Ben stood on the pavement and looked the building over, shielding his eyes from the sunlight reflecting in star-like bursts off the metal signage.

After a moment he climbed the short flight of steps and entered a reception area in which everything was chromed or in shades of grey. One wall was given over to a display of photographs of grand engineering projects – tunnels, bridges, towers – glowing with fluorescent light. Across the display there was a slogan: KENNER – ILLUMINATING YOUR VISION. Ben approached the desk where a young, stylishly short-haired Asian woman in a striped blouse was sitting, smiling blandly as if awaiting activation.

'Hello,' said Ben, as warmly as possible.

'What can I help you with?' she said, tilting her head and broadening her smile just a touch.

'I don't have an appointment but I wondered if I could speak to Leslie Reeves, please?'

She tilted her head the other way and frowned. 'May I ask please what this is regarding?'

'It's a personal matter,' said Ben.

Her frown deepened. 'May I take your name please?'

'It's Ben Hodge,' he said. 'He doesn't know me.'

She smiled again but only with her mouth. 'Let me see if he is available today – it's possible he's out of the building. Perhaps you'd like to step across to the waiting room.' She gestured towards a corner with a coffee machine, a stack of trade magazines and a large model of an oil tanker.

Ben took a seat.

He listened as she made a phone call, muttering under her breath.

When he looked up, she was glancing his way with evident concern. She hung up, stood up and walked across to the waiting area, stopping before she had got too close. She spoke to Ben as if he were a child. 'I'm afraid Mr Reeves isn't available right now but if you want to leave a number, I can get him to give you a call later this afternoon.' She flashed a false smile.

'Look,' Ben said, 'I don't want to be awkward, but can you try again, and tell him it's about Esther Garrett.'

The receptionist did not seem to recognise the name. 'Okay,' she said, 'but then I will have to ask you to leave.'

Ben nodded mildly.

This time, the phone call was shorter.

'He'll be right down,' she said, astonished.

Ben waited as visitors with briefcases, and staff with rolled-up sleeves and lanyards round their necks, came and went. After five minutes, a door swished open and a man stepped into the waiting room. 'Mr Hodge, is it?'

'Yes, that's right.' Ben stood up and stuck out a hand. Leslie Reeves regarded it for a moment and then took it and shook it, firmly but briefly.

It was difficult for Ben to imagine that the man in front of him had ever been a long-haired stoner. His head was shaved to the scalp, his eyebrows arched and neat, and his wide jaw only faintly grey with stubble. Though his features had thickened with age he had the lean build of a marathon runner or cyclist and seemed to stand lightly on his feet. He wore a plain but expensive blue shirt, grey flannel trousers and brown brogues.

'I can't spare long, I'm afraid,' he said blankly, neither hostile nor friendly, just waiting for more information. 'There's a café in the basement.'

Ben followed him through a door and down a flight of steps. They didn't speak. The basement was bright and white, filled with tables, armchairs in primary colours and vending machines. There were more huge photographs of glowing roads, cityscapes and factories overlaid with scattered words in capital letters: SECURITY, SAFETY, SUSTAINABILITY, CONTINUITY.

Leslie Reeves directed Ben to a pair of armchairs in an alcove. Ben sat down first.

'So, who are you?' Reeves asked bluntly.

'Nobody,' said Ben. 'I mean, I'm not official.' He hadn't decided on his approach and Reeves's intense stare was unnerving him. 'I've got a personal interest in Esther Garrett's case,' he said, eventually.

Reeves stared, jaw twitching. 'I'm sorry but I'm not interested in talking to you about this. Why didn't you ring first?'

'I couldn't wait,' said Ben. 'It would have been another day wasted.'

Though he had expressed his refusal to talk, Reeves had not moved, so Ben went on.

'I know that you went out with her when you were both teenagers.'

Reeves shifted in his seat and picked up his iPhone from the tabletop to check for messages, giving himself time to think. 'That was a long time ago.'

Ben nodded. 'If you're anything like me, that doesn't matter. You must think about her sometimes, especially now the story is back in the news.'

'All the time,' said Reeves, then his coldness broke. 'Listen, mate, I've got a partner and children and a career here – I can't afford to be dragged into this.'

'I understand,' said Ben, and then, before Reeves could retreat, he asked him a direct question. 'Had you split up when she disappeared?'

Reeves nodded.

'How come?'

'I can't remember,' said Reeves. 'I was only a kid.' He narrowed his eyes, thinking hard. 'I suppose she'd outgrown me.' He shook his head and waved a hand. 'Like I said, I don't want–'

'I heard she was seeing someone else – do you know who it was?'

'She didn't cheat on me,' snapped Reeves. 'She wasn't like that.'

'No, but after you'd split up–'

'I don't know anything. I don't remember anything. Sorry.'

This time, Reeves did make a move, pushing back his chair and standing upright in one neat move.

Ben felt a surge of anger at Reeves's selfish indifference. 'There are some people who think you did it,' he said. His voice was even but he intended it to wound.

Reeves's eyes widened. 'You can't come in here and say that. I don't know who you think you are.'

'Where were you between five and six in the evening on the day she disappeared?'

'You can't ask me that,' said Reeves. His voice was loud enough now that one of the women working behind the lunch counter lifted her head to look across the empty canteen. 'You're not the police.'

'But I am asking,' said Ben. 'Of course, you don't have to answer.'

'I'm going to call—' Reeves cut himself off and frowned. He lowered himself back into the chair. 'What do you mean, between five and six? Wasn't it much earlier than that, when she got off the bus from work?'

Ben betrayed his elation at getting Reeves's attention with no more than a couple of blinks. 'I don't think so,' said Ben. 'The police got that wrong.'

'I was in Exeter, I should think. I certainly wasn't in Berebroke. I never went out to those villages – I'm a city boy.' He smiled weakly and then sighed. 'All right, okay. We split up. She dumped me.' He looked around anxiously. 'Because all I did back then was smoke weed and take pills. She thought I was boring, and I probably was. She smoked a bit but she wasn't into anything else. Whoever it was she met was "mature", which is what teenage girls are always after.'

He looked at his phone again.

'Older?' asked Ben.

'I can't say for sure but, yes, I'm pretty sure.'

'Someone at college or from the university?'

Reeves shook his head slowly, pouting as he measured his response. 'No,' he said with some hesitation, drawing out the word. Before saying any more he looked at Ben, assessing him. 'Sorry about getting angry but please, before I say anything else – who are you?'

Ben decided to tell the truth. He explained to Reeves that he was a witness in the case, that he had been a child at the time, and that now, as an adult, he felt compelled to do something to get justice for Esther.

Reeves nodded. 'That's quite strange.'

'I know.'

'You should leave it to the police.'

'I know.' Ben smiled weakly.

Reeves smiled back shyly, a glimpse of his teenage persona appearing through the cracks in his face. 'This is going to sound bad.' He puffed and turned his eyes towards the floor. 'I was gutted when we split up – I thought she was awesome, basically, and I guess I'd got pretty into her. So, I sort of kept an eye on her. Like, I used to just hang around near the shop on Saturdays.'

'You spoke to her?'

'Only once when I took back some CDs I'd borrowed and a couple of books. She tried to be friendly.' He squinted and rubbed at his temples. 'Can't have been easy, though. I was angry at her, I guess.' He frowned. 'No, I don't mean that,' he said, waving an open hand as if trying to scrub those words from the record.

'It's okay,' said Ben. 'I know what you mean.'

'The thing is, I saw him once – the new bloke.'

Ben's skin prickled. 'And?'

Reeves's phone rang. He snatched it up, pressed it to his ear and said, 'Hi, yes, okay, two minutes.' He put it into his shirt pocket and stood up.

Ben stood up too.

'I didn't see much – it was raining and he had a hood up, but I could see that he was older than us. They didn't kiss.' Reeves swallowed and blinked. 'But he put his hands up to her face and I saw that he was wearing a wedding ring.'

'What about his clothes?'

'Black trousers, black shoes, as far as I could tell – nothing remarkable. Look, I'm sorry.' He gestured at his phone.

Ben didn't say anything or move and Reeves stayed rooted to the spot, too, his thoughts churning.

'So I might have seen the bloke who did it?' he said after a moment. 'I never said anything to anyone because all these years I thought that guy in prison did it. I thought they had him.'

He put his hands on his slim hips and looked towards some distant point. 'Should I go to the police now, do you think?'

'Yes,' said Ben, reluctantly. 'You probably should. But, please, do me a favour and don't tell them about me – unless you feel you have to, of course. They don't really approve of me sticking my nose in.'

Reeves nodded.

'Bloody good job you did,' he said, but Ben felt sure he'd made a mistake. It came to him that he hadn't done anything wrong, not exactly, and he would be quite happy to explain to Ewan Marwick or anyone else. That was, if a call from Reeves resulted in anything other than a Post-it note gathering dust on an Exeter CID detective's desk for a year or two.

CHAPTER TWENTY-ONE

Ben arrived back in Exeter after dark, exhausted. As he climbed the stairs to his flat, a plastic bag from the kebab shop in one hand and a bundle of mail in the other, he realised at once that something was wrong: the door at the top of the steps was already open. There was a tapering line of what seemed like bright blue by contrast with the gloom. Ben felt his legs weaken but fought the instinct to back away. Instead, he put the polystyrene box and envelopes down on the step, with only a small amount of noise from the rustling of his coat and the carrier bag, and took the final few steps towards the door with his hands compressed into quivering, tentative fists.

Ben hadn't been in many fights, and certainly none since he was at school, but he was tall and had always been able to defend himself on the few occasions anyone on the streets of London had attempted to provoke a confrontation. If there was a junkie or teenage burglar in his flat he was confident he would be able to cope, unless they pulled a knife. He did not expect it to come to that, despite the adrenaline that was raising the hairs on his neck and elevating his breathing. He was sure that whoever had been here was long gone. There were no sounds of movement and none of the strange electricity that the hidden presence of another person seemed to generate.

He pushed the door open slowly and stepped into the hall. Standing still for a moment, he cocked his ear but heard only the insistent bop, bop, bop of dripping water on stainless steel. He reached for the light switch and, counting down from three under his breath, flipped it. The light came on but nothing else happened – it did not trigger the scattering of bodies or shouting.

Moving anti-clockwise around the hallway he checked each room in turn, switching on every light. There was no one in the bathroom, not even behind the shower curtain. The kitchen, he noticed from a quick glance, had been disarranged, but was deserted. The sitting room was scattered with papers and a chair had been overturned, but the little furniture there provided no hiding place.

Finally, he turned on the light in his bedroom and checked behind and inside the wardrobe, and under the bed. He laughed nervously, almost madly, reminded of childhood and the ever-present fear of monsters. Sitting on the edge of the bed, he caught his breath and wiped cold sweat from his forehead. Then, looking up, his face became stiff and he swore: on the desk where his laptop and iPad had been was nothing but a tangle of cables.

He stood up, retrieved his dinner from the staircase outside, and closed the front door as well as he could. The latch no longer worked and so he dragged a heavy armchair from the sitting room and jammed it under the handle.

Exhausted and unsteady, sweating but still cold, he sat down in the same chair and permitted a shudder to run through his body. He had been burgled by an opportunist, he told himself, refusing to acknowledge, at first, a thought at the back of his mind.

When he had calmed down a little, he ate a few mouthfuls of greasy meat and salad with his plastic fork, devouring them messily, feeling his nerves steady as his stomach filled up and chilli sauce burned his mouth. He slowed, then stopped, then placed the carton on the floor, wiping his hands and face on a napkin.

Standing up, he walked slowly to the kitchen. His shoes tapped on the linoleum, echoing from the bare walls, as he stepped to the sink and turned the tap tight to stop the dripping. The basin was full of brown-black scraps of paper, burned and then doused. He picked through until he found a large piece still white at its centre, with legible marks. It was his own handwriting and those scraps, he realised, were the remains of pages of his own notebooks. He let the damp fragment fall, shaking it from his fingertips.

In the front room, he looked at the scattered papers: bank statements, mobile phone bills, rental contracts – all were intact, though they had been thrown about. His TV, DVD player, stereo and handful of CDs hadn't been touched.

Returning to the bedroom, he stood in the doorway, staring at the desk where his computer had been that morning. Not only were the PC and tablet gone but also the memory cards and USB sticks that had sat in a plastic desk tidy next to them. One of them had contained his own copy of the scans of Christine Kelly's notebooks.

Drowsily, he indulged the thought he had earlier unconsciously rejected: someone had broken into his flat to take or destroy all the research he had done into Esther Garrett. As he chewed the thought over, he found his face twitching until a restrained, triumphant smile broke out. This intrusion, this counter-attack, meant he was onto something. Logically, he knew he ought to be scared at the thought of having provoked contact with a murderer, or at the very least a murderer's accomplice, but the overwhelming feeling was joy. He had made a break-through – he had got something right, for once. He was, perhaps, within reach of victory.

His laughter erupted afresh when he remembered that most of his notes had been typed up or scanned and were sitting somewhere on an email server in California: apart from the clean-up job and the price of a new door lock, this invasion had barely cause him any inconvenience.

He fetched a bottle of beer from the fridge and opened the kitchen window to let in the cold air, which made him calmer yet, and blew away the lingering smell of burnt paper. He put his hand in his pocket and wrapped it around his phone. Surely, he thought, this ruled out the idea that it was anything to do with Marlon Wakefield, and he knew he had to tell Lucy Garrett. He pulled out the phone and dialled her number. As he heard the chirruping ringtone in his ear he regretted his decision at once. It was after midnight, on top of everything else, and he knew his voice would be unsteady. He took the phone away from his ear and was about to hang up when he heard her voice.

'Hello?'

'It's Ben.'

'Oh, for God's sake,' she said, the words mushy, her voice thick.

'I'm sorry to ring so late but I really think you might be in some danger.'

'Are you threatening me?'

Ben was startled. How had she heard that in what he had said?

'I was burgled tonight and whoever did it knows something about Esther. I think it must have been whoever took her, which means they're still around and here in town, now.'

She laughed harshly. 'Are you making this up? It sounds ridiculous.'

'No, I'm serious,' he said. 'Whoever did it destroyed my notebooks and files. Or tried, anyway. They took my computer, too.'

'Ben, I'm going to hang up.'

'I don't care if you hate me and never talk to me again but I'm serious,' he said firmly. 'Call someone and go somewhere safe tonight.'

She laughed again but this time it failed to chime. 'You mean it, don't you?'

'Yes.'

There was a dreadful silence on the line.

After another pause, she said, 'What's the idea? That I'll come and stay at yours for protection? That we'll make up and be friends again? That I'll fall in love with you?'

Hurt as this did, Ben spoke calmly, his voice level. 'Did you talk to your dad? Does he know I've been nosing around?'

'It's got nothing to do with him,' she said. 'I wish I'd never told you.'

The line died.

He considered going to a hotel but simply didn't have the energy, and so tried to get some sleep in the now insecure flat. He didn't undress except to remove his shoes and lay on top of the bedclothes. With no lock on the front door and the evidence of someone else's recent presence all around him, Ben felt as if he was awake every minute of the night, or at best drifting in the unsteady boundary between consciousness and dreaming. What the clock told him were minutes, felt like hours, and try as he might to direct his thoughts to happy memories or favourite fantasies, the path wound back to the same few lines of thought – an irritating loop with only minor variations. He worried not only about important questions, such as who had burgled his flat and whether they might come back, but also things that had no immediate relevance – small memories of his mother, of childhood, of his grandfather's factory-scarred hands.

When the alarm on his phone rang at 9am, he was lying with his eyes open in the cool blue morning light, feeling drained and heavy-limbed. He sat upright at once, relieved that the pretence of sleeping was over. He felt almost excited, because he could tell something fundamental had changed.

He didn't bother to shave or shower, and kept on the same clothes as the day before. The flat was cold thanks to a constant draught blowing through the half-open front door but he felt quite warm thanks to a state of near-fever. He made a litre jug of strong, burning hot coffee and drank most of it in one sitting, staring dead-eyed at the window but not beyond it. It didn't make his head any clearer and only made him feel twitchy. He stood up and surveyed the damage to his flat in daylight. It was superficial and could be put straight in ten minutes.

His entire body jolted in terror when, in the silence, he heard a noise in the hallway – a heavy step on the carpet. He looked around, unsure whether to hide or grab something to defend himself.

Whoever was there stopped moving and, after a moment, said, 'Hello?' It was a deep voice with a soft West Country accent, its tone cautious rather than menacing.

'Hello?' Ben said back. 'Who's that?'

A face appeared round the frame of the door into the sitting room – a curly-haired man with a neat dark beard. On seeing Ben, fixed in place and visibly quivering with fear, the stranger frowned and stepped into the room. He was taller even than Ben, and broad, dressed in a dark grey suit that could only have been made to fit at a specialist tailor. With a broad hand, the back of which was thick with black hair, he pulled a wallet from his trouser pocket.

'Detective Sergeant Cooper,' he said, showing his warrant card.

Ben blinked. 'I didn't call the police.'

The police officer edged into the room, looking warily about as he put his wallet away. Ben detected a sharp aroma of garlic and bear-like maleness. 'Had a bit of trouble, have you?'

'How do you mean?' said Ben.

DS Cooper frowned and looked at Ben with narrowed eyes. 'The front door, mate – hanging off its hinges.' He was close enough now that Ben could see spots of dried red sauce on his tie, which must have been at least ten years old and was missing threads here and there.

'Right,' said Ben. 'Of course.' He tried to look relaxed but was conscious of every small action from blinking to breathing.

'You all right, mate?' said DS Cooper with the mock concern police officers learned to express when they really intended soft menace. 'Hungover or something?' He was now standing inches away with his hands on his hips and Ben fought the urge to step back as the stink of Cooper's body and breath enveloped him.

'How can I help you?' said Ben, trying to smile, but managing only a grimace.

'I've been asked to pay you a visit by a colleague of mine,' said Cooper. He rubbed a finger under his nose and stepped away, beginning a circuit of the room. 'Detective Superintendent Marwick, up London way.'

Ben was forced to turn his entire body to track Cooper's movements. The detective scanned the papers scattered on the floor, prodding at them with a toe.

'We understand that you've been sticking your nose into things that don't concern you and I'm here to tell you to back off, and to let you know that we're keeping an eye on you.'

Cooper continued his circuit as if trying to sniff something out. Ben wondered why he hadn't left already, now his message had been delivered.

'I worked on the Esther Garrett case,' Cooper said after a moment, as he picked up the paperback book about the case which was lying, dog-eared, on an otherwise empty shelf.

'Yeah?' said Ben.

'I was in uniform back then, two years on the force.' He leered in disgust. 'Sorry, I mean "in the service".'

Ben waited as Cooper flipped through the pages of the book. He found the wedge of glossy photo pages at the centre and studied a mugshot of Aaron Greenslade.

'We all thought he did it. He had a bad reputation – his whole family did.'

'But he didn't,' said Ben.

'Well, that's what they say now.' Cooper tossed the book back onto the shelf. 'Human rights,' he said, sneering, without further explanation. 'Mr Marwick tells me you've been playing detective yourself.'

Ben felt his cheeks burn. His legs felt weak and he wanted to sit down but he didn't like the thought of allowing Cooper to stand over him.

'I was trying to help Lucy.'

Cooper smirked. 'You know why she wanted your help, don't you?'

Ben shook his head, slowly.

'She's writing a book herself.'

'What?' said Ben. He ran a hand through his hair and rubbed at the back of his neck.

'That's why she's suddenly interested in her big sister after all these years – because someone offered her twenty grand for her story. Only she's got to tie it up nice and neat or who'll want to read it?' Cooper laughed drily. 'She didn't tell you, did she?'

Ben tried to look disinterested.

'She only came to you, I reckon, because you're part of the story. Thought you'd have some good tales to tell. Spice things up a bit.' He looked Ben up and down. 'Except I don't think you turned out to be as interesting as she expected.'

Cooper moved back towards Ben and stood in front of him, staring him down. 'So take the hint. Leave her alone, and keep your fucking nose out.'

Ben met his gaze but his eyelid kept twitching, betraying his nervousness. 'Who else do you think could have done it?'

With a bang, Cooper slammed a hand against the wall. 'What part of keep your nose out didn't you understand?'

'What about her dad? What about Eddie?'

Cooper laughed, showing his yellow teeth. 'Still going? You're not as wet as you look.' He scratched at his beard, pulling on coiled black hairs which glistened with grease. He seemed to be struggling with himself. 'No, he didn't do it.'

The urge to gloat at Ben's ignorance overcame his obligation to discretion. He glanced over one shoulder and lowered his voice. 'We know where Eddie was for all but about five minutes that night. He left his house at 9.05, he punched a 17-year-old in the chops at 9.10 and got stopped for speeding at 9.15. One of my colleagues escorted him home.'

Cooper looked over the other shoulder and sniffed. 'So you're not as clever as you think, are you, son?'

After Cooper had gone, though his stale aroma lingered, Ben sat and simmered. He wanted to ask Lucy about the book or, more precisely, wanted to hear her say, 'No, it's not true, I didn't use you'. His anger grew until he felt it as a kind of tension in his limbs. He stood up suddenly without having decided to do so and set off into the streets.

Ben arrived at Lucy's office, agitated and anxious, and looked up at the windows, each a square of yellow light facing off the winter grey. He texted her and waited. When she appeared in reception on the other side of the plate glass doors, she said something to the security guard who looked directly at Ben. Then she came outside and faced him across the courtyard, holding her red coat in place with folded arms. She looked angry and also, Ben felt with crushing regret, a little afraid. But that didn't stop him asking, abrupt and one degree from shouting, 'Why didn't you tell me about the book?'

She whitened. 'I don't know what you mean.'

'Lucy, please – you owe me an explanation. I'll never bother you again, I promise, but I need to know if it's true.'

She weighed the question while the security guard stepped nearer the door. He had a hand on the walkie-talkie pinned to his jacket.

'It's true,' she said. Ben sensed a struggle in her. After a moment, the desire to express something deep and too long suppressed won out. 'What else do I have? I don't have family. Esther took my childhood and my parents. She's why David left me to go to bloody Hong Kong. So why shouldn't I at least get something out of it? Some money. Who cares.'

'But it wasn't her fault,' said Ben, his voice cracking. He took a step nearer and the security guard spoke into the walkie-talkie as his eyes fixed hard on Ben's face. 'He took her and he did this to you.'

Lucy smiled acidly, unapologetic and full of contempt. 'I think you'd better go, and don't contact me again,' she said.

'That's fine by me.' He walked away quickly in case she saw him break.

Whoever had taken Esther had ruined them all, he thought, and they would ruin others, and it would never end. He needed to talk to someone who would understand and, like a miracle, despite his frantic confusion, a name came to mind.

CHAPTER TWENTY-TWO

He found her number using directory enquiries and called as he walked through the park opposite his flat, beneath the crumbling brick wall of the old Jewish cemetery. As it rang, he glanced at the children playing on the swings and slides while their mothers observed from the sidelines, in woolly hats and quilted coats. His own mother's face materialised briefly from some deep memory, half-turned in laughter, and then slipped away.

'Hello?' said a woman's voice on the line.

'Hello. Is that Chelsea?'

'Who wants to know?'

Ben smiled and felt a surge of joy. Though her voice had grown deeper and her accent had softened a little, there was no mistaking her ability to make even a few words sound like a challenge.

'It's Ben Hodge,' he said.

'No fucking way.'

'Yes way,' he said automatically, just as he would have done twenty years before, a bit rehearsed, over and over again in the school playground and classroom.

'Oh my God.' She laughed with delight and Ben ground to a halt, his breath catching in his throat, laughing with her, but overcome too.

'I wondered,' he said, his voice almost cracking, 'do you want to maybe meet up?'

She did exactly what he had hoped she might, undercutting the emotion in his question, refusing to play along. 'Of course I do, you div.'

They stood on the doorstep and looked at each other for what felt like a long time, though it was really only a second or two.

She was exactly the same, and yet completely different – the same nose, mouth and eyes, but surrounded by fine lines, and beneath long, straight hair that was no longer blonde but had darkened almost to brown. She hadn't put on weight, as such, but seemed to have become more solid, somehow, as if compressed by the gravity of adulthood. She was wearing sneakers, dark jeans and a striped T-shirt, not much different to the kinds of clothes she had favoured as a teenager.

She studied him, too, and he wondered what differences she might notice. The permanent groove between his brows, perhaps, caused by frowning, or the growing together of the freckles across his nose into a single mass.

Chelsea broke the silence. 'What's taken you so long, you weirdo?'

Then she launched forward onto her toes and flung her arms around him. He was surprised to find that, after a moment's hesitation, he was hugging back – tightly, pressing his hands to her back and dipping his head onto her shoulder. Then she shoved him away, somehow affectionate even as she left him half-winded.

'Come in,' she said, 'or the neighbours will start talking.'

She took his hand and led him inside, kicking the door closed with her heel. He didn't want to let go and was overwhelmed by another long-suppressed memory: the two of them, four or five years old, in winter clothes, walking together in the park while their mothers had grown-up talk behind them. He remembered kicking fallen leaves, and Chelsea giggling.

'Do you remember when we were little,' he said, his voice just a little hoarse as she guided him to the kitchen table and pulled out a seat for him, 'that time you dared me to eat those sweets with the wrappers still on?'

Still holding his hand, she stood over him and shook her head. 'No, but it's definitely the kind of thing I would have done.'

'I did it,' he said, 'and you laughed so hard that I kept doing it, until Mum realised and told me off.' He gave a barely discernible smile. 'And you thought that was hilarious, too, so I didn't mind too much.'

Her hand slipped out of his and she stood back to look at him. He noticed, now, that there were baby food stains on her T-shirt.

'I'm not much good at this kind of thing.' She held her hands up. 'All this.'

'Me neither,' said Ben.

'Thank fuck for that. Save us both a lot of trouble, won't it? But it's good to see you,' she said. 'Since Mum died, I haven't got any family.'

'I'm sorry,' he said, sure that she would understand everything he meant by those two words.

'Me too,' she said, conveying just as much. She folded her arms. 'Anyway, if we've got talking to do we should talk now, while Jen's asleep – sorry, that's my youngest. She's sort of named after Mum.'

She pulled up a chair and sat down, quite close. There was something marvellous to him in the ease with which they were talking, despite the years.

'Got a girlfriend?' she asked, teasing, biting her lower lip in girlish fashion, amused by the audacity of her own question.

'No,' said Ben. 'Not at the moment. I lived with someone for a bit.' He shook his head.

'You're nowhere near as ugly as you were as a kid,' she said. 'Almost normal-looking.'

He smiled shyly.

'Almost.'

He shifted in his seat, leaning forward so that their heads were almost touching. He wanted to hold her hand again and so he did, and she let him.

'What about you?'

'Lee and me have been married for six years now.' She pointed at a photo on the wall. The broad-shouldered, shaven-headed man in the picture was dressed in sand-coloured army uniform, and had a warm, toothy smile. 'He's out of the forces now, working with his brother. Our oldest, Liam – he's just started school. I'm on maternity.' She sighed and pulled a face. 'Shit – is it only for another four more months?'

There was a comfortable silence during which Ben glanced around the kitchen, taking in the scrappy paintings pinned to the fridge with magnets, some expensive-looking kitchen gadgets, and a set of chef's whites, neatly pressed, dangling from a hanger on a hook on the door.

He sat back and looked her in the eye. 'Happy?'

'Yeah,' she said after a moment, sounding a little surprised.

'Good.'

Something in the way he said the word told Chelsea everything. 'Aren't you?'

He shook his head slowly and looked down at his fingers which he had tied together. He worked at his knuckles, torturing them.

'I'll make tea,' she said. 'Then tell me.'

He nodded.

While she dusted down a large teapot and boiled the kettle, Ben sat stunned and silent, watching a bird hop around the patio. The garden behind was long and well cared for even if it was plain, and was capped with several high and healthy-looking apple trees in early blossom.

With the tea and two mugs in front of them, Chelsea simply waited for Ben to speak. He cleared his throat and made a small sound of frustration, unsure how to begin. 'You know that girl who went missing, Esther Garrett? A few months ago they decided the police had probably arrested the wrong man.'

He told her about the call from Lucy Garrett, the resurgence of his teenage obsession, and everything that had happened since. She uttered the occasional encouraging word or acknowledgement but otherwise left him to unravel the words. He told her about the burglary, which made her swear in solidarity. He stuck to the facts, but paused eventually, stuck on a point.

'I guess I thought Lucy Garrett would be so grateful, or impressed, or something.' He curled his lip, appalled at his own stupidity, and then looked down at his feet, awaiting Chelsea's judgement.

'You're such a dick,' she said, but her tone was gentle.

'I know,' said Ben. He winced and swallowed, struggling over what he wanted to say next as if it was a piece of gristle in his mouth. 'I was attracted to her, I think, but it wasn't just that.' He couldn't finish the thought.

Chelsea lifted her mug to her lips with both hands and blew steam from the surface of the tea. 'She reminded you of her sister?'

Ben blinked slowly. 'Oh, God, I can't bear to hear it in words.'

'Yeah, it is weird,' said Chelsea. She frowned and turned the mug in her hands. 'The thing is, mate, everyone's weird, just some are better at pretending to be normal than others.'

She bit her lower lip and glanced towards the ceiling. 'I'll tell you about weird.' She put down her mug, stood up and said, 'Wait here,' before leaving the room and jogging upstairs. Ben drank his tea and listened to the sound of footsteps, the rattling of a loft ladder, and the clattering of the hatch into the roof.

On the table next to him, the lights on a baby monitor he hadn't noticed began to flicker as a soft, indeterminate sound emerged from the speaker. Ben watched the lights for a few moments until his eyelids began to droop. He snapped awake with a jerk: Chelsea was by his side waving something under his nose.

'Remember this?' she said.

He took the object as she began to walk up and down the kitchen with the baby in her arms, bouncing her gently. His old scrapbook.

'You kept it,' he said, running a hand over the now creased and dented orange cover.

'You asked me to,' she said with a matter-of-fact shrug. 'And, anyway, I'm terrible at throwing things out.'

'Thanks,' he said.

'What I was saying, though, about being weird. Well, look inside.'

He opened it and leafed through the pages, noting that most of the clippings had come loose and turned brittle with age. He stopped when something fell out into his lap. It was a piece of hammered, heavy cream-coloured card. He picked it up and turned it over.

'I've always felt really guilty about that,' said Chelsea. 'You're the only person I've ever showed it to.'

There was a message on the card, written in blue biro in a hand almost childishly imprecise, and riddled with spelling mistakes. Ben read it aloud, correcting as he went: 'My Dear Esther – I am so sorry. You are in a better place now. Rest with the angels my darling. You will always be in my heart.' He turned it over in his hands again.

'I took it from one of the bunches of flowers in Dodd's Wood. I don't know why. Mostly because you told me not to, I think.' She shrugged. 'But also, you know, death. Pretty girls. It was romantic. Or something.'

'It's not signed,' said Ben.

Chelsea kissed the now quietly snuffling baby's head and then glanced up at Ben. She frowned.

'What's wrong?'

Ben was gazing intently at the card in his hands, spittle gathering in the corner of his mouth, almost as if he was in the throes of a stroke.

'Ben?' she said, insistently.

He blinked at that but still said nothing.

'You're worrying me,' she said, stepping closer. The movement finally shook Ben from his reverie and he looked up, startled, as if emerging from deep water.

'I recognise this handwriting,' he said.

'Really?' said Chelsea.

He nodded dumbly.

'Where from?'

'From something I saw in Esther Garrett's bedroom – a note on her noticeboard.' He raked shaking fingers through his hair, pressing them against the round of his skull. 'From somewhere else, too.' He blinked and worked his mouth dumbly, before lurching to his feet, still holding the card, at arm's length. 'I need to go,' he said, his voice thick in his throat.

Chelsea followed him to the front door. He opened it and, as he was about to step outside, stopped, turning to face her. He gave a weak smile, undercut by his crinkled brow.

'I'm glad I came,' he said.

From Chelsea's house in Okehampton, Ben walked in a daze to the bus stop on the Exeter Road. Unshaven and red-eyed, hands dug into his pockets, he looked as if he might be drunk, high or unstable, and other pedestrians, without making eye contact, slipped out of his way so that he was able to stride unsteadily down the centre of the path. Approaching the bus stop, he saw several people waiting – a teenage boy with hair over his face and the white cords of iPod earphones dangling across his torso; an old woman with too much make-up and red shoes; and a shaven-headed man in his thirties wearing a paint-speckled sweatshirt and carrying a toolbox.

'When's the bus due?' Ben asked hoarsely as he reached the shelter, addressing no one in particular.

After a long, uncomfortable pause, the shaven-headed man answered in a thick Polish accent. 'It's coming just now.'

Ben leaned against the low, purple-grey brick wall behind the bus stop and fixed his eyes on the bend at the bottom of the hill. A minute or so later, he saw the flat front of an off-white double decker approaching and those around him at the bus stop began to shift and shuffle, gently asserting their rights in the invisible queue, preparing to board. The bus pulled in with a squeak of brakes and an elderly man got off. Ben let the others board first and then hauled himself up.

'Single to Exeter,' he said absently.

He paid and took his ticket and, as the bus pulled away, took a seat in the centre of the lower floor. He rested his head against the greasy window and stared down at the ticket.

With almost every seat taken and the scheduled 3.35 departure time seconds away, there had come the sounds of shoes slapping through puddles on wet paving, and then Esther Garrett, in shop uniform and well-worn duffel coat, had launched herself aboard with a laugh, turning to wave at someone.

Despite the rain, her lips had been gleaming and perfect; she had applied fresh clear gloss, just before boarding. As she spoke to the driver, her lips were parted – she was breathless, but not only because she'd dashed for the bus: her eyes were deep and dark, the pupils dilated. She had been excited, looking up at Peter from under her lashes.

She had handed her ticket to Peter Hodge, and he took it.

He didn't look at it, stamp it, and hand it back as he had with everyone else's – his hand reached out, enfolded it, and pulled back. The ticket didn't go near the machine, and when she walked away from the cabin, she was empty-handed.

When Ben had stared at her over the top of his comic, and she smiled at him, yes, it had been a sweet smile, but was there also something else – she was suppressing her amusement at some private joke. The smile was involuntary and not especially aimed at him.

She had sat down next to Aaron Greenslade, slouched and menacing, without any hesitation, because she didn't care – she wasn't scared, because she wasn't alone, as everyone assumed after the fact.

Ben remembered that he had stared at her and that she had smiled back at him, but that wasn't what had happened at all: she had smiled, yes, but not quite at him. Next to the driver's cabin, mounted against the big front window, there was a mirror, giving him a view of the whole bus. Ben had looked at it so many times – his father's arms stretched out on the big wheel, the top of his head, sunglasses and, when he looked up, a foreshortened, fish-eye view of his face.

Esther Garrett's perfect smile – that row of milky-white teeth – had been directed at the mirror, not at Ben. At the driver, not at Ben. At Peter, not at Ben.

When Aaron Greenslade had propositioned her and she moved to the front of the bus, Peter had spoken to her. 'You all right, love?'

Back then, lots of people were still in the habit of calling young women 'love', but not Peter – he'd never done it – it wasn't in his vocabulary. He called men 'pal', young men 'son', but young women, nothing.

But Esther Garrett – she was 'love'.

Ben hadn't registered the oddness of it at the time because the whole situation was so strange – because his father's exact words had been the least arresting part of the entire incident. But he could see now, or rather hear, that the 'love' meant something in this context.

When she had nodded in response how had her face looked? Ben had played the moment over in his mind many times but had perhaps somehow distorted it, or failed to understand what he was seeing. Were there subtle signals? Was there meaning in the dip of her head and the way she had blinked – a message for Peter that Ben as a child, whose desires were yet to fully unfurl, could never have read.

When Greenslade had come to the front of the bus, raging and fierce, Peter had kept the doors closed not out of some vague sense of gallantry towards a stranger, but because he had a particular interest in Esther. He might never have opened the doors, or at least not until she was much further away, if Greenslade hadn't threatened Ben.

'All right, keep your hair on,' Peter had said, when he needn't have said anything. It was another delaying tactic, an attempt to distract Greenslade for just another moment.

When Greenslade had disappeared into the darkness, too close to Esther for comfort, Peter had said, 'Gave that poor lass a good head start anyway, didn't we?' but, of course, he hadn't believed it – he wanted reassurance.

He had chosen Ben over Esther, but perhaps regretted it.

What had Peter said to Steven Sweetland? 'She got on at Exeter. I've seen her on the route a few times before, coming and going, like.'

It had been more than that – of course it had. In some sense, that Ben intended to understand, Esther Garrett and Peter Hodge had been together.

Peter, his own father, was Esther's Older Man.

But what could he do about it?

CHAPTER TWENTY-THREE

Ben spent most of the rest of the day sat in a pub in Exeter – the same one to which Lucy Garrett had taken him after their visit to the prison, with its dark corners and air of discretion. He sat drinking lager, several pints over the course of hours, and staring into space with an unnerving intensity which ensured he had a large table to himself, even when the pub got busy. The barman watched him warily, waiting for trouble. At 5pm Ben downed what was left in his glass and strode out of the pub, purposeful now and on the other side of tiredness, light-headed to the point of euphoria. He walked a few minutes to the bus station where he approached the Okehampton bus.

For a moment, he hesitated: he didn't know if he could handle that journey again, in the company of Esther Garrett's ghost and with the knowledge that at the end he would have to face Peter. Standing under the concrete canopy, enveloped in the smell of diesel fumes, he considered walking away and boarding a train back to London. He could delete his father's number from his phone, stop speaking to him, and wait for the police to do their jobs. But he had to know for sure – had to look Peter in the eye, and hear him confess. With a clenching in his gut, he boarded the bus and took a seat next to an obese man with a flea-bitten dog.

In the half hour the journey took Ben was quite absent, playing over the conversation he was about to have. Though the bus was warm he felt freezing cold and twitchy, his body flooded with adrenaline, readying him for a fight or to flee.

At Okehampton, he mumbled 'Cheers' to the driver, speaking automatically, as he stepped out onto the wet, black pavement, and into the country darkness. He stood and watched the bus pull away, wondering about the man behind the wheel – did he have children, a wife, girl-friends, boyfriends? He had just been a pair of hands, a pair of eyes, a uniform to Ben and to everyone else. The red tail lights disappeared into a dip in the road and Ben broke free from his haunted reverie.

At the front gate of his father's little terraced house – the one where his grandmother had brought up a family, and where Ben himself had lived, on-and-off, for so many years – he stopped again. The lights were on and he could hear the low intonation of a television newsreader muffled by the window. He looked up and down the road with its parked cars. A ginger cat prowled along a garden wall; somewhere nearby, a plastic wheelie bin rattled over cobbles; and the smell of woodsmoke, from logs freshly laid on an evening fire, drifted down on the cool air.

When Ben knocked on the door it was not his usual timid tap but a full-fisted thumping, over and over.

The door flew open and Peter lurched out ready to swear at a sales-man, charity collector or religious zealot. When he saw Ben the reflexive words of greeting froze on his lips. Something about the expression on Ben's face made him step back and at that Ben pushed his way inside, slamming the door behind him. He was satisfied at the booming sound it made, at the way it startled a still-retreating, shrunken Peter, and at the shaking of the flimsy walls.

At the end of the hall, at the bottom of the stairs with their strip of dusty beige carpet, under the dangling, dim, naked bulb, Peter stopped and set himself steady. 'What the bloody hell's wrong with you?' he said, trying to sound stern. His voice failed him and, dwindling to a whisper, he merely sounded pathetic.

'Esther Garrett,' said Ben.

'Who?' Peter snapped back without hesitating.

At that, Ben couldn't help but laugh – a harsh, fierce sound that came from a previously undisturbed pit of disdain deep inside him.

'Don't try that,' he said. 'Everyone round here knows who Esther Garrett is, and you most of all.'

'Oh,' said Peter, 'Yeah, that lass that went missing.' He scratched his head as if he'd forgotten something, or had just woken up from sleepwalking. With his shoulders slumped and bewildered, he looked small and old.

Ben stepped forward again, forcing Peter to totter backwards into the kitchen, scuffing his slippers as he went.

An empty Fray Bentos tin and an overfilled ashtray sat on the table next to a newspaper folded open to the sports page. There was also a large plastic bottle of cider, half-finished.

'Shall we sit down, son?' said Peter, gesturing at the two rickety kitchen chairs with their peeling paint, at least fifty years old.

Ben ignored the question. 'I know all about it.'

'About what?' said Peter with a whining note, his feigned confusion and innocence those of a child caught stealing from the biscuit tin.

'I know that you knew her. I know that you were with her.'

Peter collapsed into the chair and let his head hang down on his chest. His bony hands clawed at his scalp, as if trying to rub out some memory or pain. Ben was mesmerised by the sight – those hands were his hands, with the same rounded nails, same prominent knuckles, and with the familiar freckles along their sides.

'Did you kill her?' Ben asked, calmly and quietly, but with an intended keen edge.

Continuing to claw at the ridges of his skull, Peter rocked a little and a wet sound escaped from his gaping mouth.

Ben's hand whipped out to smack the back of Peter's crawling hand.

He hadn't expected to do it and the violence scared him, but it was effective: Peter stopped grizzling and looked up, flaring with anger. Ben stared back with his own pale irises gleaming cold, fists clenched at his sides, his height no longer rendering him awkward but intimidating.

Speaking slowly, separating each word, he asked again, 'Did you kill Esther Garrett?'

Peter made a whining sound.

Wide-eyed, he showed his palms. 'I swear, son – I swear on my mother's life, I didn't have anything to do with it.'

After a long, piercing look, wanting it to be true, Ben shook his head sadly and said, 'No. I don't believe you.' His mouth hung open and he swallowed saliva that was gathering at the back of his mouth, a precursor to sickness.

Sensing Ben's weakness, Peter adopted a look of mild amusement, as if the whole business was ridiculous – an interlude – and made a move to stand up. Ben clamped a hand on Peter's shoulder and pushed him down, digging into the bones and sensitive nerves with a surprising strength of grip.

'I know that you had something going on with her,' said Ben. 'That day, on the bus, she gave you her ticket and you didn't give it back.'

'Is that it? No, son, you're remembering wrong–'

'Don't interrupt,' said Ben, raising his voice just a little. 'I remember all of it, exactly. You took her ticket, only it wasn't a ticket, was it? It was a note, arranging to meet later. That's how these things were done before everyone had email and Facebook and text messages.'

Peter licked his lips nervously and rubbed at his sagging Adam's apple with the tips of his fingers, but said nothing.

'After your shift you went out, probably in Nan's car, and picked her up. Then something happened.' Ben frowned, frustrated at the gap in his story. 'And you killed her. Maybe it was an accident – I don't know – and then you disposed of the body somewhere no one's ever thought of looking.'

At that, Ben blanched as a sickening thought occurred to him. 'Not here, surely?' He pointed downward. 'Not in this house – in the garden or something?' He had lived there, played there, looked out over the back garden for all those years.

Still, Peter said nothing.

Ben pushed on. 'Then you told the police about Aaron Greenslade and faked that statement from me because you wanted him to take the blame. You let an innocent man go to prison for you.' Ben laughed bitterly. 'And it was you that burgled my flat last night. My own dad.'

Again, there was no reaction from Peter other than a blink and a suggestion of a shrug.

'For God's sake, Dad – I'm not a policeman,' said Ben. 'I'm your son.' He spat out the final word, half fury, half sorrow.

Peter brooded for a moment, chewing on his tongue.

'You're wrong,' he said. 'Dead fucking wrong. I didn't know her, I didn't fuck her, and I can tell you one hundred per cent, cross my heart, I didn't kill her.'

And yet the more vehemently he denied it, the surer Ben became. 'Stop lying, Dad – I *know*. I'm your son. I know.'

Ben took the memorial card from his pocket and held it up, watching with pleasure as Peter paled. 'This is your writing, isn't it?'

'No,' said Peter.

'The thing is,' said Ben, pressing his lips together, squeezing the blood from them, as the skin around his eyes tightened, 'maybe no one else needs to know.' Ben didn't know if he meant it or not. Part of him dreaded the thought of his father in prison and of the act of familial betrayal required to put him there. Peter, for his part, acknowledged the gesture with a grunt and a half smile, but made no commitment.

'But if you don't talk to me,' said Ben, pleading, 'then I'll have to go to the police so they can investigate properly.'

'Go to them with what?' said Peter. He tried to sound scornful but Ben could tell he had nothing but bravado to lean on now. 'Some story about something you think you saw when you were a kid but that's only just come back to you? They'll laugh you out of town.'

'Let's find out,' said Ben and pulled his phone from his pocket.

Peter leapt to his feet, pushing the chair back across the kitchen tiles with a screech, and grabbed for the phone. With his free hand, Ben pushed him away. Peter stumbled over the chair and collapsed on his back across the floor. He scrambled to right himself, cursing and grunting with pain, but only succeeded in raising himself onto his elbows from which position he looked at Ben imploringly.

'Don't do that, son. Ben. Please.'

Ben weighed the phone in his hand. 'Then tell me.'

There was a long pause in the gloomy, filthy kitchen. The fridge purred and clunked and wind whined through the pipes of the extractor fan above the cooker. Peter licked his lips, steeling himself. 'We got talking on the bus one afternoon.'

Ben put the phone back in his pocket.

'It didn't happen very often but sometimes, it was weird – there would be only one person on the bus. In the school holidays especially or Sundays. When it was like that, I always talked to whoever was there, even though I wasn't meant to, especially if they were sat close. You know, like a taxi driver.'

Peter rolled slightly and pushed himself up, dusting the knees of his jeans, and collapsing into the chair. He coughed roughly, reached to the table for a neatly rolled cigarette, and lit it with a plastic lighter. It crackled as he drew on it, the paper catching and glowing fierce orange.

'She was leaning on the luggage rack and we sort of looked at each other at the same time. I was a young man, then – I was only a kid when you were born – and, you know, not bad looking, and she smiled at me. Do you remember, son? Her smile?'

He almost choked on his words and jammed the cigarette between his lips to cover the stumble. 'So I asked her where she was going, friendly, like. Not chatting her up. And then we just got talking. Only for ten minutes before someone else got on, but that was long enough.'

He put his hands together, cracking his knuckles and tipping his head from side to side as he tried to put his thoughts into words.

'You know when there's a connection? It was just like we were mates, straight off the bat. She told me she didn't get on with her mum and dad. She told me she'd split up with this kid, whatever he was called, and that she was right off boys.'

He frowned and ran the thickened thumbnail of the hand holding his cigarette through his eyebrow.

'There was something in the way she said that. It was like an invitation, wasn't it? Because I wasn't, you know, a boy.' He waved his hand, irritated at the difficulty of finding the words. 'I can't explain it, but it was the *way* she said it. So, when she was getting off, I did something mad.' He sighed and his shoulders sagged. 'I slipped her the number of the payphone in the canteen at work, on a bit of paper, and put my name on there as well.'

'She was sixteen.'

'Fifteen,' said Peter. 'Her birthday was in September.' Peter banged a bunched fist onto the tabletop. 'That's when I went wrong, giving her that number – I wish I hadn't done it, son, I do.'

Ben nodded ever so slightly. Yes, that was the fatal moment when a line was crossed.

'She called me a couple of days after we first met and I could feel her excitement down the line – do you know what I mean?' He looked desperate and sad, suddenly. 'I'd been lonely, son. I didn't know how to meet anyone otherwise.' Peter tapped his chest with his hand, momentarily overcome. 'Even on the phone, she had this laugh. My God, it did things to me.'

Ben flinched. He didn't want to hear more about his father's arousal but didn't dare interrupt.

'We met up town, in Exeter, just for a cup of tea, like – that's what I kept saying to myself: we're just talking, we're just having a cup of tea, we're just going for a walk. No one looked twice at us. Maybe they thought we were related or something, I don't know, but no one cared, and she never touched me until there was no one else around.'

He smiled but Ben could only see it as a leer.

'She knew what she was doing. She went for me, tongue down my throat before I knew what was happening.' The smile faded from his face. 'And that was that. Afterwards, I couldn't stop it, not when I'd had my hands on her, and felt her up against me. I was gone.' He stopped and growled, 'What?'

Ben shook his head. 'It's disgusting.'

'Just because you're like your mother,' said Peter, viciously. 'Just because you haven't got any human fucking feelings doesn't mean the rest of us can just switch them off.'

'Shut up.' The muscles in Ben's jaw flexed, tightening his cheeks.

'I'm a passionate man. I have a lot of love in here.' Peter thumped a hand against his sunken chest.

'Finish your story.'

'This is difficult, son,' said Peter.

Ben said nothing, only fixing Peter with a challenging gaze.

'It got heavy for a few weeks. We couldn't leave each other alone. Up in Berebroke woods, a blanket on the ground. All I could think about was when I was going to see her, and where we were going to meet.' He waved his fingers in a circle, dispersing cigarette smoke around his head. 'It was like an addiction.'

'Didn't you try to stop?' said Ben. 'You must have known it was wrong.'

Peter cast his head to one side. 'Nah. It wasn't. You saw her – she wasn't a little kid. I wasn't some sort of paedo. She was a young woman. I wasn't the first bloke she'd been with, either. She knew her way around.'

Ben felt sick. Quietly, he asked, 'So what happened, in the end?'

Peter opened his mouth, but no words came out. His hands rose to his scalp again where they began to rake at his thin hair. 'Same thing always happens – same thing happened with your mum – I got bored. You've had women, haven't you? You must know how it is? At first, you go mad just looking at them, imagining what it'll be like to touch them, and then when you do it's electric.' He shivered. 'For a while. Then the thrill just fades away. You start looking at other women, craving them, and the one you've got don't get you going. The grass is always greener, eh, son? They start to annoy you, too, don't they? With their questions and little habits. You start to see they ain't perfect. Their fucking shit stinks like everyone else's.'

Peter stopped, breathing heavily, exhausted by the effort of the confession – more fluent than Ben had ever heard him before. Ben waited.

'I was starting to get fed up of her, but her? She was going the oppo-site way. If I tried to dodge out of seeing her she went mental. When we did meet up, however distant I was, she was only more keen. Always asking questions.' Peter put on a whining voice, and contorted his face into a mean caricature. '"What's wrong? What's the matter? Is it some-thing I've done?", like she was scared I'd ditch her. And that ain't a turn on.'

He scratched at his ear and shrugged as if her feelings were still utterly bizarre and inexplicable to him.

'All the time I was hoping she'd get fed up and move on. But what she wanted, see, was to–' he wiggled his fingers in the air, mimicking dissipating smoke '–was to run away. She hated her parents. Her dad was a bad sort. She couldn't wait to leave home and she thought we could just up sticks and go to Scotland.' He gave a wheezy laugh. 'She was obsessed with bloody Scotland – I don't know why. Because it was a long way, I suppose. But I couldn't do that, even if I wanted to. I had a job and my mother to look after.' He looked at Ben with a painful, embar-rassed expression. 'And you.'

Ben snorted and turned his head to avoid Peter's eyes.

'No, don't be like that – you were my boy,' said Peter, raising his voice. 'My little boy. I'd have crawled through broken fucking glass to do anything for you. I'd have chucked myself in front of a truck if I could save you. Still would, son. You know that.' His voice caught in his throat. 'So I couldn't just run off to fucking Scotland with a girl I hardly knew. When we actually had to pay the bills and live together, and with her dad after my guts, she'd have got sick of me too.'

'Why didn't you just say no?'

'I did – that's exactly what I did. That night, I picked her up. She knew something was wrong straight away because I was moody and she started asking me while we were still in the car and I said, straight up, like, that I thought we ought to stop seeing each other.'

Peter stopped, then, struggling to catch his breath. 'Oh, God,' he said, wrestling with the memory. He breathed unevenly and a tear ran from the corner of his eye, tracing its way over the bumps and folds of his stubble-covered cheek.

Ben pulled out the other chair and lowered himself into it.

'She was upset. She wanted to know what she'd done wrong, said she'd do whatever I wanted.' He swallowed hard. 'I ain't proud, son, but I couldn't resist an offer like that. You know what it's like when you're fucking randy – you're like a different person, aren't you?'

'You're sick,' said Ben.

'I'm normal. That's what men were put on this earth to do – look at women, and take them.'

'I'm supposed to look up to you – to respect you. How can I?'

Peter directed his glance towards the safety of the blank wall. After a moment he wiped a finger across his eye and went on. 'Afterwards, I thought, no, you can't string her along – you can't just leave it until next time, so I said, "Esther, love, this is it. We're done."' His shoulders were rising and falling with the effort of forcing out each word and his voice had become raw and grainy. 'So she said she was going to tell everyone about us. She didn't mean it like blackmail, I don't reckon, but she was hysterical, screaming. I just wanted her to be quiet, so I reached out.' He demonstrated the action, his hands rising into the air in front of him, his eyes unfocused or, rather, focused on something that wasn't there.

'You did it because she was going to tell people? To stop her talking?'

Peter shook his head furiously, waving his outstretched hands in denial. 'No, no – not that – literally just to stop her screaming. I didn't want anyone to hear her in the woods and come running. I couldn't be seen with her, not like that. I'd have ended up on some register or something.'

It wasn't convincing and Peter didn't even seem convinced himself.

'I didn't think anything. I just did it. It was what do you call it? Instinct.' He looked at his hands. 'When I realised she was dead – you can tell, you can really tell, when someone is dead – I calmed right down. And then I knew I had to get rid of her.'

He took a swig of cider from the bottle on the table and wiped his lips with his fingertips.

'I put her in the car first. She was heavy, like a sack of spuds. I got covered in mud and crap and nearly broke my fingers but I did it, all on my own, and no one saw me. Then I sat there in the car and I had a bit of a turn. Got the shakes.' He waved a hand over his chest. 'I couldn't fucking breathe. Thought I was having a heart attack. I drove around for ages, trying to think what to do with her.'

'Didn't you think of going to the hospital or the police?' said Ben, a pleading note in his voice, beginning to wish for some redeeming detail in his father's story.

'Can't say I did,' said Peter matter-of-factly.

'They might have been able to resuscitate her.'

'No, son. It was too late. And nobody wants to go to prison, do they? Have their whole lives taken away, like that.' He clicked his fingers. 'Human instinct.'

He drank more cider, just enough to moisten his tongue. 'I thought about the sea, down at Exmouth, but I didn't know the coast well enough to think where would be quiet, and I didn't have nothing to weigh her down. I didn't want her washing up. I was going to put her in a ditch – one of them ones off the main road, between the fields – but I knew someone would find her, knowing my luck. I thought about burying her.'

At this, he paused, and leaned forward to rest his arms on his knees, his face now close to Ben's. When he spoke, it was as if they were back in the pub, talking over their beers, father and son.

'You didn't really know Grampy Hodge, did you?' He pointed at a framed six-by-four photo on the wall over the half-sized dining table: it was from the 1980s, faded to shades of orange, and showed Ben's paternal grandfather, Robert, in an open-necked white shirt and braces, smiling in front of a garden fence, squinting into the sun. His hair was slick with grease or hair oil and his features were pasty and thick.

'Not really,' said Ben, looking away from the photograph and back to Peter.

'He died when you were, what, three years old? He was a bastard – a proper bastard. Not a day went by he didn't take a belt to me or your Uncle Wayne, or knock your nan about. If there was a penny in the house he spent it on rum so we were hungry and cold half the time.'

'Don't make excuses.'

'No, son – it's not that. Do you know what he did for a living?'

'He was a gardener, wasn't he? For the council?'

Peter laughed grimly, drily. 'That's what your nan always told everyone. Fucking ashamed, she was. What he was, son, was a gravedigger. He spent all day, every day, forty-odd years, digging graves in the mud and rain. And he hated every minute of it. He used to come in at night and he'd tell me what he'd been doing that day because he knew it scared me – the fucking bastard. He'd tell me he'd had to open up a grave and his foot had gone through the lid of a coffin into the rotten guts of some old woman who'd been dead and buried five years. That sort of thing. He used to think it was funny. Death didn't scare him.'

'What's this got to do with Esther?'

'He told me once that it took hours to dig a proper grave. You had to go down at least four feet, ideally six. Even if I had a spade that night, which I didn't, I knew I wouldn't have the time or strength to do a proper job of it. She'd end up a foot down, hardly covered, and then some idiot with a dog would come along and I'd be up shit creek. So, I remembered your granddad, and that reminded me of something else, so I came home.'

'Home? Here?'

Ben's skin crept at the idea that Esther Garrett's body might be concealed within feet of where he was sitting.

Peter shook his head. 'Don't worry – she's not here now. I couldn't have lived here all these years with her under the floorboards.' He shuddered. 'I came back here. You were in bed, fast asleep, and your nan was having her last cup of tea before bed. She saw the state I was in, covered in mud, shitting myself.' His face reddened as he fought to control his emotions. 'She was a saint, my mother. No woman ever loved her boys the way she loved me and your uncle, and she knew I was in trouble straight away. She looked at me, dead in the eye, and she said, "You don't need to tell me anything. What do you need?" I told her to go to bed, close her door, and leave me alone. I said it was nothing serious, but that, if anyone asked, I was there all night. She went to bed and then I went down to the shed.'

He pointed past the kitchen sink and the pantry to the glass-pane of the back door. 'I found dad's work bag, hung up on the hook there, and I got the keys.' He stopped himself. 'Look, it's easier if I show you.'

'What do you mean?'

'Let's get in the car and I'll drive you there – show you where I put her. Then you can decide what you want to do.' He reached out to touch Ben's hand but Ben pulled it away before they made contact. 'I know you'll do the right thing,' he said, resting his fingers instead on Ben's knee. 'We're family. Blood.'

He got up and opened one of the kitchen drawers where, for decades, bits of string, envelopes, souvenirs and knick-knacks had been dumped. He dug through the rubbish with his fingertips, removing wedges of paper, tobacco tins and jars, until he found what he was looking for – a bunch of three large rusty keys on an iron hoop that Ben had seen many times as a child.

CHAPTER TWENTY-FOUR

They drove in silence through empty streets, past unlit bungalows and shuttered shops. Ben kept glancing at Peter, astonished to find that, despite everything, the man in the driver's seat was still his father. Peter, absorbed for the moment in driving, looked as if the conversation back at the house had never happened. There was something reassuringly normal about being there together in the car, pop music playing low on the radio, and Ben found himself wishing, despite everything, that it might be possible to stay in that instant forever. Then on the right-hand side of the car Ben saw the last row of houses before Exeter Road cemetery – several acres of utter darkness behind a stone wall – and the tension returned. Peter slowed the car and pulled up onto the pavement in front of the gatehouse. They both sat in silence as the car cooled, clicking and creaking.

Peter spoke first.

'It looks as if they've changed the lock,' he said. 'My old key won't work.'

'Okay,' said Ben, relieved. 'We'll stay here.'

'I know another way in.'

Peter took a torch from the glove box and opened the car door. Cold air rushed in, causing Ben to shiver. Ben opened his own door and climbed out. They slammed the doors shut behind them at almost the same moment, the sound of one an echo of the other, reverberating across the open space.

Peter led the way, hands in the pockets of his leather jacket, shoulders hunched, and his breath white around him as he walked purposefully along the line of the wall. Bramble bushes had burst over the stones and their tendrils hung down, thorns snatching at Ben's hair and jacket like clawed fingers. The wall terminated at a pathway that ran uphill and Peter turned on his torch, directing the weak, white beam at the ground. The way was clear of growth and roughly paved with gravel and shards of stone. Without pausing, Peter tramped onward. In the beam of light, Ben saw their destination: a smaller side gate.

Peter stopped up ahead, breathing heavily because of the effort taken in climbing the slope, and because the frosty air was clutching at his tar-fogged lungs. He directed the torch onto the bunch of keys and tried one, then another. The gate popped open and Peter stepped through the arch. Ben followed him.

Away from the glare of streetlights, Ben could see the tops of tombstones, picked out by the moonlight. Those near the gate, in the plots by the wall, were relatively new and straight but further along the path towards the centre of the cemetery they became tilted and broken. Where the four great paths met, Ben discerned the outline of the small chapel around which were clustered the oldest, most elaborate, and most decrepit graves – pure Victorian gothic extravagance. Some had collapsed in on themselves or fallen most of the way to the ground and all were tangled in brambles.

Peter walked purposefully towards the chapel, his footsteps rasping on the gravel. As he followed Ben looked anxiously around and over his shoulder; something was rustling in the overgrown grass – birds, or perhaps rats. When they reached the building, Peter stopped with a stamp. He gave a phlegmy cough into his fist.

'She's in there.'

The chapel was a severe building, functional rather than beautiful, with only a few gothic features to distinguish it from a school house or even a barn. Its simple windows were leaded but unstained, made ugly by protective chicken wire. Areas of black paint looked hardly better than the graffiti they covered on the honey-coloured stone.

'That night,' said Peter, almost whispering, 'I got the key and I drove down here. I unlocked the big gate there—' he pointed '—and drove straight in – this is gone midnight, now, right?'

Ben detected a note of weird relish in his father's voice as he embraced the storytelling.

Peter began to walk slowly round to the double door at the front of the chapel, at either side of which sat a withered potted palm and a half-rotten bench. 'I parked up, right here, backed up to that door.' He fumbled with the keys on the hoop and inserted one into the keyhole. The lock snapped open loudly, echoing around the empty stone building. He seized the ring handle and opened the door, which cried in agony as it swung inward. As he stepped inside, he turned off the torch. 'Batteries are dying,' he said, before disappearing at once into the total darkness.

Ben hesitated, his skin crawling at the thought of what might be ahead.

He heard Peter's voice, distant now, luring him on. 'I dragged her in here.'

Ben stepped over the threshold and stopped, allowing his eyes to adjust. At first all he could see were windows, high and fogged with mould or dirt, filled with blue moonlight, but eventually he discerned a desk to his left, rows of pews, and a simple, plain altar. There were no paintings or hangings, no memorials – just whitewashed walls. The smell of damp and decay was so overwhelming that he would not have been surprised to see mushrooms sprouting between the flagstones.

Peter was waiting for him, standing in the centre of the aisle. In the dimness, his skin looked grey, and his eyes were lost in the shadow of his brows.

'Shouldn't think anybody ever uses it these days,' he said, gesturing with an open hand, which he then used to scratch his cheek. 'Expect most people have their ceremonies at the local church, if they bother at all. That's what my dad used to say, anyway, even back in the seventies.'

He stopped speaking, rubbing at his nose with a thumb, and sniffed.

'Well?' said Ben. A shiver overtook his body, working its way across his shoulder blades and down his spine.

'I was here till four or five o'clock,' he said. 'Come on.'

He moved on, towards the altar. Ben followed.

At one side, Ben saw there was a staircase with an iron railing leading into even deeper darkness. Peter took a couple of steps down before turning the torch back on, but its light was now so faint as to be near useless. At the bottom of the steps, under the altar, was another door, which Peter unlocked and opened. A pungent aroma of damp soil and rotten vegetation blew out on a chill draught. Before entering the vault, Peter reached inside and patted his hand up and down the wall. He popped an old-fashioned lever light switch, but the bulb was dead.

'Ah, well,' he said.

'Hold on,' said Ben and then turned on the small flashlight on his mobile phone, though he knew it would run his battery down in no time at all. He directed the beam at Peter, who shaded his eyes and then, as if pursued, slipped through the doorway.

Ben felt an alarm sounding through his body – a drop in temperature, the prickling of every hair. He didn't believe, or couldn't believe, that Peter would do him any harm, and yet he wanted so much to run away, into the light. In that moment, he had to decide whether he was on Esther Garrett's side, or his father's, and picked Esther. He composed the briefest of text messages: 'Ex Rd Cemetery help'.

'Are you coming, son?'

Peter's voice seemed to come from a long way away.

'Yes,' Ben shouted as he rushed to send the message. He realised he didn't yet have Chelsea's number and, in his panic, picked the first of his most recent contacts: Lucy Garrett. As he descended the steps he regretted his choice. She would either have blocked his number, or would ignore the message, or wouldn't understand it. He might as well not have bothered.

Passing through the door, in the white-blue ring of light from his phone, Ben saw that the vault was not at all gothic but utilitarian, and dirty, piled high with sacks of weed-killer, gardening tools, lawnmowers of varying vintages, and stacks of plastic chairs. He heard more scurrying and noted the musty aroma of rodents. A draught was seeping through a vent at ceiling level which had been kicked in and through which bottles and cans had been dropped to form a pile on the floor, half covered with dry leaves.

'See these slabs?' said Peter, pointing down at the floor. Ben directed his light downward at plain concrete flagstones with thick cracks between them. 'I cleared all this lot,' said Peter, pointing at the heaps of junk and old crates piled up against the far wall. 'I had light and plenty of time and all these tools.' He walked to the corner and took a pointed shovel in his hand, its tip white with lime, weighing it in his palm.

Ben tensed.

'So I took up the floor, two stones by six, nice and neat, and then I dug four foot down.' He became flustered again, running his hands over his head as if to soothe himself. His voice sank to a hoarse whisper. 'Then I just chucked her in.'

He closed his eyes.

'Jesus,' he said. 'It was fucking awful. There was this sound I can't describe. I covered her up, put the stones back, put everything back where it was, near as, and took away the leftovers from the digging in a couple of old sacks. I dumped them in a ditch. Then I came home, washed up, and had half an hour's kip before the police turned up at the house.'

Both of them were staring at the heap where the barely-there beam of Peter's dying torch met the cold circle from Ben's phone.

'Is she still there now?' asked Ben, dragging the words from somewhere deep and harsh.

'We've got to leave her be, son,' Peter replied firmly, setting his jaw and piercing Ben with a cold gaze.

'Her family.'

'Fuck 'em,' Peter shouted, his voice bouncing from the low ceiling and bare walls, sounding as loud as the firing of a gun.

Ben flinched and took a step back, causing him to stumble over a raised stone in the uneven floor. He reached for something to hold but found nothing and, instead, crashed to the ground. His phone shattered on the concrete and its light went dead.

'What about our family? What about me and you? You're my boy,' said Peter in the darkness, his voice low and trembling. 'You're my boy.'

Ben started to push himself up.

'I'm sorry, son,' said Peter.

There was just enough light through the broken vent to cast Peter into silhouette as he stalked towards Ben with the shovel upraised.

'I don't want to do this,' he said, strangulated and bitter.

'Dad, don't. Please.'

Time slowed as Ben lifted his arms to protect himself from the black figure above him. The shovel came down, finding his forearm, and he cried out as something seemed to shatter. The second time it fell, it connected with his skull, and Ben felt a pressure bear down on his brain.

'Sorry, son. I did warn you – I *tried* to warn you.'

Blood rolled over Ben's eyes and mouth and he sank into a black pit.

Ben was not sure, at first, if his eyes had really opened: the darkness of unconsciousness was inseparable from the blackness into which he was looking. Perhaps he had gone blind from the blow on the head? He blinked and felt his eyelids moving, caked with something sticky and crusting.

Though it was muffled, he could hear the sound of laboured breathing and a steady crunch and patter – someone working in rhythm. He felt as if there was a weight pressing on his body and he could taste iron in his mouth and throat. He tried to speak but his lips would not part and his tongue had dried like leather.

After a minute or so, peering along the length of his own body, he became able to discern a shape moving in the darkness, performing the same action over and over. What he could see made no sense to him – something rising, glinting, and falling again.

When it stopped, he heard a chesty cough, unmistakeably Peter's. There was a flare of orange light and then a steady glow as the smell of rolling tobacco filled the air. Ben sucked it in through his nose, delighted by its sharp sweetness. He had a startling but brief vision of a moment in childhood, sitting next to his father on a hillside overlooking a field full of cows, eating a packed lunch of cheese and pickle sandwiches while his father smoked. He felt elated, overcome, but still unable to move.

There was a sudden sucking sound, another cough, and the light was extinguished. The delicious smell of tobacco passed. Then the digging began again – yes, digging, that was it. That was what was going on over there, in the place that was just a little less dark than where he lay.

He managed to move his tongue and then to push his between his lips, but when he tried to say, 'Dad,' aloud he managed only a small sigh.

The shovel came flying out of the hole, landing with a clatter, and Ben observed Peter's silhouette as he heaved himself up, swearing under his breath. He stood by the side of the hole for half a minute, breathing heavily, before taking a few steps to where Ben lay on the cold floor.

He knelt down and Ben felt his father's breath on his face, across his ear. Two hands clamped his head and he realised that he was being kissed on the cheek. Then Peter's tears began to gather on Ben's forehead, slick and warm. Peter formed no words, merely grizzling and groaning. He planted one final kiss on Ben's forehead before standing up.

He bent and grabbed Ben's ankles, and then jerked backwards. Ben moved only a few inches but felt his arms being dragged above his head. Beneath him, his shirt rucked. Peter grunted, snivelled, and yanked again – another few inches. He kept going, heaving as if in a tug of war, until Ben found himself with clothes bunched around his head, his chest and gut exposed, and with his arms painfully extended. There was another tug and, suddenly, the floor was gone. Ben fell awkwardly, in a pile, and, at last, managed to make a sound: a lung-emptying involuntary grunt as his body folded up on itself into a near-foetal position.

He blinked. In what little light there was, he could see something lying there next to him in the dirt – something dark and faintly reflective, a curve, some sharp lines.

The world turned white, then, and the rustling, muttering, murmuring of deep night exploded into cacophony.

'Police – don't move,' someone shouted.

The text message he had sent to Lucy Garrett on his way down the steps had saved him. She hadn't ignored him, despite everything, and had instead called the police.

Then in this new, overwhelming light he saw what lay next to him in the pit. He felt no horror at the sight, only something like religious euphoria. The curve was that of a cranium, brown skin stretched taut around it, with wisps of black hair. There were black holes where eyes ought to be and bones protruding through black polyester that refused to rot.

'Esther,' he said, at some level below a whisper.

The moment was broken as shadows passed over him and hands grasped at his clothes. He shielded his eyes from the bright light. It took a long time for paramedics to lift him out of the pit, simultaneously gentle in case he had broken his neck, and robust as they strapped him onto a stretcher. He floated up the staircase, into the now brightly-lit chapel, and out in the cold air where the lights of police cars and ambulances, out of sync with each other, bounced blue from the stone and the undersides of the trees.

He saw Lucy Garrett. She had her red coat hugged close around her and was shivering.

'Can you stop a minute', he croaked.

The stretcher bearers paused.

Lucy walked across the gravel and stopped just before she reached him.

'I found Esther,' he said, a crooked smile on his face. 'I found her.'

He reached out a hand and she stepped backwards.

'No,' she said. 'I can't.'

She looked at him with absolute disgust – the son of the man who killed her sister.

He felt himself moving and watched her slip out of view.

He understood.

END

Printed in Great Britain
by Amazon